This wasn't my room. My heart began to pound in my chest. The floor was covered in scattered garbage and layers of dust. I turned and shone the flashlight around, there was old furniture stacked and long forgotten. I looked back at the floor, the garbage was covered in dust and cobwebs. Moving carefully, I walked toward a wall and held the light, so I could see it. It was a boarded up, window. No light shone through.

Lowering the phone, I opened my contacts and tapped Arius' name. I held the phone to my ear, my hand shaking.

"Second thoughts, beautiful?"

"Arius," I almost cried, "I don't know where I am."

"What? You were just in your room a minute ago."

I shook my head. "I'm not. It's dark and dirty and I don't know where I am." Tears threatened to fall.

"Paisley, listen carefully. I want you to hang up and open the app on your phone marked team. There's only one group on it, dial that, it will call all of us." His tone was so even.

I nodded.

"You got it?"

I nodded again. "Yes. Yes."

"Okay, do it now." The line went dead.

Shaking, I held the phone, so I could read the screen and opened the menu. I'd seen it and thought it was some preinstalled thing that came with the phone. I opened it and hit the only group listed 'good team'. I put the phone to my ear.

"I'm here." Arius said quickly. "Do you have your earbuds with you?"

I nodded then remembered he couldn't see me. "Yes. Hang on." I reached in my pocket and pulled them out, one fell to the floor. Clasping the other one in my palm, I lowered the phone and pushed the side of the earbud, so it would connect. It took two tries to get it in my ear properly. "Okay." I said.

"What's going on?" Victor's voice was in my ear.

"Paisley has somehow ported herself somewhere." Arius said sounding like he was running.

"How is that possible?" Chase asked.

THE ALTEREALM SERIES
1 *The Huntress*
2 *The Seer*
3 *The Empath*
4 *The Witch*
5 *The Chronos*
6 *The Warrior*
7 *The Telepath*
8 *The Healer*
9 *The Kinetic* (coming soon)

Writing As: Jacqueline Paige

Dreams
Three steamy stories that started with a dream

Curses
Two tales of curses.

After the Silence
Volume 1 Bree

ANIMAL SENSES
1 *Heart*
2 *Scent*
3 *Passion*

MAGIC SEASONS ROMANCE
1 *Beltane Magic*
2 *Solstice Heat*
3 *Harvest Dreams*
4 *Autumn Dance*
5 *Winter Mist*

SINGLE TITLES
Solitary Witchling
Salvation
Café Serenity

The Chronos

Alterealm Series

Book 5

By J. Risk

Family tree at the end of The Witch

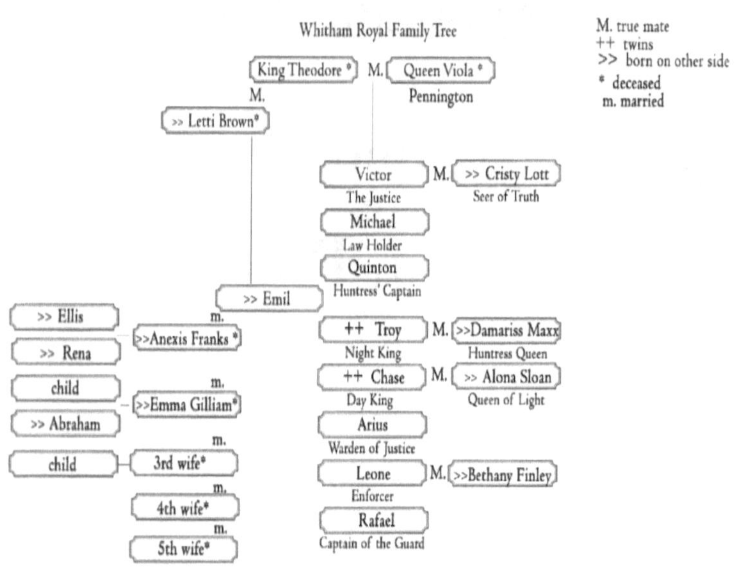

Published by FRP
Copyright © 2018 Roxane Kerr
Edited by Gaele L. Hince
Cover art by: Off the Wall Creations

Updated 2020

Excerpts from *The Warrior* by J. Risk copyright ©2018 by Roxane Kerr

ISBN (paperback): 978-1-7774387-5-3
ISBN (digital) : 978-1-7774387-4-6

ACKNOWLEDGMENTS

I'd like to say a HUGE thank you to my beta and proof readers - for finding all those places that have the wrong facts, whether it be where I've changed the color of a character's eyes throughout the book or areas that are just too chaotic for readers to follow.

Also, to my editor - without her no one would understand a thing I write! She takes those fuzzy areas and makes them clear, hardly ever swears at me (I suspect it's a good thing we live far apart, or she may come to visit just to throw things at me) and forgives (mostly) when I repeat the same grammatical error over and over.
Thank you!

Prologue

Looking over my shoulder I kept running. I didn't see anyone following me, but I wasn't taking any chances. For two weeks I'd watched, waited and planned for the opportunity to get off this island. It was now or never. I couldn't be here another minute.

I pulled at the hard, red cuff around my wrist, trying, yet again, to pull it off. If I could access my abilities I might have a better chance. It was seamless, I'd spent the last two weeks trying to get it off. Stumbling over a branch, I looked back up and tried to figure out where I was headed. There was no path, and. they never patrolled this way, ever. I didn't know why, but I intended to find out.

My lungs screamed at me to slow down, but my mind told me go, so I kept going. At any moment I expected to hit another invisible wall. I'd encountered more than one as I tried to discover how well they covered the island. I knew hitting one at this speed would probably knock me unconscious, but I had to try.

I ducked around low branches as I tried to keep going in a straight line. It scraped across my cheek. Shaking off the sting, I glanced over my shoulder when my footing slipped. I slid across the ground on my hip and landed, stunned and panting. The ground dropped off suddenly.

Getting to my hands and knees, I crawled toward the edge. Reaching it, I put my hand out looking for the barrier I couldn't see. My hand wasn't stopped by anything.

Inching forward, I leaned over and looked down. It was a straight drop into the water. It had to be at least a hundred-foot drop, from my estimate. Now I knew why no one came this way. There was nowhere to go.

Arms shaking, heart pounding I leaned over to see if there was a way to climb down. Shaking my head in disgust, I sat back on my heels. Even with ropes and a harness, there's no way I'd try climbing down that.

Now what? I looked behind me and held my breath, listening. I still heard no one. I looked around the edge of the drop off. If I took the time to look further for a way to climb down, it would give them more time to realize I was gone.

Leaning over again, I looked down. Could I jump? I was a good swimmer; I just wasn't sure I was brave enough to jump. A barrier could also be an unknown factor. If I could find the courage to jump, there was no guarantee I wouldn't hit a barrier on the way down, or in the water. I could literally be plunging to my death in so many ways.

"There's nowhere else to go this way. Head back and check in the bushes, she's hiding somewhere."

I lay flat on the ground. They knew I was missing. My heart was beating in my throat as I tried to keep my breathing quiet. I looked out over the water. It was quite a distance to the nearest land.

"Told them they needed to put trackers on them. I'm sick of wandering around here with the damn insects looking for women that think they can get off the island."

I nodded my head, I could do this. Had to do this. Getting up slowly, I stayed low and looked through the trees to see if my location was visible. I didn't see anyone. I straightened and backed up a few feet. Leaning over on my knees with shaking hands I swallowed the fear lodged in my throat.

"Fuck, I'm getting eaten alive here."

I leaned toward the edge and launched myself over the side, hoping I'd clear any rocks near the shore. I'd like to say the descent was long enough that I had time to look, but it was over in a flash. Icy water closed over me as I dropped into the depths.

The shock spurred me into kicking toward the top as quickly as I could. When my head broke the surface, I gulped in the fresh air. I'd done it! I was off the island. Bobbing around I turned to look in all directions. There were rocks sticking out, marked so boats would see them. I could rest on the other side of them so no one looking from the island would see me.

Treading water, I debated taking off my shoes, but decided when I made it to land I'd need them to put as much distance between me and these insane people. Kicking was hindered, but I started toward the rocks as fast as I could manage.

The water was much colder than I'd imagined it would be. I was already feeling my muscles start to cramp. Turning, I laid on my back for a moment to check the distance from the island. It wasn't as far as I'd hoped. I rested for a bit longer, hoping to catch my breath, while scanning along the shore to see if anyone was looking there yet. I didn't spot anyone.

Flipping back over, I pushed my body further. The shoes had to go, they felt like cement weights. I tried to keep my head above the surface to take them off. The laces were wet and wouldn't untie, so I bobbed up and down, sputtering for air several times, trying to free my feet.

I had to pause between shoes. I was wasting valuable energy doing this. Taking a deep breath, I sunk beneath the surface and fought to get the second shoe off.

Hands grabbed me, I gulped in water, trying to struggle out of their hold. Kicking out against them, I reached the surface and started swimming with all my strength. I was not going back.

I heard someone say something but wasn't about to stop and see. The sound of a boat registered, and I swam faster. My side was hurting, my legs felt like they were moving slower and slower. I went under again, and had to fight to not gasp for air while under the surface. Kicking, I managed to get my head above the surface. I didn't know how much longer I could do this.

A hand touched me again. I kicked out and connected with a body. I heard a man swear as I dropped below the water once more. He pulled me up and held me firmly with his arm wrapped around me. His grip was tight. He was swimming and dragging me. I fought, coughing and swallowing more water than air.

I held onto his arm, trying to rid my lungs of the liquid, gasping for air. He turned, and I found myself at the rock I'd been heading for. I clung to it, still trying to breathe, gathering the strength so I could get away. Large arms surrounded me, his body pressed me against the rough surface.

"I'm not here to hurt you." He said between breaths against my ear, "you're safe. We're here to get you to safety."

I turned to see a boat coming toward us. "Safe to where?" I coughed when water filled my mouth again as a wave hit the rock.

"Away from that island." He said calmly, his uneven breathing against my cheek.

I rested my face against the rock, drained, I couldn't swim any more.

"Arius, let me coast as close as I can." Another man called out.

I heard the motor of the boat stop.

"Thought she was going to out-swim you." A third male said.

He lifted his head away from me, "it was close." He huffed out a breath.

"I brought a blanket." It was a woman's voice.

I didn't know if this was another lie, or a scheme to get me back on the island. My body was numb, I was shaking from the exertion and had no more fight left.

I felt myself being pulled through the water and lifted up.

A woman's face was in front of mine. "I saw you. You are so brave." She nodded and wrapped something warm around me. "You're safe now."

That was the last thing I heard, just before I closed my eyes.

Chapter One

I opened my eyes, bolted upright, ready to run. I stumbled, then looked down. I was wrapped in a thick white robe.

"It's okay. You're safe."

I looked to see a tall man with long black hair and a towel wrapped around his neck, standing at the end of a large bed. He had his hands out to his side, showing they were empty.

"Where am I?" I looked around. The room was huge.

"You're` safe now." A small, red-headed woman came over and sat on the bed. "I'm Bethany."

I looked around, there were four more large men in the room and two women. The women were dressed in normal clothes, not grey jumpsuits. I looked down and lifted the edge of the robe.

"I tossed the coveralls you were wearing." A blonde woman told me. "Once you're warmed up, we'll find you something else to wear."

My legs were shaking. I watched as the man that had pulled me out of the water crossed his arms over his bare chest and looked at me. I should probably thank him. "Thank you." I said in a rough voice. My throat hurt, reminding me how much water I'd tried to breathe.

He inclined his head and walked over to stand with the other men.

"I'll be right back." Bethany said and walked out of the room quickly.

The door was left open.

I knew this was not the island obviously, or the women wouldn't be in here, dressed that way and free to leave. And there was no room that looked like *this* on that chunk of land filled with lunatics.

The males stood off to the side talking, I couldn't hear what they were saying, but every few seconds one of them would look at me. Except the one with the long black hair and towel wrapped around his neck, his eyes hadn't left me. Then again, he probably thought he'd jumped in to save an insane woman swimming in the bay.

The blonde motioned to the bed. "You're still shaking."

I hesitated for a moment, then decided to sit down on the edge of the bed. I turned so I could see everyone and pulled up my legs to tuck into the robe.

She sat on the end. "I'm Daxx. What's your name?"

I looked to the males, then back to her. They definitely weren't with the bunch from the island or they'd know my name. "Paisley," I said quietly, "Roan."

The men all turned to look at me. The one with the long blond hair cocked his head. "Did you say Roan?"

I nodded, not sure why that mattered.

"Troy?" Daxx turned to look at him.

He raised an eyebrow but said nothing. Giving the other men a brief glance, then he pulled out his phone.

I couldn't hear what he was saying, but the other men watched him. The two women in the room didn't seem to care what he said. I turned to look at the young one standing in the corner.

When she saw me look at her she smiled, "It's okay now." She nodded. "I'm so glad I saw you." She bit her lip then looked like she was focusing on the space above my head. Her eyes moved over my face, and she nodded again and sat down on the floor.

The petite redhead came back in carrying a tray. "I've brought you some tea, to try and take the chill off." She seemed concerned and sincere. With an understanding smile, she set it beside the bed and stood there. "I know you're probably very confused and scared right now, but it's going to be all right."

"Yes. We'll eventually get on that damn island and annihilate every one of those sick bastards." The blonde woman nodded abruptly then frowned. "Troy, she's wearing a red cuff."

Troy and the redheaded man came over.

I moved over on the bed to put more space between us. They stopped.

"It can't be ours…"

"It's not one of mine." The man that rescued me said. "But if they're illegally making those as well, then she must have some gift they don't want her using."

I looked at my wrist then covered my hand with it. Was that why I couldn't use my powers? "I can't get it off."

Bethany picked up a cup on the tray. "Try to sip this, your throat must hurt.

I took it and sniffed. It smelled good, so I took a small sip. The warm liquid felt good on my throat. "Thank you."

Troy stepped back. "I agree with Arius, if they were afraid of her…"

The small one that had been sitting in the corner jumped up. "She could use it against them. She could use it against us, but I don't think she will. There's good all around her." She nodded and sat back down.

The blond woman shrugged. "Crissy did see her and usually when she sees…"

"Where is she?" A man that looked identical to Troy, except with a goatee, came running in. He was barefoot, clad in dark jeans with a white dress shirt hanging open, his hair looking like he just climbed out of bed. He ran toward me then stopped at the end of the bed. Squinting his eyes, he studied me for a moment.

"Chase." A tall woman with black hair ran in the room. She stopped and huffed out a breath. "He ran all the way here." She held her hand over her chest and tried to catch her breath.

"I don't see it." Chase waved a hand erratically toward me. "No resemblance whatsoever." He snorted, "Which is a blessing for her, he's ugly as…" the hand waved some more, "just ugly." Moving to the side of the bed, he bent down and looked at me with a strange look on his face. "What-what is your name?"

Hesitating, I looked around, no one seemed concerned with this strung out man standing there. "Paisley Roan." I said slowly.

"Roan! Yes." He spun around and went toward his twin. "The fates wouldn't be so cruel as to bring her here and it *not* mean something." He nodded and then pointed to the woman in the corner, Crissy, I think someone called her. "She saw it. *She* saw it. So it must be…" Jolting, he paced away then paused and looked at the man with the towel around his neck. "Arius why are you standing there dripping wet?"

The serious grey eyes finally moved from me to look at this Chase man. With a jerk of his head he motioned to me. "I pulled her out of the bay. She jumped off the cliff to get off the island."

"Right." He rushed over and grabbed his face between two hands. "Bless you." When the grey eyes glared at him, Chase jerked his hands away then he spun and came back toward me. "Do you know your parents? Uncles? Aunts?"

"My parents died." I glanced around the room and all eyes were on him, not me.

"Oh." His face briefly showed sadness. "That's—I'm sorry." Jerking, he paced to the end of the bed. "When?"

Scowling at him, I pulled the large robe tighter around me. "When I was a baby. My grandmother raised me until she passed away." I looked at Bethany, hoping she'd offer some insight as to what was wrong with this man. She stood there with her eyes wide staring at him.

"Your grandmother." He moved quickly to the other side of the bed and leaned down. "What was her name?" He waved a hand at me, "other than gramma, or granny or whatever?"

"Melissa Roan." I said with hesitation.

"Roan! Yes." He straightened and crossed his arms over his chest. "Did you know your grandfather?"

I shook my head, hoping if I answered his strange questions he'd go away, and I could figure out how to get out of here. "He disappeared before I was born."

"Disappeared." He threw his hands up in the air and looked at his twin. "Vanished!"

"Chase…" Troy stepped toward him.

Chase waved it off then went toward him. "For two hundred and sixty years he's looked at me—us, like we were some sort of parasite." He turned and gave me a stern look. "King not bug!"

He laughed and went to the red headed man with the soft brown eyes— that were filled with shock right now.

"And now—*now* I have something to jam in his face that will knock him off his Elder-high-horse-never-stepped-out-of-line-in-his-perfect-life. Ha!" Pulling his phone out, he waved it around then spun back to me and shook it. "Now here *she* is in all her beautifully splendid existence-ness." He smiled at me. "His…great, great…I don't know." He turned and looked around at the others. "I need a mathematician." Tapping his screen, he continued to pace. "Michael. I need a genealogist and one of our historians." He paused. "Do we have a historian genealogist? I need one of those. *Now.*" He waved his hand around. "In the girls' room." With a sound that was close to a growl he looked around the room. "In recent months whenever one of us have referenced *the girls' room*, which room did we mean?" He shook his head. "The Huntress's room. No. Not Troy's!" He spun around and pointed to a door. "The one with the mall closet—just get here." Hanging up he turned around, looking very excited then turned again and ran out the door.

"Alona…" Troy looked at the tall woman with the black hair.

She had her hands over her mouth, her eyes huge and was shaking her head. Dropping her hands, she backed toward the door. "I'm sorry." She looked at me. "So, so sorry." Her eyes moved over everyone standing there gaping at her. "I'm afraid this is my fault." She looked back to me. "I'm an empath—he's an emotion feeder," she shook her head, her face blushing, "we were experimenting—he's a little excitable right now." She grinned, "Sorry." Turning she ran into another large man with short black hair and a scar down his face.

"Alona, what the hell is wrong with Chase?" He dropped his hands from her arms. "He orders me here and now he's running down the hall with his arms in the air doing a victory lap?"

She laughed.

"Where is my queen?" Chase's voice boomed from the hallway.

Laughing the Alona woman ran out after him.

The dark-haired man looked around. "What did I miss?"

Troy shook his head and looked at me. "I apologize for that—whatever *that* was." He smirked, "even though I'm going to play it on a loop in my head, over and over, for the rest of my life." He turned his hand slowly beside his head.

The less serious looking redhead hugged Bethany. "I don't know what he had, but I'll take two." He laughed, and she smacked him. "Sorry, but that was funnier than the time we tried…"

Troy cleared his throat.

"Never mind." He finished.

"You men are all ridiculous." The blonde woman said. "As if Paisley isn't traumatized enough after what she's been through." She pointed to the door. "Out. All of you! Out."

She looked at the one with the towel around his neck. "You too Arius, before your eyes get stuck in that position from staring at her."

The men gave me a look, then started for the door. Definitely not associated with those people on the island.

"We'll talk shortly." Troy smiled at me. "Rest and warm up."

Arius watched the others leave, then came over and stood at the end of the bed. "I will be back to take the cuff off." His haunting grey eyes moved over my face for a moment, then he held my look with a harsh gaze. "As long as you assure me my family is safe with your abilities free."

I nodded. "They're safe. I never use it to harm anyone, but as a short cut or to defend myself, yes. Never to hurt anyone."

He nodded slowly, the harsh look still on his face. "I'll return shortly." He gave Daxx an abrupt tilt of his chin and turned and walked out, closing the door behind him.

I sat there, the silence heavy in the room.

"Do you need anything?" Bethany sat on the end of the bed.

I shook my head. "The tea is fine, thank you."

"I can get cookies." The one in the corner said.

Daxx grinned. "I'm sure she's a little too shell-shocked right now for cookies, Crissy."

Crissy gave her an odd look. "Cookies help everything."

I smiled at that. She wasn't wrong. "My throat is sore. I think I breathed more water than air."

"How did you know that side of the island wasn't warded?" Daxx asked.

I looked to her. "I didn't." I took another sip. "For the last week I've been checking in all directions, that was the only one left." I set the cup down. "Did you say warded?"

She nodded. "They have mages and witches that have made barriers that act as an alarm, all around the island."

"I don't know about mages and witches…"

"They have purple eyes. I don't like purple eyes." Crissy said.

I'd seen a few like that. I still didn't understand the various eye colors, but I knew enough to know they weren't average people. "Okay. Then yes, they have those there. But these barriers actually stop anyone from crossing, or at least any of us girls."

"You're taking this very well." Bethany said. "When I started to discover things, I wasn't nearly as calm."

I blew out a breath and looked at them. They knew what the red thing on my arm was, and mages and witches... I looked at my hands. "I'm not exactly an average girl, so just knowing that there are others out there that aren't—makes me feel less like a freak."

Bethany nodded and held up her palm. There were sparks and streaks that looked like flames around it. She gave me a slight shrug.

I smiled.

"What is your ability?" Daxx asked quietly.

That was a question that had never quite worked out for me when I answered it. "I manipulate time." I shook my head. "Not like time travel, I can stop people, objects, slow time around me."

"The frozen clocks!" Crissy jumped up. She looked so excited. "You're the frozen clocks."

I looked from her to the other two.

Daxx smiled. "Crissy has visions. That's how we knew you were in trouble."

I gave Crissy a wide-eyed look. "I thought you meant you saw me in the water."

Crissy nodded. "I did," she tapped her head, "here, and then when we were in the boat."

I sat back and wrapped my arms around my waist. "I would have drowned if you hadn't." I shook my head. "I knew it was a long shot, but I was out of options." I looked to Bethany then Daxx again. "A few of the girls were taken off the island and didn't come back. I didn't want to wait and see if I was next and if where we'd be taken was worse."

The soft look she'd had hardened, and in it's place was anger.

"We've been trying to find a way on the island." She shook her head. "With no luck."

"You know what's going on there? Those people on it?"

She shook her head again. "We have an idea and have been trying to stop them." She sighed. "It's a lot to explain." She waved her hand around. "All of this, and what's going on."

Bethany held out a phone. "First, do you have anyone to call and let them know you're all right?"

I looked at the phone. "No. There's no one." The expressions on their faces told me they understood all too well. "I don't even know if I still have a place to live."

Daxx stood up. "We'll worry about that after you rest."

I nodded. "Is there a bathroom?"

She motioned to the door.

I stood up and walked slowly toward it. The muscles in my legs were still shaky. I went in a started to close the door.

"Paisley."

I looked to Daxx.

"There's no windows in there to escape through, and even if there was, you're not where you think you are."

I paused and gave her a confused look.

She smirked. "I just know the look of someone about to run."

I didn't say anything, just turned and closed the door.

The bathroom was larger than my room. I didn't know where I was, but everything here was expensive and matched. I went over and looked at the tub. It was huge, like a baby hippo could hang out kind of huge.

Shaking my head, I paced a moment, then stopped and stared at myself in the mirror. I had definitely looked better. My short dark hair that usually fell in place was standing straight on end. Showering with strange men wandering around had been a real concern for me. I looked like a mad scientist. Stepping closer, I touched the bags under my eyes. I hadn't slept much in the past few weeks.

Turning away from that sad image, I spotted the shower stall in the corner. Did I want more water? I touched my dirty hair.

Chapter Two

I stood in the closet with the women. For whatever reason, this closet could have been several stores filled with every size, style and accessory possible. I'd discovered, while showering, that during my slide I'd taken several layers of skin off my hip and leg, so the fact that this closet had loose-fitting workout clothes in my size was a plus.

Daxx held up a pair of black sweatpants. "These look about right."

Taking them, I held them against my waist, they'd work. I pulled them on under the robe.

Pulling a top off the hanger, I glanced at her. "The woman with the crazy man, she said she was an empath?"

Daxx laughed and glanced to the other two women, who were also grinning. "Chase is going to *love* knowing he met you in that state." She sobered, "but, yes she's an empath."

I turned the top around and held it up against me. How I was dressed was the last thing on my mind at this point. I just wanted clothes on before the men came back. After that, I needed to figure out how to get home. I didn't even know where I was. "I always wondered if there was such a thing." I shrugged, "with what I can do, I suspected the stories about others were true,"

Turning, I dropped the robe and pulled the shirt over my head. Pulling it down, I turned to see the not just the women standing there, but Arius in the doorway of the closet.

His brows were furrowed. "Did I put that bruise on you?"

I'd seen it when I showered, the mark from his arm wrapped from my collarbone to under my arm on the other side. I shrugged. "It's no big deal. If that bruise wasn't there, I would have drowned." I touched my forehead. "This one is from bouncing off one of their invisible walls a few days ago." I shrugged, "thought I'd found a spot without one." I touched my cheek, "this is from branches."

His grey eyes flicked to mine briefly, he didn't look placated by that reasoning. He looked at Daxx. "Have you discussed anything with her?"

She shook her head. "Not really."

Closing the distance between us in a few strides, he stopped in front of me and leaned down. "I can take the bruising away."

I gave him a surprised look. "You have a healing touch?" I'd never heard of something like that, but wouldn't that be cool.

He shook his head. "No, blood."

My eyebrows shot up. "That's a little too vampy for me, but thanks I can live with a bit of bruising considering it saved my life."

He made a sound of displeasure in the back of his throat and rested his hand on my shoulder as he leaned down and looked at me.

I waited for the words, something like 'please let me take them away', but he said nothing. His eyes were haunting, but nice to see the pale grey this close. I felt a pressure in my head, a new weird feeling I'd never felt before. I frowned, "are you trying to mess in my head?" I stepped back so his hand dropped. "That's kind of an invasion of privacy, you know," I nodded, "please don't."

Straightening he gave me an odd look. "You felt that?"

"Yes."

Daxx came over. "Has that ever happened before?"

Arius shook his head, "not that I know of." He shrugged, "Troy would know, or someone with a similar ability—" he looked down at me. "What is yours?"

I held up my arm with the red cuff on. "Take this off and I'll show you. It's not dangerous."

His gaze moved over my face slowly, emotion moving through his eyes, but he didn't say anything. I held his gaze, so he could see I wasn't scamming him. Looking down, he lifted my arm and pulled something out of his pocket. It looked like a barcode scanner. "This one may not work on an illegal device. If not, I have some older models we can try."

I nodded and held my breath as he turned my arm over and held it against the cuff. I wondered how he knew where to hold it.

"Your pulse is what closes it." He said then pushed the button.

It zapped my wrist. I jumped but didn't pull my arm away.

Moving the scanner, he pulled the cuff off my arm. He looked at it, turning it slowly. "How would they know how to make these? This is almost flawless."

"We need to figure that out." Daxx said not sounding happy.

I rubbed my arm where it had rested since I woke up on the island. "Thank you." I looked around for something to use. I wanted to show them that I wasn't dangerous. I remembered the cup from my tea. "Come out here." I walked out of the closet and went over to the bed. Picking up the cup, I drank the last sip as I walked to the middle of the room. I turned to look at them. Tossing the cup into the air, I held my hand up toward it. It stopped falling halfway to the floor, and was suspended in the air. I kept my eyes on it. "I didn't stop the cup. I manipulated the time around it. It's hard to explain."

"Cool is what it is." Daxx said.

"Where is she?" A voice boomed from the door.

I jolted and a second later heard the cup break.

"Don't move." Arius came over and picked me up by the waist and set me on the bed, so I wouldn't step on the shattered china. He stood against the end of the bed, almost blocking me.

I looked to the door to see a man standing in it—he looked very similar to Arius.

He started toward me in long strides. "You were on the island?"

I continued to kneel on the bed, wondering if I should stand to even the field with the size of these people.

Arius straightened, took a pose that a man getting ready to fight would.

Two others came through the door. "Dad." The blond said, reaching the angry looking man and grabbing his arm. "They're going to ask her. Calm down."

Troy and the tall, cold-looking redhead came through the door next.

"Emil." Troy didn't sound pleased. "She's barely regained consciousness."

The man, Emil, shook his head. "If she got off the island, then we know how to get on."

Arius shook his head, his hands on his hips. "She dove off a cliff, barely missing the rocks at the bottom."

Eyes wide I looked at him. I hadn't seen rocks.

"Did you see this woman on the island?" He pulled out his phone and tapped the screen a few times. Coming over he gave Arius an odd look, then held his hand out toward me.

I took the phone and looked at the screen. My heart beat harder. I nodded. "Yes, she's there." I straightened my arm, giving him back the phone. "She's only been there a few days. She's treated better than most of the girls though." I looked to Daxx, then Bethany. "I don't know why some are treated better than others."

Daxx sighed. "I think I do." She turned to Troy. "I'm willing to bet those *with* changing eyes are prized more than the others."

"What does that mean, exactly?" I climbed off the bed.

Arius put his hand out, so I wouldn't move toward the glass. With his boot, he pushed a piece further from me.

I turned and looked at Crissy, "if the mages and witches' eyes are purple, what is the significance of the others?"

"She's human." Emil said looking at Arius.

Arius nodded. "She is."

"She doesn't have to wear a device?" The tall blond next to Emil asked. "So, she was born on this side?"

I frowned. "What device? He just took the red bracelet thing off."

He held up his arm, a small watch-like thing was on his wrist. "One of these."

I shrugged slowly. "No idea what that is." I looked to Arius. "This side, where?"

He rubbed the back of his neck and looked over at Troy.

Troy sighed. "I think we should go to the dining room and get comfortable." He offered a small smile. "We have much to explain."

I looked down at my feet. "Can I get some shoes first?" The sooner I got to see where I was, the faster I could figure out how to leave.

I stared down the table, my mind was trying to process everything they'd just told me. So many eyes and they were all on me. The scary redhead, Victor sat at the opposite end of a huge table with at least twenty chairs. Currently all were filled but six. It had been decided that they would let the crazy man and his wife Alona, sleep. I wasn't sure why he'd been so super-charged, and what it had to do with her being an empath, but not having that distraction was good. I was trying not to have a meltdown at the moment.

Emil and his two sons seemed interested in the explanations I was getting. Unlike me. they accepted everything that was said.

I held up my hands to the thirteen people looking at me. "I just need a minute." I stood up and looked at the wall lined with portraits. Putting my hands on my hips, I lifted my chin and looked at the ceiling. Blowing out a breath, I tried to stop the information from swirling in my head. "Where to start?" I whispered more to myself than anyone in the room.

Dropping my hands, I glanced back down the table. "So all of you, except," I pointed to Emil's two sons, "are brothers. Including the crazy twin." I glanced to Troy, his lips quirked but he still nodded. "And you are *both* kings?" I looked to a few of the others. "Is that wise? I mean I know it's not my place, but a leader with…" I paused, "issues. Have you tested him for ADHD, because you may want to think about it."

There were several snickers and snorts of amusement around the table.

Emil looked at them. "I feel like I've missed something."

"I will fill you in later, brother." Rafael said.

At least I think it was Rafael. I went over everything flying around in my head, trying to grasp at just one thing that I could ask. "This," I motioned in the air, "other side is actually another realm? And no one in *my* realm knows it exists." I shook my head, "Clearly the government doesn't know, or the whole planet would be aware and taxed for existing." I paced away from the table then turned to see all were nodding. I paused, noting that Arius' gaze never left me. His family looked to one another often, but he was like a breathing statue. Unmoving.

Turning on my heel, I looked to Victor. "You'll understand if I'm struggling with that."

He inclined his head. "It is quite a lot to grasp at once."

I nodded. "Quite."

I put my hands over my mouth and moved just my eyes to study them. Checking and waiting, hoping one of them would crack a smile and tell me this was an elaborate joke of epic proportion. Then I remembered waking up on the island. I dropped my hands. "I'll come back to the realm issue in a minute." I glanced around then went back to Victor. "That island—of insane people you are fighting and trying to stop? Because they are, aside from kidnapping women, trying to bring down some barrier—between realms which is very bad for both sides."

Their relaxed expressions changed to hard looks, some lethal and cold, so that conclusion was, at least, very true.

I tilted my head and huffed out another breath, still trying not to freak out. "I am all for stopping them after the last few weeks of complete insanity." Pausing, I rubbed my hand over my temple. "So, aside from people with other abilities," I pointed at no one in particular, "and I must say this is a huge selling point for me in this entire scenario— because as you know I have a little something extra myself…"

"Oh? Like?" Michael asked.

Daxx grinned. "Watch this." She grabbed a glass off the table and glanced at me.

I nodded.

Pushing her chair back, she tossed it in the air.

Lifting my hand, I made it stop before it crashed down.

"She manipulates the time around it, not the object, Victor. Isn't that fascinating?" Crissy sounded very excited.

"Indeed, heart, it is." He replied.

"Someone catch it." I dropped my hand and looked down.

Troy caught it before it hit the table.

"Can you do that to something living, or only to inanimate objects?" Quinton asked.

"Both. If I can see it, I can stop the time around it." I shrugged. "There's a distance and size restriction, but for the most part I can manipulate time for just about anything."

"I've never met a Chronos before." Leone said. "I've read about them…"

"Since when do you read?" Rafael smirked.

"Not now, brothers. Paisley wasn't finished speaking." Arius told them with barely a glance to them.

I took a deep breath, finding my place again. "Right, then aside from not being the only freak for once—the changing eye colors feels about the same as when I tell someone I can manipulate time." I held up my hand. "So, purple is magic for your people." A few nodded. "And Chase, the crazy king his are yellow which signifies he *feeds* on emotions. I can't even think of the how of that right now."

More heads were nodding. That did provide more clarity to what Alona had said, before chasing after her husband down the hall. "Right. Red eyes are essence *feeders*?"

More nods.

"Okay, so that feels like a soul sucker. A person's essence is their actual *being*, and that goes soul deep to me."

"From a philosophical point, one could say that." Victor nodded slowly, "but the essence we're referring to could be more accurately described as the energy or vitality in a person's veins."

"But not blood?" I really needed clarification. I put my hands on my hips and stared at him.

"No. Not blood. It's carried through the body in their blood, but we do not feed on that blood." Victor held my look.

I nodded slowly. Then shook my head. "I'm still stuck."

"It's quite complex to accept and rationalize." He sighed. "Of course, with the vast number of vampire and horror movies in the last millennium, minds are programmed to accept a certain image, making the reality even stranger."

I nodded. "It's very hard to erase and rewrite the things etched in my head."

"I would think it would be."

"I think I'll just shelve the eyes and feeding topic for the time being and move on." No one said a word, so I decided to proceed. "You speak of millennia or," I point to Troy, "your rambling twin said for two hundred and sixty years—

that, that ah," I motioned around the room, "you clearly live a lot longer to speak of time as if it is infinite."

"Not infinite." Troy said quietly.

"Okay, so ballpark number here. Who is the oldest in the room?" I crossed my arms and looked around, none of them looked that old. All eyes turned to Victor. I raised my eyebrows.

"I'm five hundred." He said.

"Five hundred? Five. Zero. Zero. Five hundred?"

He nodded.

I slowly looked around the table. "You're all in your— *hundreds?*"

Bethany shook her head. "It's hard to grasp. When I found out how old Leone was, it was," she looked at him, "shocking."

I huffed out a breath. "Yeah. So, you're…what?"

"In my twenties." She answered quietly.

I puffed out my cheeks, trying to sort that. "Well, that takes the May-December thing to a whole new level, doesn't it?"

She smirked and nodded.

"Paisley?"

I turned to Emil.

"I realize this is a lot to take in. I recently had to sort through it myself, am still sorting through it, but if you could explain how you got on that island…" He gave me a strained look. "My daughter, I'd like to figure out how to get her off."

I put my hands over my face for a moment. Then dropped them. "I don't know. I woke up on it, with that red cuff around my wrist."

Victor looked to Troy. "If they knew she had an ability…"

Troy nodded, "they've been observing her."

"What do you mean you woke up on it?" Arius asked, his voice low.

I waved my hand around. "I feel like a complete idiot. For not seeing the signs that he was some sort of—" I sighed,

"I don't even know." I sighed. "I thought," I shook my head, still mad at myself over it. "A guy—I thought was into me and loved music as much as I do," I motioned in the air, "I thought I was going to a private, invite-only performance." Frowning, I stared at the floor, "he was totally sweet and didn't appear insane," I shook my head and looked up to Daxx, "until I woke up and he had done a complete three sixty, and was nothing like the guy I'd met at the coffee shop."

"He drugged you?" Arius asked.

I shrugged, "I guess. I don't know when or how. One minute I'm walking to the pier, the next I'm waking up on that island." I scowled. "I've had no music since. I don't know where my phone or tablet are, but I've been losing my mind with no music."

Arius made a sound in the back of his throat that sounded like a growl, then turned to look at Michael. "Are all the photos processed and on file now?"

Michael nodded.

Arius pulled out his phone and tapped out a text message.

"You think we may already have him?" Daxx asked.

Putting his phone down, Arius took a deep breath and exhaled slowly. "We can only hope."

I looked from one to the other. "Wait, you-you have some of these people?"

Daxx nodded. "Yeah in our prison."

Relief flooded me when I saw they really were trying to stop them. "I just have one more—," I snorted, "okay I have hundreds of questions, but I there's just one I need to know," I looked at Emil, "and then I'll draw a map of the island if it will help. I was all over the inside of the building we were in, except on the top floor."

"What's the question?" Troy asked.

"Your crazy brother, what is his thing with my name?" I shrugged, "he was quite..."

Troy nodded. "Yes, he was." He glanced at Victor slowly, then back to me. "One of our elder's surname is Roan."

My eyebrows went up. "So you think we're related?"

He shrugged. "It could be coincidental." Glancing to the others, his gaze came back to me. "But recently, we've discovered nothing has been placed in our paths that is a coincidence."

I opened my mouth, then closed it and gave him a stupefied look. "I might—I could have relatives?" I blew out a breath, "I don't even have friends. It's just been me for ten years."

"Warden, here is…"

I jolted and spun around and threw my hand up. A large man carrying a tablet stood frozen on the spot. I lowered my hand and he took a step then paused and frowned. "And *that* is why I don't have friends." I said quietly.

Arius appeared beside me and held out his hand to the man. "Thank you." He took the tablet.

The man was still frowning but turned and left.

"Sorry." I said quietly. "I'm a little bit jumpy."

"With good reason." He motioned to the chair. "Please, sit. I'd like you to scroll through some photos, maybe identify the man responsible for you being on the island."

I sat down and watched as he set the tablet in front of me. I leaned forward and then stopped and looked up at him. "Do you think, at some point I can go see if I still have a place to live? I just rent a room, but I'd like…"

He leaned one hand on the table, hovering over me. "We'll go check on that once you've eaten and aren't so shaky."

I lifted an eyebrow at him. "The shaky is more from the information overload than diving off the cliff."

Amusement briefly flashed through his eyes.

"Oh, good you're still here." The sweet redheaded lady came into the room. She held up a small jar. "It's ointment, love, for your scrapes." She set it on the table beside me. "Just to help them along." She gave me an understanding smile. "Until you're able to grasp and accept blood healing." With a quick nod, she turned and walked out just as quietly as she'd entered.

"Thank you." I wasn't sure how she knew, but had noticed when I sat down that the scabs on my hips pinched with the movement.

"You're injured?" Arius asked frowning down at me.

I shrugged. "It's nothing, just slid across the ground a few feet when I was running."

He continued to look down at me for a moment, his jaw clenching. Giving me an abrupt nod, he motioned to the tablet. "Please." He turned and walked to the other end of the table and leaned down to speak to Troy.

I looked down at the tablet and tapped the screen to start scrolling through the photos. I don't know what I expected to see, but the first few photos were very angry, scary men. I looked up to see most eyes were on me.

There were so many faces, I focused on each one seeing if there was anything familiar about them, drowning out the conversation around me. More questions were forming as I looked, like how had people with glowing eyes not been noticed in all of time? They walked among us and no one knew it. I looked up around those in this room, they seemed normal. Maybe a bit larger than average, but still. Glancing back down, I tapped to go back to the previous photo. His eyes were yellow, but his face looked familiar. I looked up to Daxx.

"You see him?" She stood up.

All conversation in the room stopped. All eyes turned to me.

I looked at it again. "I'm not totally sure. His eyes were not yellow…"

"Shit." Arius said venomously.

"That would explain it." Quinton nodded, looking around.

I looked to him. "Explain what?"

"If he feeds off emotions, how he was able to know what you were feeling and adjust his behavior accordingly." Victor said while watching Arius.

I opened my mouth to deny, then realized they were right. "He always said—did the right things." I sat back feeling completely defeated. "I'm such an idiot."

"It's not your fault." Arius came down the table in a few long strides and picked up the tablet. He studied it, a nerve in his jaw clenching as he did. "Come down to the cells." He turned and walked out of the room.

I watched him leave and then turned slowly to look at Daxx. "The what?"

Everyone stood up.

She motioned to the door. "I guess he wants you to be sure that's him." She gave Troy an odd look as she came towards me.

"Oh." I stood up. "Okay."

Chapter Three

I followed the others through carpeted tunnels, down sloped floors and around several turns. The whole time, I was thinking it was a good thing I didn't bolt like I had intended when I woke up, or I'd still be running up and down these halls trying to find a way out.

Several of the others went into a room with a wall of screens, I went with Victor, Troy, Michael and Daxx to weave through walls of plexiglass, or I think they were. The cells were a giant rat's maze.

We stood in a large room. Arius came toward us down a narrow hall, he turned and then disappeared from our sight.

"He's in a mood." Daxx said quietly.

Victor inclined his head and looked at the floor. "There's only one thing I know of that can set off one of my brothers in *that* way."

The others all turned to give him a surprised look.

"Really?" Daxx looked to him, then to me, and then back to Victor.

Troy appraised me for a moment. "The fact that she doesn't need a device…"

The wall to my right suddenly became see-through. I stepped back and watched Arius shove a man into a small room on the other side. He stood there looking angry for a moment, then walked out. The door he went through closed and then he was standing in the space with us.

"Is that him?" He asked in a low tone.

I turned, eyes wide and hesitantly glanced through the wall.

"He can't see you." Victor assured me.

Knowing that, I stepped closer. Hugging my waist with my arms I studied the man pacing around in the small space he'd been tossed into. He was wearing a blue cuff, similar to the red one I'd had. "What does blue mean?" I asked without taking my eyes off him.

"Not to get too close." Daxx explained, standing beside me. "Sometimes it's because of an ability, sometimes their feeding category. Yours was a magic jammer, at least that's what I call them."

I took a ragged breath. "And his means?"

"Feeding." Arius said with disgust. "He has no abilities."

I snorted, "He excels at acting and lying. That's an ability." Taking a deep breath, I turned and watched him more. "I can't be sure, he's not standing still long enough to..."

Arius made a noise of exasperation and stomped out. He appeared in the cell with the man. I don't know what he said, but his mouth moved. The guy stopped and looked at him. With a scowl on his face, Arius went over to him and grabbed him by the back of the neck and turned him, holding him inches from the wall I was looking through.

"Well." Daxx said under her breath.

It took me a moment to look away from the angry man, whose grey eyes were locked on the wall. I knew he couldn't see me, but it was like he could. Dragging my gaze from him, I studied the man he held and then nodded. "It is him."

Victor reached over and touched a panel beside him. "Arius." He said.

With a jerk of his arm, Arius shoved the man, so he smacked up against the wall face-first. He left and came back in the room with us. His eyes were locked on me as he entered.

I nodded. "It's Martin, it's him." I paused for a second, wondering if that was even his real name.

"I'll go take a look at what's in his head." Troy said and went to move past Arius.

Arius held up his hand. "In a moment."

Troy gave him an odd look and then glanced to Victor, who shrugged.

Arius came over, leaving mere inches between us, he leaned closer, his pale eyes locked on mine. "Did he touch you?" His tone was so quiet I barely heard him. "Paisley, did he *touch* you?"

I blinked and then shook my head. "He scared me when I woke up, but, no, he never really made any advances, just lied his ass off to get close to me." I hugged my waist, watching the emotions going through his eyes.

Straightening, he spun on his heel and left again.

Before I could ask, he was in the cell with the Martin again. Arius said something and closed the distance between them in one long stride. I don't know what the guy answered but whatever it was, Arius wasn't happy with the response. His eyes went red and he picked him up by the throat, whipping his feet right off the floor as he slammed his back against the wall. Martin struggled against the hand gripping his neck. I was momentarily stunned by the fact that Arius' eyes were red, and without any apparent effort could hold the weight off the ground as Martin wasn't a tiny man.

Reality came rushing through the awe. "Please go and stop him." I looked up to Victor.

He glanced down at me, then nodded to Troy. They both left and were in the room with Arius. Victor grabbed Arius as Troy pried his hand from Martin's neck. I couldn't hear what they were saying.

"Usually Arius is the quiet, calm one." Daxx said sounding shell shocked.

Someone chuckled. "Not when he's in here, kitten, this is *his* domain."

I turned and gave a wide-eyed look to the crazy twin, as he stood behind us, arms crossed over his chest.

"What has Arius so riled?" He asked, not taking his eyes off the commotion in the cell. He sighed and walked out.

I turned to see him enter the cell as well. He leaned against the open door and said something. His brothers stopped and looked at him.

"I'd turn the speaker on, but I have no idea how." Daxx said softly. She glanced to Michael who gave a quick shake of his head and looked at me.

"I'm sure there's nothing pleasant being said." He said.

I turned to stare at Chase. He stood still and seemed bored with the whole thing, nothing like the lunatic that I'd met earlier.

Arius threw his hands up and backed away from Martin. He motioned to Troy, who nodded. Chase, Arius and Victor left the cell. Arius stomped by where we stood and kept going. I watched until he turned and vanished in the clear tunnels.

"I'll go make sure he doesn't kill someone." Michael jogged after him.

I watched Victor glance to Troy, then in the direction Arius had gone in.

Chase leaned against the entrance, his hands tucked in his pockets. "I haven't had nearly enough sleep or coffee to apologize with my usual flare," he motioned a hand toward me, "but I deeply regret our first meeting earlier."

He was so not like the man she'd met earlier. "We all have moments." I said with a slight shrug.

He laughed, "It was a moment all right. Naughty mate of mine." He glanced to Victor, "while I ingest copious amounts of caffeine, perhaps someone could fill in the details of what I've missed." He motioned in the direction Arius had gone. "And what is going on with the pretty one."

Daxx turned from the cell Troy was in and nodded. "We should get Paisley something to eat anyway. At some point all this is going to sink in and a full stomach will help her pace while trying to sort it out."

Victor nodded, glancing away from Troy. "I'll stay and wait for Troy." He looked to me briefly, "or stop Arius from choking him."

Daxx hadn't been kidding. I was pacing around the large room I'd awakened in earlier. The others had gone to have a nap, although I had no idea what time of day or night it was, sleep was a long way off for me. I'd been brought back to this room, even been allowed to lock the door. I stopped and stood in the middle of the room. This was a far cry from the room I rented. The bathroom alone was twice the size of my room.

Mentally recapping time. I was in another realm. I shrugged, that was cool, in a never-dreamt-possible sort of way. Huffing out a breath I walked toward the amazing closet—that I was told to pick whatever I wanted from… In another realm of good people, as opposed to those controlling the island. Daxx referred them as team bad, I had other descriptions for them, but hers seemed more polite. So the good people… were they even people?

I shook my head, I'd come back to that. The good ones from this *realm* were working to stop *team bad*. I could live with that. I'd even help if I was able. The idea of me, literally stopping those jerks in their tracks so they could be tossed off the island, held a great appeal to me.

Taking a deep breath, I turned and walked in the other direction. The good people in this other realm were old, very old and their eyes changed colors because they fed on—more than food. I stopped, put my hands on my hips and stared at the carpet.

Yeah, this was so far from mental digestion, it wasn't funny. Music. I needed music to process. I'd searched the whole room for a radio, but there wasn't anything. Music was my—everything. When I was happy, mad, when moments were too heavy, or I needed an escape—music was the answer. This was definitely in the too heavy, bordering on crushing me flat category. It had been the longest two weeks of my life without my music. The island had been so silent that a few times I was tempted to run around screaming, just to have some sort of sound.

Sighing, I turned back toward the bed, then stopped and looked at it. The bed may, in fact, be bigger than my entire room in *my realm*. Groaning, I walked toward it, now I was back to step one all over again.

A knock on the door had me jumping so high, I probably looked like a startled cat. Going over, I unlocked it and opened it enough to peek out.

Arius stood there, his face completely void of expression. He held up a phone then held out his other hand.

Wireless earbuds. I gasped and flung the door open and took them. He continued to hold the phone out, so I took that too.

"Bethany and Rafael loaded plenty of music onto it. They didn't know what your preference was."

More excited than a child on Christmas morning, I opened the music app and started scrolling. "I like all kinds." I recognized many songs. "Oh, this is great." I was nodding.

"Bethany said wires were annoying, so she got you earbuds."

I opened my hand and looked at them. "They probably cost more than a weeks' rent." I mumbled. "I don't have any money, but…"

He shook his head, "We don't expect you to reimburse us."

"Oh." I looked at the phone again. "Thank you." I waved my hand around, "I've been losing my mind in the silence. Thoughts in my head are often at full volume."

Tucking his hands in his pockets, he leaned against the doorframe. "I can imagine it's a lot to take in."

I nodded. "It is, but at the same time, it's not."

His eyes searched mine as I spoke.

"Some of it just clicks, like I should have known all along." I motioned for him to come in, finally realizing he wouldn't unless asked. Despite the rage in the cells, he didn't feel like he was a threat. I smirked at the thought as he walked by, because I was such a good judge of character that I'd let some jerk lure me to be held as a prisoner on an island.

I left the door open and went toward the couch. "If you go all red-eyed rager on me, I swear I'll stop you in your tracks and leave you there until I'm too exhausted to hold my hand up any longer." I warned him, only half joking.

He inclined his head. "Fair enough, warning received."

This man was far calmer than the one that dangled Martin by his throat. "You kind of freaked me out earlier." I sat on the couch, pulling my legs up to tuck under me.

He stood there for a moment, his grey eyes moving over me, then sat in one of the big chairs across from me. "I'm sorry about that." His jaw clenched. "It wasn't my intention." He motioned to me, "the idea of an innocent, one not even aware of our world being held against their will," his large shoulders shrugged slightly, "it upsets me."

I snorted, "Yeah it upset me too." I sat there looking at him, trying to see how old he was. With his long black hair, not so much as a single grey showing, no wrinkles—I had no idea. "So, how old are you?"

"Two hundred and fifty," he smirked, "well almost fifty-one if we're counting days."

"That could get exhausting, counting days." I studied his face for a second. "You don't look at day over twenty-nine, if that helps."

His mouth quirked again. "You'd be surprised how hard it is to look old around here."

I laughed. "Yeah, that's a problem most can relate to." I rolled my eyes. "Aside from the whole other realm thing, the eyes and odd diets, the age thing is right up there on the list of the hardest to grasp things."

He made a motion with his hand. "If you have any questions, I don't mind answering them."

I opened my mouth then closed it and thought for a moment. "Honestly, there's about a hundred that are all knotted in a big mess," I tapped my head, "up here right now." I shifted, so the cloth wasn't rubbing against my hip. "Earlier when you offered," I swallow, wondering how to word it, "blood," I said slowly, "for the bruises…"

He nodded.

"I honestly thought, vampire."

Arius smiled, a real smile, changing the whole appearance of his dark, brooding normal resting face. "That's a common misconception."

"No doubt." I fidgeted with the phone in my hand. "So how do you guys do that? I mean emotions, essence," I blew out an exaggerated breath, "because I'm telling you, I've imagined some pretty freaky methods."

He clasped his hands in his lap, looking regal. "I'm afraid explaining would only fuel your vampire theory."

Raising one eyebrow I tilted my head. "Answers like that only make me want to know more, but not, all at the same time."

"If you wish to know I will tell you," he held up a hand, "if you promise not to run away screaming."

I frowned, "had that reaction often?"

He nodded. "More often then we'd wish it."

I looked down at the phone in my hand, debating if I really needed to know. How bad could it be? I sat back, my eyes connected with his. "Okay. Go for it." I nodded, more to myself then him.

"Very well." He looked down and didn't move, just sat there with his hands clasped in his lap.

I guess he had to think of the best way to word it. When he looked back at me his eyes were glowing red, like they had been in the cells. I swallowed and made myself keep looking at them. "That's going to take some getting used to."

He tilted his head but didn't speak.

"Are you breaking me in gradually here?"

He grinned, "Something like that."

I almost dropped the phone. Leaning forward on the couch I looked at his mouth, he even opened it slowly, so I could see the fangs. Fangs. Pointed, scary-ass fangs. In his mouth. "Yeah, so," I swallowed nervously, "that might make someone think vampire." He closed his mouth while I was still looking at it. When I looked back to his eyes they were grey again.

"You didn't jump up or scream." He smirked.

I nodded in slow motion. "Yeah, I think stunned best describes my current state." I looked at his mouth again. "Could be a delayed freak-out, not sure right now." Sitting back, I hugged my knees to my chest. "So, fangs." He nodded. "I'm guessing there is biting involved."

"For essence feeders, yes." He was so calm, his voice quiet.

"No fangs for the others?"

He shook his head.

His lack of emotion and movement was starting to get to me a bit. "You know if you blinked or moved more often, that would help discredit the vamp thing." I nodded. "Okay, so, fangs." I looked at his mouth again. "You just, what, bite someone to get essence?"

He inhaled deeply, his large chest rising. "There's more to it than just biting, but for the sake of an easier explanation we'll go with that."

"As the one without fangs, all I'm saying is ouch."

Arius smiled. "We can make it not painful, if we chose to."

I frowned, "is that right?"

He nodded. "It is."

"Okay." I looked down at the floor briefly. "We'll just file that for later discussions."

"If you wish."

We sat there for a few moments, just looking at each other. I don't know what he was trying to see, but I knew I was trying to see if he looked like something other than a large, quite good-looking man. "Today when I refused the blood *thing*, what were you trying to do in my head?"

He cleared his throat, "persuade you otherwise."

I raised an eyebrow at him, "and you were hoping to do that how?"

He actually moved and leaned forward, resting his elbows on his knees and looking at me. "I have an ability. I can touch someone and look into their eyes and *suggest* they do what I wish."

I opened my mouth, then closed it when I realized he was serious. "Well that would be a handy thing." I smirked. "So it doesn't work on me I take it, or we wouldn't be having this talk."

He shook his head slowly. "It doesn't."

"It only works on some?"

The nerve in his jaw twitched. "There are very few it doesn't work on."

I frowned. "Really. I guess that's good for me, my head is hack-proof."

He smirked, but his eyes were still studying me. Sighing, he sat back again. His dark mood returned that quickly.

"I don't think I'm going to settle down any time soon, so I was wondering," his grey eyes flicked to mine, "if I had paper or something I could draw the layout of that building on the island." I shrugged, "I can give a rough description of the building and areas I tried," I rolled my eyes, "before I jumped off the cliff."

"I watched you jump." He said quietly. "I was on the other closest island, facing those rocks you were trying to reach."

I gave him a shocked look. "You must be a fast swimmer."

"Fast enough." His eyes moved over me slowly, "I was swimming as soon as I saw you go over the edge."

"I did say thank you, didn't I? For getting to me. I doubt I would have made it." I winced, "sorry about the whole struggling and kicking you part."

His look lightened. "It's understandable to fight when you're grabbed in the middle of a swim."

I heaved a big sigh. "I'm still shocked I did it. Considering that's my biggest phobia."

"Swimming?"

I shook my head. "Heights. It took a lot to jump," I shrugged, "but when I heard them looking for me, it gave me the shove I needed."

His eyes held mine for a moment. "I will take you to Victor's office, there's a white board that you can use to draw the building's schematic." Standing, he stood there and waited for me to get up.

I got up and went over to the bed to sit down, putting my shoes back on quickly. Getting up I grabbed the jacket I'd picked out of the closet. "Should we leave a trail of crumbs?" He gave me an odd look. "So I can find my way back here again."

He smiled, "that won't be necessary." He motioned to the phone as I picked it up again. "All of our numbers are programmed in. Alona and Chase are awake right now, so if you need help you can call either of them."

I followed him to the hallway. "Everyone else went to sleep, shouldn't you be sleeping?"

He sighed. "All of us are used to broken sleep, I'll go after I check in at the cells again."

I gave him a hesitant glance.

"I won't go near him again, if that's your concern." He walked slowly beside me.

"It's just harder to get information out of someone that has stopped breathing." I tucked the phone and earbuds into my pocket.

"I don't usually lose control, but it's been a day of," he looked down at me, "unexpected events."

I chuckled. "That's putting it mildly." I glanced at his long hair that moved as he walked. "I'm jealous."

He gave me a confused look.

I motioned to his hair. "Your hair is prettier than mine."

"When you have so many brothers," he grinned, "standing out is important."

I looked at the long ebony hair again. "I'd say you succeeded there," I shrugged, "but if you want my opinion, your eyes are what make you stand out from the rest."

Those very eyes moved over me as we walked. "I always thought they made me stand out in the wrong way."

I shook my head. "No. I like that mine are different. Some people have brown eyes, some have a lighter brown. Mine are a pale amber." I gave him a small smile. "I like them. They're uniquely mine."

Arius paused in step and looked down at me. "So do I." Clearing his throat, he motioned to a door. "This is our private practice room, so if you work out and need somewhere with space, this is the place to come." He stopped and pushed open one of the double doors.

I stepped in and stood there. "Oh." I didn't know what to say. It was bigger than most gymnasiums, and one whole wall was lined with weapons. Every kind of weapon possible, except guns, as far as I could tell. "What do you *practice*?" I gave him a wide-eyed look.

He smirked. "Whatever we want." He motioned to the large mat covering over half the room. "Alona practices Tai Chi often, so if you ever can't find her this is usually where she is."

"I guess picking up emotions from everyone is hard, I can see needing a quiet place."

"Yes." He motioned to the hall again.

I went back out. "These halls are endless."

He chuckled. "I'm still not sure I know each one, and I grew up here."

I looked at his feet and back up to his face as we walked. "You mastered the growing part."

"That is Michael's office," he pointed to a door, then motioned to the one just down from it. "That is Victor's office."

I nodded. "He won't mind me in it while he's not?"

Opening the door, he held it for me. "No, especially if you can shed light on the island. We've been trying for some time to figure out how to get on it."

I snorted, "Well I figured out the off part, so hopefully you can find the way on." I looked around the large room. There was a table in the middle, like it was used for meetings. A big desk was over in the corner with bookshelves along one wall. Turning, I walked over to a large map on the wall. "Is this where we are? The other realm?"

Arius came over and crossed his arms over his chest and looked at it. "That's Alterealm."

I glanced at him. "Creative name."

He laughed. "It was named that long before anyone I know existed."

"It's huge, like whole other country kind of huge." I don't know why I thought it would be otherwise. "And your brothers are kings of all that?" I moved my hand in a circle over the map.

"They are." He pointed across the room. "There's the board." He went over and looked in a drawer in the desk. Pulling out some markers, he came back and set them on a table beside the large board.

I looked up at it. I was only five foot three and it had to reach at least seven feet up the wall. "I might have to stand on a chair to reach all of it."

He smirked and looked down at my feet. "Just don't fall." He turned and leaned against the board, crossing his arms over his chest. Hesitantly he reached out and brushed the hair back from my forehead. "I can't persuade you to let me help heal this, and your other injuries?"

I touched the bruise on my forehead. Pain was in his eyes as he looked down at me. "I don't think I'm there yet." He continued to look at me. I didn't know what it was like when he used his ability, but looking away from his eyes was still hard for me. I felt drawn to them. I swallowed nervously. "If I ever get there, I mean, I don't have fangs to bite you with to get blood…"

He pulled a short, very sharp looking knife from somewhere behind him.

I winced. "You cut yourself? Ouch. You guys into pain or something?"

His lips quirked. "I don't think any of us are." He shrugged those large shoulders of his. "A little bit of discomfort to help someone else is a small sacrifice."

"So, you cut yourself and drip blood into my mouth?"

He grinned. "We really need to expunge all the alternate 'facts' you've picked up from the movies from your mind."

I gave him a playful sneer. "I'm sorry, until today the only people I knew of with fangs were actors in movies." I looked at the knife again. "How much blood are we talking about?"

"Quantity and frequency depend on the injury and it's severity that requires healing." He brushed the hair back from my bruise again.

"For mine?" I wasn't sure why my voice sounded breathless.

"Very little. I haven't seen the cuts from your fall, but Daxx assured me they weren't serious." He glanced at my mouth and lingered for a moment before holding my eyes in his gaze. "Are you there yet? I can almost hear your mind processing this."

I smirked. "I'm a very curious person that likes to have the facts."

He made a quiet noise in his throat. "Here's a fact for you. Outside of my family, no one has held my gaze as often, or as long as you do. They all fear me."

"That sounds lonely. I think eyes are the most beautiful part of a body. No two pair are the same. Even with twins, the pattern in the irises are different."

"What are mine like?" He leaned down slightly to close the difference in our height.

I studied his eyes for a moment. They were pretty, but I certainly wasn't using that word with a man as virile and masculine as him. "They're very deceiving, in a gorgeous way. They appear to be so pale, but the irises actually have fine black lines throughout them. They are uniquely yours."

"You're forgetting how much my brother Emil and I resemble each other."

I shook my head still looking at his eyes. "No. You have similar coloring, but your eyes are silvery-grey, where his are closer to blue."

"When did you have time to study Emil's eyes to notice such detail?" His brows furrowed.

I shrugged. "Immediately, it's what I notice first about a person."

He straightened up slightly but didn't look away. "Let me heal your injuries, please. I'm responsible for one, and after being the only person in my life to look me in the eyes—since I was fifteen—I want nothing more than to do anything in my power to make your life perfect.

I smiled. "Perfect? Not just better?"

He shook his head. "You deserve perfect."

"Because I complimented your eyes?"

His lips quirked. "That certainly didn't hurt."

I watched his gaze move over my face again. There was something in the way he looked at me, but I wasn't sure what it meant.

"Paisley, please let me."

My breath hitched in my chest. "Okay, but only because you asked, and didn't try to *persuade* me again."

He touched my chin lightly with his finger. "Trying that again, with you—felt wrong." Leaning back, he pulled his shirt over his head.

I took a mental picture of the perfectly toned muscles in front of my eyes. So that's what an eight-pack looked like. Across the side of his ribs he had a long-jagged scar. I touched it softly. "How did you get this?"

He put his hand over mine. "My job isn't always dealing with scrawny con artists." He released my hand. "A prisoner managed to get a weapon in that wasn't metal—it had some sort of chemical or poison it that prevented me from healing. Even with my blood."

"Is he still alive?"

Arius gave me an odd look. "Yes, he is, and still a resident in my cells."

"Cutting yourself for me, it will heal?" The idea of adding a mark to such a work of art bothered me.

"It will, in less than a minute."

I met his look. "That's handy."

He smiled. "Very."

"Okay," I bobbed my head quickly, "let's do this before I chicken out." I couldn't believe I was about to drink blood. Then again, on the scale of strange new things, this wasn't close to the top of the list.

I turned my head when he lifted the knife to his chest. Just because I knew how the blood would get there, doesn't mean I wanted to watch. When he gently grasped the back of my head, I looked to see blood running down his chest.

"Less than a minute." He reminded me softly.

Leaning closer, I licked the blood off his chest and then put my tongue against the cut.

He inhaled deeply, his hand flexing against my head.

The cut healed, and I was almost disappointed. Apparently, my palate was okay with blood. I looked up at him. His red eyes were watching me.

"I didn't realize I'd have this reaction." He whispered.

"You don't normally when you do this?"

He shook his head slightly.

"Why with me?"

"Everything with you is different." He moved my hair from my forehead and rubbed his thumb lightly over where the bruise had been. It didn't hurt. His hand trailed down the side of my face to cup my jaw.

"The black lines are still in your eyes." I said quietly, "I thought they'd be pure red."

Those red eyes flicked back to mine. His chest rose and fell under my hand.

I looked at his mouth and wondered if I was brave enough to look at his fangs this close up. I reached up and touched his mouth, so he'd open it more. He did, with his red eyes locked on mine.

Heaving a sigh, he lifted his head and straightened. Pulling out his phone, he looked at it. "I'm sorry. I'm needed in the cells."

I dropped my hands away from him. "Something wrong?" I watched his eyes change back to the grey. It was the coolest thing I'd ever seen.

"Someone was brought in that is not being cooperative."

"You don't have guards to deal with that sort of thing?"

He put his knife back into the case. "I do, but all citizens on this side know me. Fear me. So quite often, I just have to be present and they cooperate, fearing I'll look them in the eye."

My heart pained for him. "Arius, that's so sad." Hugging my waist, I watched him pull his shirt back on. "I get it, though." I whispered, "The few times in my life I've told someone what I can do, they never look at me the same again."

He gave me a tender look. "I will never look at you as they did." He stepped closer and touched my chin gently. "Draw your map, do not fall off the chair, and call if you need me."

"I thought you were going to sleep soon."

He grinned, "I don't have a problem answering the phone knowing there's a pretty woman on the other end. My brothers, however, I can ignore and go back to sleep." Slowly, he stepped back from me, then turned and left.

I stood there for a moment. Reaching down, I pulled the waist of the track pants open. The scrapes along my hip was gone. I opened my mouth to voice my thoughts out loud, then realized I had none. There was nothing I could say to that.

Chapter Four

I stood back and looked at the map. It was more detailed then I thought I would manage. The more I drew, the more pieces I remembered. Hopefully it would be helpful.

Turning off the music, I checked the time. I'd been here for 6 hours? As if prompted by realizing the time, I yawned. Looking at the map once more, I picked up the red marker and stood in front of it. It was a long shot, but my gut still told me to mark it down. There was one place I suspected would be a way onto the island. I didn't know it for certain, but the guards got antsy anytime one of us had gone near it. I marked a big X with a question mark at that spot.

Standing in the hall, I looked both ways. Now, to figure out how to get back to my room. Heading in the direction we'd come from, I stopped outside the practice room. Biting my lip, I opened the door and looked in.

Alona was in the middle of the large mat, going through a series of graceful moves, holding them frequently. I stepped in quietly, not wanting to disturb her.

She paused and looked at me, then smiled. "Can't sneak up on an empath." She motioned all around her. "In a body free space like this, the moment any emotion steps through the door, I'm aware."

"Sorry, I didn't mean to interrupt you."

She waved a hand at me. "It's fine. I'm just taking a short break from searching." With long, graceful strides she walked toward me. "In case I was remiss during our first meeting," she smirked, "I'm Alona, Chase's mate."

I nodded. "I know."

"I am sorry about Chase's—episode. You probably thought we all were lunatics when you woke up to that."

I grinned. "It was touch and go for a few minutes."

"I'd imagine so. I'll have to remember to turn our phones off next time, so his brothers can't call him." She sighed. "How are you doing?" She tilted her head, "your emotions are all over the place."

I touched my head and faked a wince, "I'm still processing all of it."

She nodded. "I understand. I was a little lost when I found out." Alona laughed, "Imagine living almost a hundred years, and knowing nothing about your own heritage."

I gave her a surprised look. "Oh, so you're like," I lifted my hand, "them." I couldn't help but hope I looked that good at a hundred.

She sighed. "Mostly. My mother was human though, so I'm missing out on a few of the perks like quick healing and the healing blood."

"Your eyes go…"

"Red." She nodded, "and I have the fangs as well."

"Wow, that's—" I paused. "I'm still having trouble with that."

She gave me a look, a gentle expression in her eyes. "I'm sure you'll manage to sort through it." She pulled out her phone and checked it. "So are you just out wandering?"

I shook my head. "I was in Victor's office drawing a map of the island."

She cringed. "I was on it, they all gave me the creeps."

"They took you too?"

Shaking her head, she went over and picked up her boots. "No. They wanted to recruit me to help them raise funds for their cause."

"Really? So it's an organized group of insane people?"

She chuckled, "unfortunately, yes." Straightening, she motioned to the door. "I'm going to meet Chase at the dining room, if you'd like to come."

"I'd like to tag along… in hopes that I'll find the room I'm staying in somewhere in our travels."

She grinned. "These halls are dreadful, they go on forever. Our side isn't as bad, with all of the offices being over here, but I still have to pause and ask my guard, Sith, where we are from time to time."

I looked around the large room. "You have a guard?"

She nodded. "Yes. Currently he's at my apartment, on our side, tearing up the carpeting for me." With a smirk she put her hand to her mouth. "Shh, don't tell my king. Sith is supposed to be with me at all times." She mimicked in a low voice.

It hadn't occurred to me. "I guess that's part of being a queen."

She sighed and turned to the door. "I suppose. I don't blame the men for assigning guards to us women. There have been some incidents that warranted that action."

Following her out into the hall, I tucked my hands into my pockets. "Incidents?"

She nodded. "They're quite determined to get their hands on as many women as possible. "She hissed out a breath. "The idea of them trying to breed their own army is just—"

I stopped, my eyes bulging and looked at her. "Excuse me? Breed? What?" My heart was pounding inside my chest. I put my hands over my cheeks. "I'm so stupid. How did I not see that?" Dropping my hands, I turned to face the wall and leaned my head against it. "I could have been… those poor women."

"Paisley? I'm sorry, I didn't mean to upset you."

I turned to see Alona looking as distressed as I felt. "Empath." I whispered. "Sorry." I inhaled deeply and closed my eyes. Blowing the breath out slowly, I tried to calm down.

I looked at her. "Just back away—however far you need it to be." I nodded. "I just need a minute."

She started backing up.

Turning away from her, I held my hands over my face. "If I hadn't gotten off that island, I could have been..." I shook my head. I couldn't go there. I'd have a meltdown. Bending forward, I rested my hands on my knees and inhaled slowly, trying to slow my racing heart down.

"Paisley?" Alona called out.

I looked down the hall to see Alona standing about thirty feet away.

"Are you all right? I didn't mean..."

I waved a hand at her. "It's fine. It's not your fault." I stood up and held a hand over my churning stomach. "I just—I was so caught up trying to find a way to escape, I didn't put the pieces together."

"I'm terribly sorry." She put her hands over her mouth then dropped them. "I feel ridiculous right now, yelling at you from down the hallway."

I shrugged. "Hey, you do what you do to survive, right?"

She nodded. "Yes, that's what you did—on that island. What you needed to in order to survive."

"*What* are you two up to?" Chase came around the corner and stopped in front of Alona.

She motioned to me. "Having a conversation."

He looked down at me and then tucked his hands in his pockets. "Later after this is sorted, we'll discuss your invisible guard." He sighed. "I felt the spike in emotions, my beloved, what's happened?"

Brushing her hair over her shoulder with an annoyed expression on her face, she motioned to me again. "I upset Paisley by blurting things out. She told me to step back so it wouldn't affect me as much."

Chase nodded and held his hand over his brow and looked at me. "You can come closer now. I'll aid my lovely mate with coping."

I started walking closer, not sure how exactly he was going to do that. I still stopped leaving several feet between them.

Chase looked from me to Alona. "What's the problem?"

"That's what I'd like to know." Arius came from the same direction Chase had. He looked like he'd just woken up.

Turning, Chase gave him a curious look. "Trouble in the cells?"

Arius shook his head, his eyes looking at me only.

"Have you slept yet?" Alona asked sounding concerned.

"I think so, briefly." His grey eyes moved over me in a slow appraisal. "What's upset you, Paisley?"

I gave him a startled look. How he could know at a glance that I was upset, was a first for me. No one had ever cared enough to notice before.

Chase looked from his brother to me, pausing on my forehead for a second. "Oh this is intriguing." He said in a hushed voice.

"I'm afraid it's my fault," Alona said quickly. "I blurted out something about those lunatics trying to breed an army."

I looked up at Arius. "If I hadn't—" I couldn't say it.

Stepping closer, he pulled me into his arms and hugged me. "You got off before anything could happen. They won't get their hands on you."

I leaned back and looked up at him. "You don't understand. They took two women—they never came back. What if…"

Alona made a sound of distress. I turned to see Chase holding her. He glanced to Arius with a hard look, his desire for retribution plain to see.

"We're going to find them." Arius touched my chin, so I'd look at him again. "We already found three recently. Troy is pulling as much information from the heads of those we've locked up as he can. We still have several locations to check."

I nodded. "I finished the map. There may be a weak spot in their wall, or whatever it is. I marked it."

His eyes flicked to his brother for a moment. "You can explain it to all of us in a few hours. Right now though, you need to rest. I can—see how tired you are."

I sighed. "I just want to get the other women off the island."

"I know," he gave me a soft look, "but you're no good to anyone if you drop from exhaustion."

I nodded slowly. "You're right. Okay. I'll go lay down for a bit." I rubbed a hand across my brow. "I don't even know when I slept last, really. I was afraid to sleep on the island, woke up constantly—" I looked up to see his pale eyes watching me, unwavering, he was listening to every word I said. "I don't know how to find that room with the closet." I motioned to Alona, "she was taking me there."

He smiled. "I will take you there." He looked to his brother. "We'll see you in a few hours. Let the others know we'll have breakfast in Victor's office, so we can study Paisley's map and see where we stand."

Chase smirked and bowed his head. "As you wish."

Alona rolled her eyes and smiled at me. "That's twice now, perhaps our next meeting will be less eventful than the first two."

I looked at Chase and smirked. "The first one was very memorable."

Chase pointed a finger at me. "We are *not* discussing that." He turned and pulled Alona along with him and went down the hall.

"I didn't mean to upset her." I said going in the direction Arius motioned to.

"She has bad moments, lets her guard down too much. Did you find her in the practice room?"

I nodded.

"That's why then. That's her quiet time and Chase stays out of her head when she's there alone. So he probably hadn't realized what was going on, so she was left to her own defenses, and you getting upset caught her off guard."

"Chase can get in her head and help her?"

He sighed quietly. "Through their mating bond." He held up his bare arm. "The tattoos on the couples, it's the mating mark. Once it's complete it forms a bond. My brothers and I have a mental connection that's similar. We can sense what each other is feeling at times."

I paused. "Is that how you knew what was going on? That Alona and I were upset?"

His grey eyes connected with mine briefly, then he nodded to walk again. "Something like that."

"That's kind on amazing. To be connected to your family in that way."

He smirked. "It has its moments, but at other times it's like having someone nagging you relentlessly." Stopping, he motioned to a door.

I looked around. "We're here?" I opened the door and it was the room with the closet.

Arius leaned against the door frame. "Please try to rest."

I nodded. "I will. You need to as well."

He took a deep breath. "I've been trying to, but my mind has other ideas."

"It's so annoying when that happens." I hugged my arms around my waist. "I guess your job is hard to get out of your head."

He grinned. "My work never interferes with falling asleep. They're confined to a cell where no magic works, only those with pure intentions can access the doors, so there's no chance for escape."

"I don't understand the door part, but it sounds secure."

"It is."

I yawned and covered my mouth quickly.

"Enough distractions. Go get some rest. I'll come and get you later when we're meeting everyone.

"Ok." I started to turn, then paused. "Can you explain why we're eating breakfast in the evening?"

He grinned. "Yes. Later I will, only if your brain can cope with more information."

I gave him a serious look. "Always."

Chapter Five

I stood looking at my reflection in the mirror. I looked like a different person after Alona had done my makeup. I don't know what she did to my eyes, but the liner made my eyes look exotic and pretty.

Behind me Alona stood smiling. "I knew it would be your color. It was too dark for me. I'm much paler. Burgundy plum." She nodded.

Moving my eyes back to look at myself. "I've never really worn lipstick, always thought it made my lips look big."

"If I had your lips, I'd be wearing every dark shade out there."

"You look great." Bethany said, getting off the bed. "If I wore a short-pleated skirt, I'd look like a middle grade student."

"That's because you are the epitome of petite." Alona sighed, "What I wouldn't give to be your size. Do you know how many boots I could buy then?"

"Because you need more boots." Daxx snorted, coming out of the closet. "I'm not a fashionista, but I think these will work." She held up a pair of black leather boots that looked like a fancy work boot to me.

"Oh, yes." Alona rushed over and took them from her.

I looked down at my skirt and at how much leg was showing. "I could never wear something like this when I work."

"What is it you do?" Bethany went over to the mirror and pushed her hair back from her face.

"I'm a deejay. Amateur stuff, whatever I can find." I looked back down at the skirt. "Wearing this while on a platform or stage—wouldn't work."

They laughed.

"Okay. We need to get to Victor's office. If we're lucky we'll get to kick some ass today." Daxx grinned.

Crissy jumped up from the chair she'd been kneeling on. "That's what Daxx does."

Doing up the second boot, I stood up. "Are we meeting the others there?"

Daxx snorted, "They've probably been there for hours and dissected ten different plans by now."

I followed them out into the hall. "That's good though, right? Them having a plan."

Alona shook her head. "No. It will be a plan excluding us."

I frowned, "you *want* to go with them?"

"Not entirely, but being there means not waiting and worrying—"

"And saving their asses when needed." Daxx added.

"At least there's no tunnels on the island." Bethany mumbled.

"Or mud pits," Daxx said with a sneer.

"There's trees. I like that I can climb." Crissy added quietly.

"There's guards, invisible barriers and alarms." I looked to each woman, "and a cliff."

"Hundreds of stairs to climb." Alona added.

I pointed to her. "That too."

Daxx sighed and motioned down the hall. "We'll figure it out."

I stopped when four large men came around the corner. Three of them looked like pirates and the other one was just plain scary.

"It's all right." Alona said beside me. She motioned to them. "These are our guards. Sith, Bronx, Tim and Mac."

One looked at Crissy. "I found those books and put them by the ladder to your tower."

"Oh." Crissy looked excited. "Thank you, Bronx." She turned to Daxx. "I need to know more about herbs." She nodded and started walking again.

"Herbs?" Alona asked in a hushed voice. "She actually researches what she sees?"

Daxx sighed. "Yes and with a photographic memory, that makes her…"

"Our internet." Bethany shrugged.

Daxx nodded. "Sounds about right."

They started walking again.

I looked over my shoulder to see the large men following us. I'd feel safe with someone that size too—after I was no longer afraid of them.

Breakfast was busy and loud. Large bodies passing food around, talking, eating. The brothers spent more time debating and arguing ideas about getting on the island than anything else. Victor and both kings spent a lot of the time standing while eating, then explaining why their ideas wouldn't work.

I kept my mouth shut and listened. I had no experience with any of this.

Arius didn't talk much either. Every time I glanced in his direction, he was looking at me.

I sat by the desk with Crissy and Beth, watching the men stare at the map and pace around. Victor shook his head to something Michael said.

"Can you get in touch with Kinsley and confirm a time that would be best to try? She's there, she'll know if anything has changed since Paisley got off."

I looked from Daxx to Victor. "You have someone *on* the island?" My heart sped up.

Victor nodded. "Yes, she's been sending me information."

With my eyes wide I looked to Arius, then back to Victor. "Who?"

Michael picked up a tablet and tapped the screen a few times as he walked toward me. When he reached me, he turned the tablet around to face me.

I looked at the screen and recognized the woman. I nodded. "I saw her. She's one that's treated differently than the rest."

"Is she wearing a cuff?" Michael asked.

I shook my head.

Michael turned back to Victor. "That confirms they have no way of scanning to detect other abilities."

"How many had cuffs on?" Troy stood up.

"Maybe four of us." I shrugged. "I really wasn't paying attention to that." I pointed to the tablet. "But, she doesn't have one." I looked to Arius, who stood leaning against the wall with his arms crossed over his chest, watching me. "When I pushed the guards by getting too close to the barriers, she implored me to just lay low and act compliant."

Arius turned to Victor and gave him a hard look.

Victor sighed. "I told her to try to preserve life, without raising any suspicions."

Getting up, I moved through the tall bodies and stood in front of my map. I tapped the board beside the red X. "Is there a way to see if this has one of those barriers?" I looked to Arius, "without setting off the alarms in case I'm wrong?"

Victor came over and stood beside me. "Why do you believe there is no barrier there?" He turned to look at Troy. "I went to look earlier. On the outside of that location it is an outcropping of rock." He shrugged, "it would be an easy enough climb or even to go around if needed, there's a worn trail leading up to it." He looked down at me. "What's on the other side?"

"Rocks. It goes up about twenty, twenty-five feet and is climbable without ropes or help." I turned and glanced at Arius. "Anytime one of us went in that direction, the guards herded us back."

Arius looked at me for a moment, then turned to Rafael. "Think Clairee can test it from a safe distance?"

Rafael came over and looked at the map. He pointed to a spot on it. "We could port to here and as long as we stay in the trees, I think she can."

Troy nodded slowly. "Raf, you and Quinton take her there and see what she can find out. Take Romulus as well. We're going to need to know if he can bring the barrier down."

Quinton made a noise of annoyance. "Can I duct tape his mouth?"

Troy smirked. "Rather hard for his incantations if his lips can't move."

"Fine." Quinton went over to the table and grabbed a biscuit then turned to the door.

"I'll send a message to Miss Hinton." Victor pulled out his phone and went over to the corner near Crissy.

Chase turned to Emil and his sons. "We'll get her off there, brother. We just have to take precautions, so the women aren't endangered when we go."

Emil scowled, "I understand. Doesn't mean I have to like waiting."

A man with long white hair and eyes almost as pale came in.

"Welsley, what did you find?" Daxx stood up.

He inclined his head to Troy and Chase briefly. "I spent the last twenty-four hours watching, huntress. They're using that building. Small groups in and out every few hours."

Michael rubbed the back of his neck. "That's going to be hard to get into."

Welsley nodded. "They use a side entrance instead of going in through the lobby." He pulled out his phone and tapped the screen and held it out to Daxx.

Alona looked over Daxx's shoulder. "That's a high-rise, on my side of town." She looked at her mate. "What are they doing there?"

Daxx handed the phone to Troy.

I watched the brothers crowd around Troy, trying to see the screen. Sighing, I picked up the tablet Michael had set down. I opened it, enabled the blue tooth connection and set it on the table, then pushed my way between Victor and Arius to reach Troy. I smiled up at him and took the phone out of his hand. Enabling the Bluetooth, I waited a moment, selected the tablet then pointed to it on the table. I set the phone beside it and backed out of the crowd of bodies.

Chase smirked down at me, "you and I need to chat about a few electronic issues I have."

I shrugged, "I'm not very tech savvy, but I know my way around short cuts."

"Beth isn't allowed past the first floor." Leone stated in a low tone.

"Relax, superman. This is not a run-down dump with broken fire escapes." Bethany told smiled at him.

"She fell out of a building." Crissy said standing beside me. "You're going to have to like high places." She smiled and went back over the desk.

I followed trying to figure out what that exchange meant.

"I think we should wait until dark." Chase said as he moved back from the table. "That's a lot of ground for our witches to cover. If we wait until dark, they won't have to."

"How do we get in? We can't just walk in the front door and ask the front desk if team bad has an office in the building." Alona said glancing to the others. "And there will be cameras in the lobby for sure."

"We?" Chase gave her a hard look.

She nodded. "We." She pointed to the tablet. "That is not a tunnel, run down building or a cave, therefore I'm going."

Arius came over and leaned against the desk beside me.

Daxx held up her hand toward Troy. "Don't even think it."

Troy looked over to Victor. He sighed. "My only fear is Cristy will try to climb the damn thing."

Crissy laughed. "Don't be silly. It's all glass. Nowhere to hold onto."

I gave Arius a wide-eyed look.

His look told me not to ask. "I have a few things to take care of in the cells then I'm taking Paisley over to see if she can get any of her belongings from where she was staying."

I gave him a surprised look.

"Daxx can you give me a hand if I don't know the area?"

Daxx nodded. "Just let me know."

"I'll go with you, brother." Victor told him. "No one goes anywhere alone, remember?"

Troy nodded. "Just because we thwarted their ransom plans, doesn't mean they won't try it again."

Crissy leaned closer. "Bethany kidnapped Leone after talking in his head for weeks." She nodded.

I looked from her to Bethany and Leone standing close together.

"I agree, brother." Chase said looking to the guards around the room. "And the women go nowhere outside these chambers unescorted." He looked at Bethany. "Or next time sparky may do more than bounce someone like a ball."

Crissy looked at then to me. "Men got into Alona's apartment following the dart in my bag. Beth smacked them around with energy."

I waited for more of an explanation. It didn't come. I stood there for a moment trying to decide if I wanted to know more.

Arius looked down at me.

"I used to be the weirdest person in the room." I told him quietly.

He chuckled. "You're not even close in this group."

I looked around at the others in the room. "I'm not sure if that's a good thing, or just frightening."

He grinned and looked at his phone. "I'll come find you when we're ready to go over."

"I'll take her down to the cells and wait in your office, Arius." Victor said as he kissed the top of Crissy's head.

She smiled up at him. "I'm going to read in my tower."

He smiled back at her. "Bronx can wait by the ladder."

She nodded. "I know."

I tried to remember all the turns on the walk to the cells. "Anyone ever think of putting up signs in these halls?"

Victor glanced down at me. "That has been mentioned a few times recently."

"Just recently?" I glanced down a hall we passed.

"Mmm," he inclined his head, "it was just my brothers and I, and others that know them well for the last few millenniums, so directions weren't required until the mates appeared." He smirked. "Except Cristy, she doesn't need directions."

"I'm not surprised, she has a photographic memory?" I tried to keep up to his long stride.

"She does, but she also saw these halls years before she was in them." He said with a proud expression in his eyes.

"I'm lucky if I remember what day it is." I shrugged. "Unless it's lyrics to a song, it's touch and go."

"We all have our strengths."

He really wasn't a great conversationalist. "What's yours?"

He glanced at me briefly. "Justice." He said without further explanation.

It felt like that was one of those things I didn't want to know more about, so I didn't say anything. I followed him through doors, then recognized where we were. The human rat maze.

He opened another door and motioned for me to go in.

I stepped in to see monitors along one wall. They were all focused on the cells. All of them full.

"Arius keeps the ones he wants to monitor in the cells with cameras." He offered. Pulling out his phone he glanced at it. "I will leave you here. I'm needed elsewhere. Tell Arius to let me know when he's going over."

I nodded.

He left without further comment.

I turned back to the monitors and walked over to them. Most of the people were just lying on their bed, doing nothing. I wouldn't be able to do that without music, I thought. Movement on one caught my eye. I went closer.

Arius was in a cell with a man just as large as he was. He stood there, almost looking bored as the man paced back and forth. There was no sound, so I couldn't hear what was being said, but Arius was speaking. Without warning, Arius moved and grabbed the man by the face. I didn't know what he said, but the man lifted his hands like he was giving up. Arius released him then turned and walked out of the cell.

I glanced at the other monitors, trying to see where he'd gone, but he didn't appear in any of them.

"I thought Victor was waiting with you?"

I jumped and turned to see Arius standing in the door. I hadn't even heard him open it. "He had to do something, said to let him know when we were going."

He stepped in and closed the door, then stood there his gaze moving over me slowly.

My stomach filled with butterflies, the look on his face making me both nervous and excited. I smoothed my hands over the skirt. "Alona thought it would look good on me."

His grey eyes flicked back to my face. "She was right." He took two steps toward me then stopped. "I generally give more input on planning our strategies, but I wasn't able to think clearly when you walked in looking like this."

I touched my mouth, "I felt like it was too much."

He tilted his head, looking at my mouth. "It's very distracting, is what it is."

"Distracting?"

He moved closer, his grey eyes holding mine captive.

I'd never had a reaction like this from just a look. My heart was racing.

"Yes. Every bite you took, every word you spoke, every time you licked your lips—" he was right in front of me now, "distracting." With barely a touch, he tilted my chin up. "All I could think about was this…" leaning down he kissed my mouth so softly I wasn't sure if I'd imagined it.

His breath caressed my mouth, his eyes watching mine like he was waiting for me to look away. With a soft growl, he grasped my waist and lifted me to sit on a cabinet that I hadn't noticed behind me. His large hand cupped the back of my head as he kissed me again. Soft hesitant kisses, slowly tasting my mouth.

I wrapped my arms around his neck, burying my hands in his thick hair.

He lifted his head, red eyes moving over my face, before his mouth covered mine again. The hesitation was gone. His tongue invaded my mouth, exploring every corner. Without thought, I ran my tongue over his sharp fangs and felt the heat move though me.

He growled in the back of this throat and the kiss changed, demanding my compliance. I'd never been kissed like that in my life. I clung to him for fear I'd slide to the floor.

Tearing his mouth away, his lips traveled down my throat. At the base of my neck, he nipped gently with his fangs.

I fought to breathe.

"I want to taste you," he whispered against my skin. His breathing was as erratic as my own.

I leaned my head to the side, exposing my neck. When he bit into me, I gasped. It wasn't what I thought it would be. It was the most intimate moment in my life.

Lifting his mouth, he licked over the bite and grasped the back of my head. His mouth returned to mine in a passion-heavy kiss.

Voices in the hall had him jerking his head up.

I looked over at the door and held my hand to stop the door from being opened. Our heavy breathing echoed our emotions.

His hands wrapped around my waist and he lifted me down. I didn't look away from the door. Resting his head on mine, he continued to hold me.

Someone knocked on the door. "Arius." It was Victor.

"We'll be ready to go in a minute." Arius said loudly.

"I'll be at the intake cells."

Dropping my hand, I looked up to see his eyes were grey again.

"I didn't mean to get carried away." He whispered.

I shook my head. "Don't apologize." Reaching up, I wiped the lipstick off his mouth.

He kissed my hand and motioned to a door. "Bathroom, if you'd like to straighten up before we go." Releasing me, he stepped back.

With shaking legs, I went in and turned on the light. My hair was a mess. Patting it in place, I leaned in and fixed the smudges of lipstick by my mouth. "Not so smudge-proof after all." I said quietly.

Arius chuckled from the door. "We may have tested it beyond their expectations."

I blushed. Tilting my head, I wiped the lipstick from his mouth off my neck. Then touched where he'd bit me. There was no mark.

"Healing saliva." He said quietly.

"That's handy." I turned and smoothed my skirt down.

"Nearly as handy as holding the door closed."

"I actually slowed time down to the point that it would open so slowly, it would seem closed." Straightening my top, I glanced at him. "Will I do?"

He growled, "Yes, you will."

My cheeks heated again. He stepped back and motioned for me to go.

Chapter Six

"Keep your eyes closed and breathe slowly for a minute." Arius' hand traveled up and down my back.

My stomach started to settle. Opening my eyes, I held onto him and stepped back. "That wasn't as fun as I'd hoped." I looked at Victor, his expression was sympathetic.

"You're doing better than most."

I took another slow breath. "Really? That's something, I suppose." I glanced up at Arius. "Neither of you look as dizzy as I feel."

He smirked, "we've had a few more years to practice."

Victor chuckled, "a few."

I looked around. "I still can't believe in seconds we went from the door by the maze to beside my building."

"The maze?" Arius gave me an odd look.

I shrugged. "It reminds me of those little mazes you put rodents in to see who reached the finish line first."

He laughed. "I'd like to make some of them race through it."

Victor shook his head. "Don't tell Chase or Rafael that—or we'll be chasing prisoners around."

"True." Arius motioned toward the street.

I nodded and walked that way. My stomach was tight. That feeling of dread told me this was going to turn out the way I feared.

Five minutes later I stood outside the place I used to live. "I can't believe he threw all my stuff out." I looked at Victor. "Where's Arius?"

His eyes flicked to the door briefly, "he'll be out momentarily." He continued to scan the street.

I frowned.

"He's finding out who told them you weren't coming back."

I held my hand over my throat. It felt like my heart was in it. "I really did almost vanish for good, didn't I?"

He nodded. "You were lucky. My fear is for those we don't reach in time."

I nodded, unable to speak while keeping my emotions from overflowing.

Arius came out the door, a scowl on his face. "It was Martin." His tone was low and lethal.

"Can I go back and kick him?"

Arius raised an eyebrow.

I shrugged, "I didn't say where."

He smirked.

"Paisley?"

I turned to see my neighbor—ex-neighbor, Mrs. Stein coming toward us. She moved slowly, shuffling with her walker.

She smiled. "I thought it was you." She stopped and looked from Victor to Arius.

I nodded. "I've been staying with some friends." I motioned to the large men standing behind me.

She sighed, "I'm glad you're not with that Martin. There was something off with that one, lurking around all the time." She shook her head. "I heard him tell Mister Timbly you weren't coming back, and to toss your belongings, that you didn't want them." She leaned closer, "I didn't believe that."

Shaking her head, she motioned to the alley. "I couldn't reach much, dear, but I did get your bag."

My eyes widened. "You did? Oh, thank you." I frowned. "You could have been hurt though."

Mrs. Stein tsked, "Nonsense. You've always been good to me." She motioned to the door. "I'll go get it." She moved toward the door.

Arius rushed over and opened it for her.

She smiled up at him. "Nice to see a gentleman with Paisley." She pouted at him. "She's a good girl."

Arius nodded. "Yes ma'am."

Victor looked at his brother. "I'll wait here." He looked slowly to the street.

Arius glanced around and nodded.

The walk to her room was painfully slow. I was thankful she lived on the first floor. She came back to her door carrying the pack I used for work. At least I'd have my music and a few portable speakers. I took it from her.

"Thank you so much, Mrs. Stein." I pointed to the end of the hall. "Do you need me to run to the store for anything before I go?"

She patted my arm. "I can't afford many things at this time of the month, but thank you." She smiled at Arius. "It's good to see you with a nice man."

Arius inclined his head at her compliment. Reaching into his pocket, he pulled out a handful of money. Leaning down, he touched her shoulder and looked at her for a moment. Placing the money in her hand he straightened up.

She smiled at him, then looked at me. "I can't believe we actually won that raffle. Are you sure you don't want to split the prize?"

I shook my head quickly. "No. No, that's fine, Mrs. Stein. I have some work lined up."

She smiled and held her hand to her chest with the money clutched in it. "I'm going to call Grace and tell her."

"Okay. Bye and thank you again for getting my bag."

I stepped outside and stopped. Placing my hand on Arius' arm, I looked up at him. "Thank you for that. She's a sweet lady."

His pale eyes moved over my face. "You can come check on her from time to time if you like."

Reality hit me then. "I have no home." I whispered and looked back at the door.

Victor cleared his throat. "I think, until we've closed down that island, you're safer staying with us."

The brothers looked at each other over my head for a moment.

"You're sure I'm not taking up too much space? I mean that room could be used for an entire football team or something."

Arius shrugged. "Not big on sports." He pulled his phone out and tapped the screen, then put it to his ear. "Yeah, we're still here." He gave Victor a serious look, then glanced down at me. "I can take—" he frowned. "How many?" Placing his hand on my back so I'd start walking, he nodded. "Yeah. We'll meet you there. Bring our gear." He hung up. "They're heading to the building now. Welsley says a large group left and right after that several more went in."

Victor's expression hardened. "Sounds like they're setting something up."

Arius nodded. "That's what Michael thinks." He looked down at me. "We'll find somewhere safe…"

I shook my head. "Don't worry about me. If these people are working with the ones from the island, I'll stop time around each and every one of them so you can lock them in your maze."

Victor's lips twitched.

Arius glanced down the street and then stopped and looked down at me. "I'm not putting you in harm's way."

I sighed. "Fine, I'll stand in a corner out of the way."

He motioned to an alley. We went in and stopped. Putting his arms around me, he gently held my head against his chest. "Close your eyes, take a deep breath."

"Oh. We're doing that again." I leaned into him and closed my eyes.

A moment later my stomach churned. I inhaled through my nose and breathed out slowly. "This part is a bit anticlimactic if you ask me." I said quietly.

I heard someone make a sound of exasperation. "At least you don't throw up."

I opened my eyes to see Leone and Bethany a few feet from us.

She rolled her eyes, "Porting and I don't get along well."

Holding onto Arius' arm, I stepped back. "I suppose considering we're doing something that should be impossible—it could be worse."

"Uh," she held her hand up in the universal gesture of 'stop', "figures you'd be an optimist."

I grinned and looked around. We were on a roof. A roof! I reached out and clung to Arius' arm again.

He put his hand on my back. "Sorry, I thought if I told you before we ported, you'd freak out."

I nodded. "Good call."

Michael appeared a few feet away.

I jumped and moved closer to Arius.

"Sorry," he shrugged, "you'll get used to it." He held a large leather case out to Arius.

Arius took it and looked down at me. "Just sit tight for a moment and I'll get you off here."

I nodded and sat down right where I stood, not caring that the gravel from the roof was digging into my leg.

"We're going down." Leone said quietly.

I didn't turn to see where they went.

"You are not carrying me. This one is not broken." Bethany hissed.

I watched as Arius took off his shirt and put on a black leather vest, then pulled a leather jacket on. He pulled weapon after weapon out of the bag, strapping them to his body. With the speed he put them on, I knew that was something he could do in his sleep. What I didn't understand was why he was dressing like this, and carrying a weapons store on his body.

With fast movements, he pulled his long hair around and braided it. I'd never seen a man braid his hair before. He probably did it better than most women, then again, he'd had a few centuries to learn.

Flipping the braid behind him, he pulled two large swords from the bag and put them in cases strapped to his back. Picking up the bag, he held his hand out to me.

I looked up at him. He'd transformed into a warrior right before my eyes. Taking his hand, he pulled me to my feet.

"You're not going to like this next part." He said when I stood up.

"What part?" I squeezed his hand as we walked across the roof, toward the edge. That's when I noticed rails sticking up. The kind that went with ladders. Ladders, those torturous devices that you climbed in the air on.

He went over. "Come on. It's only ten feet down then there's a fire escape." He gave me a soft look. "You jumped off a cliff. This is nothing compared to that."

I took a shaky breath and forced my legs to move. The other alternative was to be left on this roof alone.

"Give me your bag."

I reached and held it out to him. He put it over his shoulder.

"Turn and step over."

I did, moving a few inches at a time. When I was on the ladder, clinging so hard my hands hurt, he moved up so our heads were level.

"It's okay. We'll do this together."

I moved down one rung, keeping my eyes straight ahead, staring at the dark wall.

"If it helps, this is torture for me, being this close to you." His breath brushed my neck. "Smelling you."

I went down another rung.

"I can still taste you," he whispered next to my ear.

I moved down one more. "Are-are you trying to distract me or turn me on?"

"I was going for distraction, but it's still the truth."

My foot touched something solid. I'd done it.

He put his arm around my waist and hugged me into him for a second. "We have to go." Bending down, he picked up the bag and took my hand.

He held my hand as we ran down the fire escape. I was still reeling from coming down the ladder, so it didn't even register that I'd run down two flights of stairs on the outside of a building. He released my hand when we reached the bottom, and ran along the edge of the building.

As we got to the corner, I noticed the others waiting for us. I stopped and looked at them. All the men were dressed as Arius was. I remembered the wall in the practice room, I'd honestly thought those were just to help keep them in shape.

"It's like a barbarian movie, right?" Bethany whispered.

Arius handed me back my pack. I gave her a quick nod, still trying to catch my breath.

A few of the men were squatting down looking across a parking lot.

I turned to see what they were looking at. The building was at least thirty stories high.

Arius squatted down beside Michael. "That door?"

Michael nodded.

I turned to see an emergency exit door on the side of the building.

"I could go in the front…"

Michael shook his head cutting Arius off. "We didn't bring the witches, so no cloaking. With the way you're dressed, you wouldn't make it five feet before alarms went off."

"Beth can you blast the lock?" Leone glanced at his mate.

She blew out a breath. "If it's wired, I could set off the alarm."

"We could make a run for it the next time someone comes in or out." Daxx suggested.

I looked around the parking lot, noting the lighting and where is was lacking. If I stayed to one side, I could get almost to the building before I would be seen. Biting my lip, I moved away from the others and started in that direction.

"Paisley." Arius hissed. "What are you doing?"

I turned and put my finger to my lips for a second, then ran to the spot the light didn't hit. When I reached it, I squatted down, making myself as small as possible. I was close enough to the door now. I turned to see everyone watching me. Victor held Arius' arm so he couldn't come after me and be seen.

The door opened. A man came out, then said something over his shoulder. He quickly shut the door behind him. I raised my hand, waiting. He hadn't been talking to himself. The door opened again and two more came through it. When the second one let go, I waited until it was almost closed and stopped it before it would latch.

The men's voices faded as they went around the corner of the building. Crissy raced by me toward the door. She grabbed it then nodded to me. I dropped my hand and went toward her.

Right behind me was Arius. He gave me a stern look but didn't say anything.

Rafael went by next, he grinned. "Nice move, sister."

Quinton ran up and chuckled as he noticed Arius' unhappy expression.

Daxx appeared beside me. "You're coming with me next bounty I go after—save me a lot of running." She whispered, then went in the door.

Arius grabbed my arm gently and pulled me in the door.

"Do we know the exact floor?" Leone started up the stairs.

"No, but there will be guards when we find the right one" Michael went up after him.

"They always leave a trail of guards." Chase rushed after them. "Like bread crumbs to follow."

I tugged my arm from Arius' grasp and motioned to the stairs. "Go. I'll stay at the back with Alona and Bethany."

His eyes moved over my face slowly for a moment, then he released my arm and went after his brothers, taking the steps three at a time.

Bethany rolled her eyes. "Show off."

We followed along behind the men, Beth going last as she was keeping an eye on the stairs behind us. I glanced to Alona, she held her hand over her ear.

"Sixth floor." She whispered. When she started walking again, I noticed the ear bud she wore, and realized they all talked to each other.

Beth smirked. "We're still on the stairs, and so safe we could have a tea party right here."

Alona nodded. "I'll stay at the door on the sixth floor, just pay attention to what you're doing, Chase."

We reached the landing to the sixth floor. Bethany stood by the railing looking down, there was no way I was doing that.

"Someone is coming up." She said quietly.

Alona opened the door and motioned in a direction for me to go. I stepped through the door and Crissy came running toward us.

"This way." She ran by us down the hall.

I looked at the door. "Do you want me to hold it closed?" I lifted my hand.

Alona winced and shook her head. "Arius is definitely against that idea."

I followed the direction Crissy had gone. We ran around a corner and into a large conference room. Alona closed the door behind us.

Bethany went to another door and opened it a crack. "They have so many computers."

Alona rushed over and looked. "That's how they're finding them." She bit her lip. "Try not to destroy the computers, I want the information off them." She frowned. "Unless they come at you with a weapon, leave the machines be."

Bethany pulled her ear piece out and held it her palm. "They could have files about where other women are being held."

Alona bit her lip and nodded, not saying anything.

I remembered my pack and pulled it off. Opening it I pulled out my hard drive filled with music. "We can download the files." I looked from Bethany to Alona.

Crissy came over and bent down, pulling the knife from the case on her leg. "It's wrong what they're doing." She nodded and moved to the door.

Alona looked at Bethany as she put the ear bud back in. "Change of plans, gentleman. We're coming in and getting the files from those machines." She reached behind her and pulled out a pair of nun-chucks.

My heart lodged in my throat.

"Last I checked I was a queen and allowed to make such calls." She said with a smirk and motioned to go through the door.

I rushed in behind her and then stopped and looked around. It was a large empty room except for a few tables and six computers lined along one wall, complete with monitors. That wasn't the part that had my heart lodged in my throat. The brothers and Daxx were fighting a dozen men. Not with fists, but a full-on sword battle. I gave Alona a wide-eyed look. She shook her head then grasped my arm and started for the computers.

Chase appeared in front of us, a blade in each hand. "Beloved, not happy." He almost sang.

I turned to see a man rushing at him with a knife. Putting my hand out, I focused on one of his feet. It stopped as the rest of him kept moving, I dropped my hand and he hit the floor, face first.

"Not a scratch on that body, my king." Alona said and turned toward the computers.

We reached the tables. I held out the hard drive to Alona. She took it and gave me a worried look. "Plug it in and select the computer and copy all." She nodded and turned around.

Crissy rushed over and pulled out the first tower.

I turned to see Bethany standing a few feet from me, she had her hands up, sparks moving between them. Backing up a few feet, I held my palms up and watched with her for anyone that headed our direction.

A large man came running toward me with his arm in the air. I looked at his feet and stopped them mid-step.

"Release him." Bethany said.

I blinked and a bright ball of red hit him in the chest knocking him back.

"Mine." Daxx ran over and held a box toward him and he vanished.

"Look out." Bethany said.

I turned to see a knife flying toward me. I raised my hand then felt the sting across my cheek. A hand appeared beside my head. I looked up to see Arius there holding the knife. He looked at my cheek and growled, then spun away heading for the one that had thrown it.

They met with a loud clang of metal clashing. Arius blocked his sword's swing, then kicked him in the chest and the man stumbled back. He raised the sword above his head and stepped toward him.

"I have him, brother." Victor stepped in his path and swung a thin blade at the man.

Arius spun around and went toward the next one.

I glanced over my shoulder quickly to see Alona and Crissy plugging into another tower. Huffing out a breath, I turned back, hands out and tried to watch all the movement around me. Later, when it was over I was pretty sure I was going to have a not-so-small mental breakdown.

Bethany moved closer so she could nudge me. "The door. Don't let anymore come in."

I turned to look at the one she referred to. A man on the other side looked in through the glass. I ran toward it, ducking under Rafael's arm as he swung. When I was close enough, I held out my hand and focused hard on the door. The man on the other side banged his hand on it.

"I'll go out the other one and get him." Michael said from behind me.

"Right behind you, brother." Quinton said.

I didn't take my eyes off the door. I jolted when the sound of metal rang out beside me and heard the grunt from the effort it had taken.

"Release the fucking door and get back over there." Arius growled beside me.

Michael's face appeared in the glass on the other side of it. He nodded.

I dropped my hands and turned to see Arius right behind me, his stance daring anyone to just try and come in my direction. I looked around and there were only the brothers and women in the room.

Alona lifted her head and smiled at me. "One more to go." She frowned, "Do you know how to delete the information from their machines?"

I nodded and went back over. Going to the first keyboard, I brought up the prompt and typed the command to reformat the entire drive. I hit enter.

Victor looked over my shoulder and gave an abrupt nod of his head.

"What kind of information are you getting?" Michael called from where he stood watching out the door.

"Addresses, names," Alona told him, "I don't know if it's contacts or people they're searching for, but we may have just found what we need to stop them."

I moved to the next keyboard. Arius appeared beside me and titled my chin, so he could look at my face. His jaw clenched.

"It's not serious, brother, just a scratch." Victor assured him.

Arius' head jerked around to glare at him. "An inch more and she wouldn't be standing here." His tone did not hide his anger.

I touched his hand, so I could move my head. "I'm fine." I looked back to the screen and brought up the prompt.

"Are you ladies ever going to listen?" Chase said looking over Alona's shoulder as she transferred the files from the last computer.

Alona turned her head and gave him an amused look. "We listen to every word you say."

He snorted. "Listen, yes. Do, no."

Daxx sighed. "If they had of stayed out of the way we may not have gotten this." She turned to Chase, "maybe you missed how Beth and Paisley tag-teamed that slime?"

Chase shook his head. "No, I caught it." He looked from Beth to me. "And I've decided I'm giving them both a wide berth from now on." He sighed, "All I'm saying is…"

Beth looked at me and smirked. "Can you stop someone from talking?"

Chase's mouth dropped open, his eyes huge.

I shook my head. "No I don't think so. Hands, feet, whole body, but not just a mouth because it's part of his face."

Daxx sighed, "That's too bad."

I moved to the last keyboard.

"I'm being abused." Chase mumbled.

"You love the attention." Alona said handing him my hard drive. "We'll give it back after they've copied all the data." She told me.

I nodded. "Just don't delete my music."

Arius moved over, my pack in his hand. "Are we done here?" His eyes were hard.

I nodded. "Yeah, the last machine is erasing now."

"Good."   Rafael raised his sword above his head and beat it on the keyboard, keys went flying.

"We'll see you at home." Arius pulled me against his chest.

Chapter Seven

I was about to ask how we were getting back when my stomach gave a violent heave. Clinging to the front of Arius' jacket, I looked to see we were in my room in the other realm. "A little warning next time." I took a deep breath.

"Sorry." He titled my chin up, his eyes filled with pain as he looked at my cheek. "I couldn't stand there and watch blood run down your face a moment more."

I touched my cheek carefully and winced when it stung. "It was so much to take in, I didn't react fast enough."

He made a sound of frustration. "You shouldn't have been there to begin with. I was going to bring you back first, but my brothers felt it was imperative we act right then."

I stepped back, checking my balance. "I'm glad I was. My hard drive came in handy." I turned and went to the mirror to check my face. Reaching it, I leaned in closer. There was a gash more than an inch long on my face. "That's going to leave a scar." I turned to see Arius taking weapons off and dropping them on the floor.

He glanced at me. "There will be no scars to mar your beautiful face." His jacket landed on top of the weapons. Moving toward me, he unbuttoned his vest.

I stood there, my heart racing as this man stood in front of me. "There won't?"

He shook his head slowly. Reaching down, he scooped me up and carried me into the bathroom and set me on the counter. Stepping over, he turned on the light and came back to kneel in front of me, resting one of my feet on his hand as he looked at my leg. With a gentle touch he brushed the gravel from the roof from my leg.

As he stood up, his braid hung down his chest. I reached up and pulled the tie from the end of it, separating it with my hands so his black hair hung over his shoulder. I don't know what possessed me to do that, I just preferred his hair loose.

His jaw clenched, his eyes searching mine. Reaching behind him, he pulled a knife out and lifted it to his chest. "Let's take care of the bleeding."

Before I could speak, he sliced into his chest and set the knife on the counter. I leaned forward and licked the blood before it could run down his chest. His hand cupped the back of my head as he stepped closer. Closing my mouth around the wound, I sucked gently hoping it didn't hurt him.

He sucked in a breath and wrapped his other arm around my waist.

When it healed closed, I lifted my head to see his red eyes watching me. Leaning down, he tipped my head up and licked slowly across my cheek.

A shiver went up my spine from the tenderness of the gesture.

Lifting his head, he watched me as he reached over and flipped the water on in the sink. He knelt in front of me again and wiped the dirt from my leg with a warm, wet cloth. When he finished one leg, he did the same to the other.

I swallowed, unable to think of a single word to say. His eyes changed slowly back to grey and moved over my face, a softer, caring gaze. When he released my leg, I slid to the edge of the counter until my feet touched the floor. He knelt there in front of me, his eyes holding mine. My legs were shaking as I bent my knees and lowered my body, to rest on his knees. Wrapping my arms around his neck, I pulled his head down so I could kiss him.

Grasping my hips, he pulled me tight against his body as his mouth covered mine.

There was no hesitation from either of us as our mouths clashed, trying to consume one another. With a low growl, he turned and lowered me to the floor, moving to lie beside me without breaking the kiss.

My hands ran over any part of him I could reach as he raised over me and pulled my leg to rest over his hip. I felt surrounded by him, his hands molding my body, his hair enclosing our faces, so it was just us. Not caring if I could breathe or not, I grasped his hair and held his head so he couldn't pull away. I ran my tongue along his fangs, then pulled my head back and looked into the red eyes, heavy with passion.

"Paisley?"

Daxx called out in the room.

Arius rolled and kicked the door closed with a bang.

"Paisley, I'm going to leave Tim outside your door to take you to the dining room when you're ready." Daxx said through the door. "I don't know where Arius is, probably glowering at the new prisoners and scaring them into compliance."

I looked to see Arius laying on his back, his arm over his eyes, his chest rising and falling rapidly.

"Okay. Thanks." I said loud enough she could hear me.

We lay there panting for a few moments.

"First my office, then a bathroom floor." He said quietly.

I opened my eyes and looked around. "It's the nicest, cleanest bathroom floor I've ever seen."

He snorted and dropped his arm to look at me. "It's a first for me, to lose control to the point I forget my surroundings."

I grinned. "I'll take that as a compliment."

Rolling, he got to his feet and held his hand down to me. "Unraveling a man who has spent a few hundred years holding his composure? It is a compliment, or a threat, I haven't quite decided which." He smiled.

I took his hand, and he pulled me to my feet before looking down at me for a moment. Leaning down, he kissed me softly. "I'll grab my gear and pop to my room, so Tim can escort you to the dining room."

I hugged my waist and nodded. "I'll see you there, unless you have glowering to do."

His lips quirked. "Plenty of time for that later."

I sat across from Arius at the large table. He would glance to his siblings, then his eyes moved back to me each time. I looked down to try and pay attention to what Michael was saying.

"We haven't gone through all of it yet, but we're setting up teams to go and get the women at those addresses listed, once we know everything we need to."

"Is the safe house going to be big enough? Shall I set up another location?" Alona sipped her wine and looked to Victor.

"It may be prudent to set up a few more, just in case. You can always liquidate them at a later date." He looked to Troy then Chase, who both nodded.

Setting down her glass, she picked up her phone. "Okay. I'll get Liza on it now."

Daxx sat back and sighed loudly. "I feel like we're finally in the lead after tonight." Leaning over the table she looked down to me. "Thanks to Paisley having mad skill with computers."

I shrugged. "I'm sure if I hadn't been there the towers would have just been brought back."

"Still," she nodded her head, "they could have been damaged before that without your help."

Victor picked up his phone and read something. "Miss Hinton has confirmed the guard's schedule." He looked at Quinton. "Clairee said Paisley is correct, there is no ward on that section of the perimeter?"

Quinton nodded. "None. Romulus is working to figure out a way to bring the entire barrier down," he sneered, "says it will take a handful of mages working simultaneously."

Rafael leaned forward and looked to Victor. "He's going to let us know when they have it figured out."

Victor nodded slowly and then glanced to Arius. "We'll start preparations for a full-scale assault."

Arius' look was hard. "I'll prep the intake cells."

Troy held up his hand. "My concern is, each time we've brought full teams in on the planning, they've known we were coming."

Chase nodded. "He's right. When we keep it among ourselves and have to act quickly we succeed without a hitch."

Crissy looked over at Victor. "I haven't seen anything."

I glanced at her, then shrugged. "It's easy enough to find out." Everyone turned to look at me. "Just tell small groups different things and see which one has the leak."

"Oh. Yes." Bethany pointed at me. "Like that movie. What was the name?" Leone took her hand and held it on the table.

Arius tilted his head and studied me for a moment before looking across at Michael, "it could work, and I'd feel better knowing before we hit that island." He shook his head, "too many variables there."

Michael nodded. "We'll sit down and make a list of groups and set it up, starting tonight." He set his fork down and leaned on the table. "We're digging into the history on our science team as well right now, to find out who is helping them make those cuffs and devices."

Arius nodded, but didn't say anything.

Quinton grinned at me. He raised his glass and motioned around the table. "To sisters with skills."

Mitz came out, carrying another urn of coffee.

Chase smiled at her. "You look very pleased today, Mitz."

She set it down on the table and nodded. "I am very happy." She smiled. "We've solved the color problem with the gowns." She nodded. "Each will be black then trimmed with various colors, the men will wear a cummerbund in the color that matches their mates' trim." Excitedly, she covered her cheeks, her eyes huge. "I'm so excited I haven't slept in two days." Turning she went back out into the kitchen.

All eyes turned slowly to look at Daxx.

She groaned and leaned back. "I'm going to have to do it aren't I?"

Troy leaned over and kissed the top of her head. "I'm afraid so."

She sighed. "When is it?"

Troy gave Chase a hesitant look. "Soon."

She groaned again.

I looked at Arius, my confusion plain.

He smirked. "The yearly ball to commemorate the coronation of our kings."

I sat forward. "Ball? Like a dance with music?"

Arius nodded.

I almost jumped out of my chair. "Who does the music?"

He looked at Troy, who shrugged and glanced to Chase, who smirked.

"I can do it." I nodded. "You don't have to pay me," I rolled my eyes and looked at Arius, "you did pull me out of the bay." I covered my mouth with my hand. "Gowns—so we'll start with formal music," I looked at Rafael, "does it turn into a party or is it all stuffy and official."

He shrugged, "the start is painful, but by the end everyone's feeling good."

Quinton snorted.

Rafael pointed to him. "*You* get to go this year now that you're all handsome again—you can help keep Michael from drinking too much and threatening to cut the men's legs off."

Michael made a sound of exasperation. "It wasn't legs, it was a much more personal part of his anatomy."

I stood up, then sat down again. "This is awesome! How many people attend?"

Michael frowned, "all of Alterealm is invited, only about half show up."

I covered my mouth with my hands. "Really? Wow, my biggest gig ever." I nodded and pulled out my phone, opening up a note to start a list, "I'll start with formal and gradually turn it into a well-rounded party…"

"Paisley."

I looked up from typing my list to Arius. He looked at me with his head tipped to the side.

"You can't deejay when your part of the royal family—and guests." His grey eyes held mine, a vulnerable look in them.

My eyes went bigger. He wanted me to be his date. I smiled, then bit my lip. "Well, I'm still making the play list." I waved the phone around, "just make sure the deejay is someone I can work with."

He smiled back at me. "I'll make sure he follows your every instruction, without hesitation."

Michael coughed.

Rafael laughed.

Victor cleared his throat. "It's going to be a security nightmare."

Rafael's expression sobered. "Quinton, Ira and I have been working with the guards to set up a secure watch."

"You guys all suck." Daxx said quietly. She pointed to Alona and jerked her thumb at me. "She's clearly on your side with this dance, and gowns stuff."

I looked from Arius to Alona. "I'm in a gown?"

She nodded.

I opened my mouth and then closed it. "I've never been that dressed up in my life."

Daxx snorted. "Wait until they squish you in a *bodice* and see how happy you are about it."

Troy started laughing.

Arius grinned and looked at him. "You get to make sure she doesn't hide weapons under the gown this time."

Chase stood up and held his phone up. "The surprise is ready." He looked at his brothers.

"Surprise?" Alona frowned.

Daxx looked at Troy as he stood up. "If this involves anything girly, I'm stabbing you."

Troy grinned and held out his hand. "Nothing girly, I assure you."

Bethany stood up with Leone's help. "Surprise for all of us?"

"Just you ladies." Michael got up as well.

Arius grinned and looked around at the other women before looking back to me. "It's been hell trying to keep you from finding out."

"Really?" Crissy got up then looked at Victor. "I didn't see anything."

He took her hand. "I've been holding my breath for weeks to keep it out of my head."

"Sneaky men." Daxx said following Troy out.

We stepped out into the hallway, the four guards stood there smiling. Tim, motioned to the wall.

I turned to see a large pink cardboard arrow taped to the wall. I glanced and saw more arrows going down the hall.

Daxx looked at them and then to Alona. "What is this direction?"

Alona shrugged, "I have no idea, other than the landing room and armory."

Chase took her hand and started walking. "The problem was finding a space to use."

Troy nodded. "We have no idea what some of the rooms down here are for."

I followed along behind them, Bethany beside me.

She laughed. "Bright pink arrows aren't quite what I had in mind for directions, but they work."

We went down a long corridor and then stopped at a door. A sign was hung on it that read 'girl cave'.

Daxx gave Troy a cautious look then opened the door. Everyone filed in behind her then stopped. It was larger than the dining room. There were a few desks and computers, a long table lined the wall with a map placed on it, like the one in Victor's office.

"Is that a wine fridge?" Alona glanced to Chase and went over.

He smiled. "Of course." Motioning to the loveseats in the center of the room, he shrugged. "You ladies won't drown sitting on those."

She laughed.

Troy pointed to the far wall.

Daxx ran over. It was a large target, knives sticking out of it. She turned and smiled up at him. "You know how to make a girl feel loved."

Crissy's laughter made me turn and look.

She stood in a corner lined with plexiglass, similar to the cells. She looked at me. "My own corner to bounce and fit pieces together."

I had no idea what that meant, but she jumped up into Victor's arms and hugged him, so I assumed it was a good thing.

Leone walked over and pulled a cloth covering a large t.v. on the wall. Then he picked up wireless headphones and held them up.

Bethany raced toward him and grabbed them. "It's heaven." She put the headphones on and hugged him.

Arius touched my back softly. I looked up at him. "I figured you'd be helping track down women, so," he motioned to a stand beside Bethany's t.v., "you'll have to set it up however you prefer."

My jaw dropped. I looked back up at him, he nodded. Going over I ran my hands over the stereo system, then the speakers. I pulled it out and leaned to look at it. "I can just jack my phone in." I straightened and ran my hand over the speaker, a few pairs of wireless headphones rested on top. Covering my mouth, I spun and looked at him.

He looked relieved.

"I don't know what..." I looked at it again. "I'm..." I rushed at him and wrapped my arms around him. "Thank you."

"We may never see them again." Troy said, looking concerned.

Daxx turned with knives in her hand and walked back toward him. "At least you'll know where to find us." She spun and flicked the knife at the target. It hit it with a *thunk*.

Quinton covered his mouth and chuckled. "Somebody's getting lucky tonight." He said quietly.

Rafael looked at Alona and Chase, "a few somebodies."

"We're having the data we got off the hard drives put on the private server, so you can access all of it." Victor said still carrying Crissy.

Alona smiled, "that's perfect. It will save a lot of time."

Crissy kissed Victor then squirmed, so he'd set her down. "We can print and sort according to area and date, then have a list of locations to go to." She ran down the length of the table looking completely hyped.

"Warden?"

Arius turned to see two men standing at the door. Straightening, he went over and took the tablet from them and looked down at it. His brow creased as he looked at it then glanced back to them. "Did you double check the scans?"

The one guard glanced to him fleetingly then back to the floor. "Yes, sir."

The man beside him didn't even look at Arius. "We've called the science team to confirm it."

"Is there a problem, brother?" Victor came over and looked over his shoulder at the tablet. He scowled.

Arius looked at the men, his jaw clenched. "There may be." He looked from one man to the other. "Is there just the one?"

They both nodded, still not looking at him.

I know he'd told me no one met his look, but this was the first time I'd seen it with my own eyes. I looked at everyone standing here, they didn't seem to notice. It had been happening for so long it was just accepted. Something inside of me snapped. I stomped over and pushed between Victor and Arius, I stepped close to the first man and glared up at him. "I may not know a damn thing about rank and placement around here, but I do recognize disrespect when I see it." I jabbed him in the chest with my finger and sneered at him. "When speaking to a superior, you look them in the eye, not at the pattern on the carpet."

Stepping over, I got in the other one's face. "If he wanted to harm you, he wouldn't need to use his eyes to do it." Turning, I grabbed the tablet from a shocked Arius and smacked it against the man's chest. "Go do your job." I waved a hand at them. They both looked at me, then inclined their heads slightly and backed out of the room, quickly.

Someone started clapping. I turned to see Chase looking thrilled. I looked around to see expressions of approval and shock in the room. I took a deep breath and exhaled slowly. Giving Arius a soft look, I bit my lip. "Sorry—it just…"

Chase walked over and patted me on the shoulder. "Don't apologize, sarg. *That* was fucking beautiful." He walked out of the room. "I'll be in the cells when you're done staring at her with your gob hanging open, Arius."

Quinton stepped around me, a smirk on his face. "Vicious little thing."

Rafael just laughed as he walked by. "Sisters with skills." He winked.

Victor cleared his throat and turned to Arius, "I'll go see to the science team's tests."

Arius nodded, his eyes still looking at me.

One by one they filed out of the room.

I clasped my hands in front of me and looked at him, I wasn't sure if he was angry with what I'd done.

He stepped closer, reaching over my head, he pushed the door closed.

I bit my lip. "I'm sorry…"

Grasping my waist, he lifted me, pressing my back against the door before his mouth crushed mine in a rough kiss. I wrapped my arms around his neck, trying to keep up with him.

He growled in the back of his throat and lifted his head. "If it wasn't important," he kissed me again, "I would continue this," he growled again and nipped my lip. "No one has ever done anything like that for me before."

I remembered where it all started. "Is it bad? Why they came looking for you?"

He lowered me to the floor. "They found some sort of tracker on one of the men from the office earlier." He gently brushed the hair back from my forehead.

"To track them here?" It was hard to focus on words with the way he was looking at me.

He shook his head. "Nothing can lead them to the cells or any of the chambers, they have to know that by now."

"So why are they tracking him?"

"Exactly." Leaning down, he kissed me so tenderly my breath hitched in my throat when he raised his head. "I don't want to let you go."

I bit my lip. "I'll come with you and wait in your office."

He kissed me quickly, the backed up so he could open the door. "This time we're locking the office door."

We almost ran to the cells. When we reached them, he looked both ways, then grabbed me and kissed me hard. When he released me, he was smiling as we walked into his maze.

I stepped into the office to see the women all looking at the monitors. I stopped.

Daxx shrugged. "We didn't know where else to go, you were in our new cave."

Alona smiled. "First rule, no sex in the girl cave."

Crissy giggled.

I blushed.

Daxx nodded to the monitor. "Arius has a spring in his step."

Bethany turned and held her hand up for a high five.

I grinned and tapped my hand to hers.

"That was great." She smiled.

"Yeah." Daxx glanced at me, "putting them in their place like that."

"It's horrible the way everyone fears Arius." Alona stated quietly.

"Does anyone know if there's a sound button on this?" Daxx looked down at the buttons.

Bethany leaned over and looked. "I'd probably hit the wrong one and release everyone."

Daxx nodded. "Yeah. Well, we'll just go see what's going on." She turned to the door.

I hesitated. "Are we allowed to?"

She snorted. "After earlier, you could release the worst of the criminals in here and Arius would buy you flowers."

"Uh," Alona cringed, "don't mention flowers. I still shudder after the incident in my apartment."

"Yeah." Bethany agreed as she walked by.

I followed as they weaved through the cells. I looked straight ahead, not wanting to see who were behind the clear walls.

We walked into a space similar to the one I'd stood in to identify Martin. On the other side of the wall stood Victor, Arius and Troy. They watched a man run some sort of device over another man.

Alona stepped over to the panel and looked at it. She pushed a button. Daxx gave her a curious look, she shrugged. "I listen in when the doctors are with my father."

"Your father's in here?" I stepped over to the wall.

She nodded. "It's a long story that requires wine to be told."

Crissy giggled. "Everything with you needs wine."

Alona shrugged again. "We all have our vices. Yours is climbing, Bethany needs movies," she motioned to me, "Paisley's is music. Daxx is…"

"Kicking ass," Bethany and Crissy said at the same time.

Daxx laughed, "It works for me."

"This is your job." Arius' voice came over the speaker.

We all turned to watch in the cell.

He was leaning against the wall, his arms crossed over his chest, glaring at the man with the scanner. "If you don't know, who will?"

Victor and Troy stood watching the interaction.

The man lifted his hand and mumbled something.

Arius straightened away from the wall. "Then I suggest you go get them—I have better things to be doing than standing here waiting for you to do your job."

Troy grinned and looked at him. Victor's lips twitched as he motioned to the door so the man would hurry.

"I can take a look, brother." Troy offered.

Arius stood there looking at the prisoner. He walked over and stopped in front of him and leaned down. "Do you know who I am?" The man nodded. "You will behave, or deal with me." The man nodded. Arius straightened and looked at his brothers. "We'll move him to the room that blocks all tech first, just to be sure until they figure it out." He nodded to the guard near the door.

"Wonder why he's in such a mood." Alona said with a smirk, "what would he rather be doing?"

Daxx snorted.

I blushed. "He's so sweet." I said trying to voice how he made me feel. "It's like he's completely in tune with my emotions." I looked back at him. "I *know* he's not an emotion feeder and cheater like that Martin creep."

"He doesn't need to be."

I turned to see Chase leaning in the doorway.

"A blood bond is idiot proof," he winked at Alona, "even I can't screw that up."

Alona laughed. "No, your mouth does that for you, my king."

Chase shrugged, "It's part of my charm to throw you off guard.

I looked from him to Alona. "A blood bond?"

Alona's amusement faded.

I glanced to Daxx.

She sighed. "I'm telling you we need an introductory manual for this place."

Bethany glanced to Arius then me. "He didn't tell you before using his blood to heal you?" She motioned to my cheek.

I shook my head. "Explain what?"

"Shit," Chase whispered.

Alona crossed her arms over her chest. "When you exchange blood, or even just ingest theirs," She glanced to Daxx, "it creates a bond, a link with them."

Daxx nodded. "He'll know what you're feeling." She frowned, "be damned if I can figure it out myself, but the men are pros at it." She looked at Chase. "Depending on who it is, they could tap into all your emotions or only the strongest ones."

Chase looked at the floor. "It's Arius, Daxx, he controls thought…"

"He's in my head all the time?" Hugging my waist, I glanced back at Arius. "So, he's no better then Martin." I said, trying not to acknowledge how much that hurt.

"There's a reason, Paisley, and I'm guessing he hasn't mentioned that either…"

I held up my hand cutting Daxx off. "No reason excuses deceit." I looked at her. "Can you please get me out of this maze?"

She nodded and motioned to the door we'd come in.

As we stepped through the main door back into the hallway, she looked at me. "Want to go to your room or the girl cave?"

I heavy a shaky breath. "My room please."

We went about ten feet down the hall when Arius burst through the door.

"Paisley."

I turned around.

Chase was beside him saying something I couldn't hear.

Arius shook his head and started walking toward me. "Paisley…"

I shook my head and held my hand out, focusing on his feet to stop him. I backed away, holding him there. "I don't want to talk, Arius." Dropping my hand, I looked at him. He watched me back away but didn't move this time. I shook my head and then turned to follow Daxx.

Chapter Eight

I listened to loud music, cried, listened to sad music, cried, then listened to no music and cried. I felt stupid. I was lying on the bed staring at the ceiling in the silence when someone knocked on the door.

"Paisley, it's Daxx."

I looked at the door, then rolled off the bed and went over and unlocked it.

She gave me a meek smile and came in. "I told them this wasn't a good time to meet with the Elder that may be your relative, but," she shrugged, "they're men."

I took a deep breath and exhaled slowly. "Elder?"

She nodded, "there's an elder's council." Her eyes widened, "they're all over a thousand years old," she waved her hand, "but they need to meet with him to get permission to do a DNA test."

I tucked my hands into the jeans I'd put on. "I honestly don't know how I feel about that." I ran my hand through my hair. "I'm kind of emotionally spent right now."

Daxx nodded. "I know." She motioned to the door. "I can go tell them to get stuffed and reschedule it."

I shook my head. "No. I think scheduling time with someone that age shouldn't be postponed." I motioned to my face. "How bad do I look?"

She bit her lip then winced. "Like a train wreck."

I nodded. "Give me two minutes to slop some makeup on."

She nodded.

I went into the bathroom and gave myself a moment to look in the mirror. Train wreck didn't exactly cover it, it was worse.

"I don't want to mention his name right now, but there's more that he who-we-won't-be-named hasn't told you."

I paused and looked at her in the mirror. "Bad?"

She hesitated. "Not really, but among the men, they've managed to screw up in some pretty epic ways." Huffing out a breath she shook her head. "We'll talk about it later. Have a girls' get together, because honestly, if you wait for him to explain you could be in your eighties."

I blew out a breath and turned back to try to cover up my puffy eyes. "I don't know if I want to know, when you put it that way."

She grinned. "These guys have live hundreds of years without women guiding them…"

I laughed and turned to look at her, "right—when you put it that way." I nodded. "Okay, we'll have a meeting and you ladies can fill in *all* the blanks."

As we stepped out the door, Alona jolted. "I was just coming to find you." She held up her phone. "I was told to meet at Troy's office." She pouted, "I don't know where that is."

Daxx pointed, "We're headed there now."

"Are we meeting Elder Roan at Troy's office or in the council room?"

Daxx shrugged. "No idea. I just agreed to come and get Paisley because the men are afraid of her."

I gave her a shocked look.

Alona grinned. "Milk it for all it's worth, I say."

Daxx motioned to turn, we went around the corner and she held up her hand and pointed to a door. It was open a few inches. She glanced to Alona and then walked quietly toward it.

"...that's not what we're saying, Arius." Chase said sounding frustrated. "Just stay away from her until the blood bond wears off."

"How did that work out for you with Alona, Chase?" Arius growled.

"Arius, how long have you known?" Troy sounded calm.

Daxx and Alona both glanced to me, I held my hand to my mouth. I wanted to hear what was said as much as they did.

"I knew when I pulled her out of the bay." Arius said, sounding so upset. "Holding her against that rock to keep her from drowning, and all I fucking wanted to do was mark her. Right there. Right then." He made a sound like a wounded animal would. "Her essence—fuck."

Daxx raised her eyebrows and glanced at me.

I frowned. I didn't know what he was talking about.

"It's hard, I know..."

"The fuck you do, Troy." Arius hissed. "You fucked it up with Daxx so badly we thought she was going to let you die when you got hurt."

"He has a point." Chase agreed.

"Fine." Troy sounded annoyed. "All we're trying to say is give her some space. We'll look out for her interests when she meets Elder..."

"I'm going." Arius insisted. "Don't even look at me like that, or I will have you both on the floor mewling like cats without another thought." He warned.

Alona covered her mouth. I wasn't sure if she was laughing or crying.

"Arius..."

"Chase. *My* mate. You have no say."

Alona tapped Daxx on the shoulder.

Daxx nodded and knocked on the door. "We're here." She went in.

I walked in behind them and then stopped to see what looked like a table in pieces on the floor.

"Excuse the mess, Arius was offended by its existence." Chase said kicking debris to the side.

Troy motioned to come all the way in. "We'll be meeting Elder Roan in the council chambers." He tucked his hands in his pockets and glanced to Arius.

"You coming with us, Arius?" Daxx asked quietly.

He nodded. "The more of us there, the less chance that Chase tears his head off."

Chase snorted. "I'd never—" he shrugged, "okay, I may have thought it a few times."

I gave him a startled look.

"He can be a bit of…" Troy waved his hand around.

"An asshole." Chase finished for him.

The silence was awkward. I tried to avoid looking at Arius. He looked nowhere but at me.

Chase clapped his hands. "Shall we go? Don't want to keep him waiting." He ushered me toward the door, giving Arius a quick look as he did.

The walk was quiet for several minutes.

"We didn't dress formally." Troy said glancing to Chase.

"No we did not, brother." Chase grinned.

"You're loving this aren't you?"

Chase nodded. "Immensely."

"Is it the whole council?" Alona asked.

Chase shook his head. "No. Just the stuck up one." He glanced to me. "Sorry. I know you may be related to him, but he's…"

"Been looking at you for two hundred and sixty years like you're a parasite." He scowled at me. "You are a king, not a bug." I tried not to smile, but I needed to do something to distract myself before I walked in to meet a man that may be a relative I never dreamt existed. Never mind that he'd existed for over a thousand years.

"Figures you'd remember word for word." Chase said while giving his mate a hard look.

Alona covered her mouth. "You asked to try it, just remember that when someone reminds you that you were running victory laps through the halls."

Troy chuckled.

"Shut up cave man." Chase said, "At least I didn't carry my mate slung over my shoulder like a sack of feed."

I gave Daxx a curious look.

She shook her head. "I'll explain later."

The men stopped walking, I almost walked into their backs.

Alona took a deep breath and took Chase's hand. "You're not even going to try to behave, are you?"

He shook his head slowly. "Not a chance in hell."

We walked into a room with two long tables facing each other. I didn't stop to count the chairs, but there were a lot on the side we were on. I stood in front of the chair beside Daxx. Arius stood beside me. I didn't want to admit it, but I was glad he was there. My stomach was tied in knots.

A man in a black robe came in. He was average height, by Alterealm standards, with sparse grey hair. He stopped at a chair and bowed his head formally. "Your majesties."

The four to my left sat down. Arius put his hand in front of me to stop me from sitting, then moved it once they were seated. I glanced to him, and sat as he did.

The man across from us squinted and glanced from Chase to Arius slowly. He paused then looked back to me. "It has been some time since I held a lone council." His squinted his brown eyes in Chase's direction "Perhaps I've missed something in the hasty request that was made," he looked pointedly at me, "but I do not see a royal medallion adorning this woman's neck."

I looked at Daxx and then Arius, they both wore a chain and pendant.

Chase leaned forward. "We could have partitioned the council to bring Paisley before you, but we are paying you the courtesy of keeping family business—" he glanced down to us, "private."

The Elder gave him a startled look. "What family business could possibly be…"

Chase raised his hand and motioned to me. "I'm so sorry, I've been quite remiss." He smiled in a mocking way. "May I introduce Miss Paisley Roan."

I looked from him quickly to the man sitting across from us.

"Did you say Roan?" He squinted at Chase.

"Why, yes, Elder *Roan*. I did." Chase said, with a real grin this time.

Elder Roan looked slowly from me to Troy. "May I implore, you Day King to shed some light on what this," he motioned to me, "woman has to do with this council?" He gave me a haughty look.

"Careful." Arius warned in a low tone.

Elder Roan looked shocked but bowed his head politely to Arius. "I apologize Warden of Justice, I'm quite taken aback by this."

Troy sighed, "Paisley was recently—" he looked at me, "recovered from one of the factions being led by Mister Hubert."

"She's from the other side?" He asked, looking serious.

Troy nodded. "She is, and we believe there may be more of a connection as Cris—The Seer of truth saw Miss Roan prior to that point."

The man bobbed his head. "That is quite certain. We've been going through the relevance of the visions that have come to pass from The Seer."

Chase nodded slowly. "Paisley's past and family story has a few suspicious rings to it." He grinned a wide grin.

"Such as?" Elder Roan asked.

"Her parents passed away when she was a baby, she was raised by her grandmother—her grandfather, a Roan, vanished before she was born."

Elder Roan looked from Chase to me, and sat there for a several moments not moving or speaking. "Paisley?"

I nodded.

"How old are you?" He squinted his eyes and waited for my answer.

I cleared my throat. "Twenty-six."

He leaned back, a frown on his face. His eyes flicked to Chase, then back to me. With a different light in his eyes, he studied me. "My son disappeared on the other side." He said quietly.

"We don't wish to bring up any disagreeable memories, Elder Roan," Alona said quietly, glaring at Chase so he would stay quiet, "what we'd like is permission to do a DNA test on yourself and Paisley—"

He looked at Alona. "I suppose," he nodded slowly. "Yes. I would be remiss if we didn't."

Alona smiled. "That was my mate's feeling as well."

Elder Roan looked back to me. "You're not wearing a device, so you were meant to be in our realm."

"She has an ability as well, Elder Roan." Daxx added.

He looked intrigued. "Oh, which is?"

"She's a Chronos." Arius said with a hard look, almost daring the Elder to say something a wrong.

"A-a chronos? That's—so very rare." He motioned to me, "may I see?"

I looked to Daxx, she nodded. I glanced back at him. "Yes." I stood up slowly, trying to figure out what I was going to stop.

Arius got up. "Use this." He pulled his knife from his back and held it out.

I nodded. "Okay." I backed up a few feet and held my hand out. He tossed it above the table. I focused, stopping it in mid-air.

"Oh my. That's marvelous." The Elder said.

I lowered my hand the watched as Arius caught it before it hit the table.

I turned to see Elder Roan looking more animated. "That was something." He stopped and then looked at Arius. "She holds time."

Arius inclined his head. "She does."

Troy and Chase both looked at each other. Daxx frowned and looked from them to Arius.

I gave her a curious look, she shrugged quickly not knowing what it meant.

"I will contact the lab about the tests." Elder Roan nodded, then looked to me. "The sooner, I believe, the better." He smiled and glanced at Arius. "So we can put this matter behind us and move forward." He stood up and bowed his head. "I look forward to seeing you at the ball, your majesties." He turned and quickly walked out.

Daxx looked at Arius then to Troy. "So why did he change his tune so fast? She keeps time?"

Arius cleared his throat. "It could have gone much worse."

Chase stood up, "I wanted much worse."

Alona took his hand as she got up, "we know you did."

"Okay," Daxx said and stood up, "we have a girls' meeting to get to." She pulled out her phone. "I'll message Criss."

"We do?" Alona asked.

Daxx nodded. "I promised Paize some answers." She looked at Arius and tucked the phone back into her jeans.

Chase and Troy both looked at Arius.

"We have to catch a spy." Chase said quickly.

I looked at Arius, and then turned toward the door.

"Arius." Troy said with a sound of authority.

I glanced over my shoulder to see Troy with his hand on Arius' shoulder as he watched me walk away.

Chapter Nine

An hour later I sat there staring into the glass of wine in my hand. I didn't know what to do with the information.

"I think we broke her." Daxx said quietly.

I came back to reality and looked at her. I shook my head. "No. Not broken, just—" I opened my mouth then closed it and sighed, "I don't know what I think."

"It's a lot to take in." Alona agreed getting up to get another bottle of wine. "I already knew I wasn't normal, per se, but the mate thing was a horror story for me." Opening it she came and sat back down. "We need to personalize this space a bit more, the men did well, but they have no concept of Feng Shui at all."

Bethany laughed, "Eight men decorating a room, what could go wrong?"

I looked at them, then to Crissy. "You're sure this," I waved my hand around, "prophecy is about me?"

She looked up from the cracker she'd been studying and nodded. "The brother that controls thought will stand stronger when his mate, that holds time, is found." She shrugged. "Who else could that be about if not you and Arius?"

"It's true." Daxx nodded, "and at least yours makes sense—mine was cryptic mumbo jumbo."

Setting the glass down, I decided alcohol was not going to help me figure this out. Pulling my feet up, I turned so I could see the other four women. "Let me get this straight." I looked at Daxx. "There's a prophecy about the brothers—no one knows how old it is…"

"Centuries and centuries," Crissy said softly.

I nodded, "Older than time," I paused looking for the words, "and in this prophecy you could have been mated to either twin king?" Daxx nodded and sighed. "But Troy marked you when Chase resisted the," I waved my hand around, "pull?" She nodded again. I leaned back. "That—I mean, Troy seems so…"

"Well, he's not." Daxx said then emptied her glass.

"You don't regret it?" I motioned to her arm. "Completing it."

She looked at her arm and tilted her head. "No, well, eighty—ninety percent of the time I don't." She gave me a bored look, "Only when I'm confined to quarters and pissed off, so I don't even think that counts." She pulled out her phone. "Update. All traps are set. First group in an hour." She tucked the phone back in her pocket.

"I hope this works." Alona said leaning over and filling Daxx's glass, again.

"Me too." Crissy nodded. "I don't like things I can't see and not knowing."

Everyone nodded. I wasn't sure what she said, so I didn't. I studied her. "You agreed to sleep with Victor but not be his mate…"

"I knew I was his mate, I didn't want him to mark me and be stuck with someone that just *is*." She frowned.

"Right. Then he took you to a butterfly migration," I grinned. "I still can't believe those photos, they're amazing." I shook my head, "then you knew it was going to be all right?"

Crissy grinned, her head nodding quickly. "Because I'd seen it for a long time."

Alona picked up her phone and sighed as she looked at it.

"Is it important?" Daxx asked. "Because I may not be able to kick ass right now." She raised her glass in the air.

Alona shook her head, then grinned. "No. Chase is pouting because I'm here and he's on Arius watch."

"Arius watch?" I looked from Daxx to Alona.

"Mmm," Alona set the phone down, "they get a little out of hand and…"

"Rampage." Crissy finished.

Daxx nodded, "when they're close to their mates but can't have them."

My eyes grew huge.

"Oh. No, no, not like that." Alona laughed, "She means before the marking and bond is complete." She rolled her eyes, "not after or we would…"

"Kill them and bury the bodies." Daxx added.

Alona smirked, "Not quite what I was going to say, but close enough."

Grabbing my glass, I drank back what was left in it, then paused and looked over at the stereo. I hadn't even realized the music had stopped. Putting the glass down, I got up and went over. Picking up my phone, I scrolled through some songs and selected a few that would be good background sound for this discussion. I noticed I had messages and opened them before turning the music on. They were from Arius.

"He's sending you messages?" Alona inquired leaning over the back of the couch.

I nodded. "He's sorry." I opened the next one. "He wants to talk." The next one. "He's an idiot and handled it all wrong." I closed the message app and started the music.

Daxx shrugged, "at least he's admitting it."

I went over and sat back down.

Bethany turned and looked at me. "Just don't agree to anything without clarification first."

I watched Alona fill up my glass then looked at Beth. "So you thought you were going to jail but in the meantime the secret he was keeping was you were his mate?"

She nodded, "and thought I was agreeing to sex with him, not the insta-tattoo." She held up her arm.

I slumped down on the couch. "Why don't they just explain it first?" I motioned around the room. "All of it."

Daxx leaned forward, taking her phone out and setting it on the table, then sat back again. "Except for Alona, I'd say it's because all of this is so far from the normal we grew up with, they're afraid we'll run the other way."

Bethany sat forward and picked up some crackers. "It's true."

I sighed and picked imaginary lint off my jeans. "I really thought Arius was…" I snorted, "I don't know exactly—different then all the lying, cheating, pervs out there."

"Well, he is," Alona said quietly, "he just didn't go about gaining your trust very well."

Crissy nodded. "Victor doesn't lie. He blurts out the truth even if you don't want to hear it."

Alona leaned forward and looked at her phone and smiled. "Chase is very persistent tonight." She sat back and shrugged.

I sighed. "Okay, define mate. What is the difference between this and marrying someone you love?"

"Aside from living longer…" Daxx mused.

Beth gave me a curious look, "and the insta-tattoo."

"Or the mental connection?" Crissy asked frowning.

I waved my hand around. "Yes, other than all of that."

Beth smiled, "That's easy. The completeness you feel."

Crissy nodded. "Forgiveness. It's not defined."

"Oh, fidelity." Beth nodded. "They can't cheat."

I gave her a look, "can't?"

She nodded. "They'll never want another woman." She looked at the other women. "I don't know about you, but I've had my heart crushed more than once by a boyfriend who couldn't keep it in his pants."

Daxx shrugged then nodded slowly.

"That's…" I just nodded, I couldn't argue with that being a big plus.

"Understanding." Alona said with a soft look. "Understanding, not just what you like, but who you are."

Daxx snorted. "That's pushing it."

Alona turned to her. "He doesn't look at you and just know where you're going with your next thought?"

"Okay. Dammit. You're right." Daxx sighed.

A knock on the door had all of us turn.

"Who is it?" Alona asked.

The door opened and a hand holding a bottle of wine appeared.

Alona grinned. "Oh. I do love when a bottle of wine is at the door."

"Come in Chase." Daxx laughed.

He stuck his head in, with a cautious expression on his face. "I've come to lure my mate away—so we can sleep for a few hours before we have to run a kingdom." He stepped inside. "My brothers want practice tomorrow, so I need sleep to beat their asses." He nodded.

Alona stood up.

Daxx gave him an odd look. "What are you going to do when we take down Hubert and you can sleep during the dark again? We'll never see you."

Chase gave her a shocked look. "How boring would your lives be without me?" He shrugged, "Relax. Regardless of what is going on, our lives have always been days and nights broken, one overlapping the other."

"I don't know if that's a good thing or not one right now." Daxx stood up, then grinned. "We need to limit your mate's pouring speed."

Chase chuckled, "she's very efficient at keeping the glasses full."

Alona picked up her phone and turned to smile at me. "I'd ask if we helped at all, but I know the endless processing that goes with all of this."

"Don't remind me." Chase said coming over and setting the bottle on the table. "It's a very fine line we walk," he leaned down and whispered, "us males." He nodded. "The pull to ensure our mate is healthy and happy versus the urge to make them ours unequivocally." He winked. "I am thrilled I only have to go through that once—" he pulled Alona against his side and kissed her, "and never again."

Daxx waved a hand at him. "Stop soapboxing for the men's team."

Bethany laughed, "Don't make me blast you, Chase." She motioned to me. "She has to make up her own mind."

Chase sighed, "I know, sparky, but have you ever *seen* Arius when he's in a mood?" He cringed. "I don't know how long we can contain that."

Daxx lifted both hands and then dropped them. "Wouldn't be a normal day around here if one of you weren't raging."

Chase raised an eyebrow at her. "Pot, kettle." He smirked.

She waved him off, "go."

He inclined his head and took Alona's hand. "See you ladies later." He looked over his shoulder at her as he opened the door. "I hear the gown fittings are tomorrow." He grinned and stepped out.

"Ugh. There goes my wine buzz." Daxx mumbled.

Crissy jumped up. "I'm going to my tower."

Bethany nodded, "I'm going to start printing out the data on the server, see if we can sort through some of it later."

I looked at Daxx. "Can you help me get back to my room? The pink arrows only go to the dining room and after the wine, I just want a nap."

She nodded. "Sure. I'll drop you off then I'm going to see if I can get in on some of the trap missions."

Bethany glanced up from the computer. "Good luck with that. I think we're all grounded."

She laughed. "They can try."

The walk back was slow.

I glanced to Daxx. "This has been quite the day." I frowned, "night."

She snorted. "I'd like to lie to you and say you get used to the day and night thing, but you don't."

"I found out I lost my apartment, helped sneak into a building, confiscate data, fight a bunch of scary men, I may have a great, great grandfather? Alive. And a man I really like turned out to be a cheat like the last one that got me into all of this." I sucked in a breath.

Daxx made a strange face. "Some of that is good, though." She shrugged. "On the larger scale of things."

I sighed. "I suppose, but it's been a long day-night." I stopped walking when I saw the door to my room. A small package sat outside.

"He's wasting no time sucking up." Daxx went over and picked it up and held it out to me.

Frowning, I looked at it then opened it slowly. Inside was a tube of dark purple lipstick.

"Uh, that's an odd suck up gift. Purple lipstick." Daxx tucked her hands in her pocket. "I'm assuming it has some sort of significance."

I remembered Arius' reaction to my wearing lipstick. I glanced at her. "I think he's asking me to torture him by wearing it."

"That's way more than I needed to know about Arius." She shook her head.

"It's hard to explain." I looked at the tube in my hand.

"So are you going to?" She motioned to it. "Torture him by wearing it?"

I bit my lip. "I'm not sure."

"Get some rest. The next few days are going to be crazy. I'm hoping by morning we have an idea of when we'll be hitting the island."

My heart sped up. "I'd forgotten about that."

"Understandable." She shrugged. "But if we get on it, it's going to be all hands-on deck—regardless of what the men want."

I nodded. "I'll help. Anything to stop them from taking more girls."

Chapter Ten

I found my way to the dining room without help. It wasn't exactly a defining moment, but I was happy. Victor, Crissy, the two kings and their mates were the only ones there when I walked in.

Daxx grinned. "The small victory of finding a room in this place for the first time."

I laughed and sat down beside her. "Yes."

Chase lifted his mug to me. "Morning, sarg." He smirked.

I rolled my eyes. "I am so far from a person that normally gives orders, it's not funny." I nodded when Alona held up the coffee urn. "Normally I prefer to be invisible."

She smiled. "Nice shade."

I licked my lips, tasting the lipstick Arius had left for me.

Crissy nodded. "Go up. No one ever looks up."

I cringed. "I'll keep that in mind."

"If you deejay, how is that being invisible?" Chase asked.

I shrugged. "I don't mind then, but it's not about me it's all about the music."

He paused on me for a moment then looked at Troy. "How did you make out watching over the pretty one?"

Troy paused in taking a bite. "He had a few moments and revelations."

"Oh?" Victor gave him a concerned look.

Troy glanced to me briefly and then cleared his throat. "Had to take some time to settle down, the sensors wouldn't let him open a cell."

Daxx frowned, "the warden not being able to access a cell, must have been…"

"Mmm, indeed it was." Troy added before she could finish.

"An appropriate time to change the subject." Victor cut in, nodding toward the door as Arius walked in. "I believe we have found out who has been helping make the illegal cuffs and devices, brother."

Arius paused and looked at me for a moment, his eyes noting the lipstick I wore, then he walked to the other side of the table and sat down in his seat. "I don't have any new residents in the cell." He looked at Victor.

"We haven't made a move yet, thought you may want to be in on that." He leaned back and watched his brother.

Arius nodded slowly. "I do."

"So who is it?" Daxx looked from one to the other.

"An assistant in the science department. We had thought he was just a paper pusher, but it seems he's far more advanced than we thought." Victor motioned to me with his eyes. "Rafael and Leone used Paisley's trap idea to figure it out. Had Clairee put a magic tracker on some mock plans for a new device then followed to see where it went."

"Where is that?" Arius asked, dragging his eyes from me.

"Back to his place to copy them before handing them in to the department supervisor." Michael walked in and sat down. "Quinton and I went in after he went back to work. They're all there. Our plans and schematics for authentic devices and the redesigned plans for the illegal ones." He shook his head. "We're going to have to go through the information and try to figure out how he managed to bypass the porters showing up on our system—but he's definitely working for Hubert and his fanatics."

"Where is he now?" Chase leaned on the table.

"Welsley is keeping an eye on him. He'll let us know when he'd leaving to go home."

Troy rubbed a hand over his brow. "Do we want to let it play out and see how he contacts them?"

Victor shook his head. "The damage has already been done with what he created." He looked to Arius for a moment and then back to Troy. "I'm sure you can pick the details out of his head once he's in our brothers' care."

Troy nodded and looked to Arius, who had a serious look on his face. "I can and I will."

Leone stood in the door with Bethany. "Does that mean they'll know about the two new port devices for Michael and I?"

Victor shook his head. "They will not. I have the original creator making those. Elder Arian." He nodded to Michael. "She requires both of you to drop in so she can calibrate the boxes to your touch only."

Leone grinned and Michael. "We can do that."

Michael toasted Bethany with his glass. "Yes we can."

As the remaining brothers arrived, I tried to listen to everything being said. Much of it I didn't understand. I could feel Arius' eyes on me, no matter who was speaking or what was being said. Each time I glanced at him, his eyes were moving over my face pausing on my mouth. A nervous reaction to someone looking at my mouth had me licking my lips each time, then his pale eyes would snap to mine and hold me captive.

Quinton reaching in front of me and snapped his fingers. "Earth to Arius."

Arius' eyes went cold as he looked to his brother.

Quinton made a sound of exasperation. "Welcome back. Your input is required."

Arius' brow creased as he looked around the table. "Regarding?"

Victor cleared his throat, a slight smirk on his face. "We'll come back to that shortly. Emil will be here at any moment—I asked him to come." He paused to see if everyone was paying attention. "I've had emergency correspondence from Miss Hinton."

All movement around the table stopped.

Emil walked in, his gaze immediately going to Victor. "It's true. There are more women, visibly so, in the past twelve hours." He sat at the end of the table.

Michael glanced to Chase then Troy. "Emil has been lurking on the nearby islands tracking any movement."

"I saw Rena this morning." He said in a low voice. "Just standing there staring out over the water. She looked haunted and empty." His jaw clenched a few times. "It was painful to witness." He looked at Arius. "I did not share that with her brothers."

Arius glanced at me briefly then to Victor. "What message did you get?"

Victor sat back. "Since we found those files on the computers there have been more arrivals on the island." His jaw tensed for a moment. "Including visits from Hubert and his leaders—" he lifted his hand, "I had Miss Hinton memorize any and all faces involved, before she allowed herself to be recruited. She has also overheard that they are setting up a new base of operations."

"Shit. That means those files had to have the location Willis was holed up in." Rafael growled.

Victor held up his hand. "Most likely. This still gives us the upper hand. Their ranks will be in chaos at the moment, tossing about all their carefully laid plans." He looked down the table at Emil, then to Arius. "Miss Hinton believes we should delay any attempts to take the island for at least a day, possibly longer. It is too heavily secured presently. We will only get one chance to breach it, if we go in with it like this, we could fail."

"Fuck." Arius stood up and paced down the length of the table.

Michael shook his head. "Romulus isn't one hundred percent sure he's got it right—" he waved his hand around, "whatever he needs to do, to take down the barrier. So this just allows us the time to be sure."

Arius heaved out a breath and looked at me. His anger was plain to see. He motioned to me. "Paisley said girls were being taken off and didn't return. We can't wait too long."

Emil stood up. "They're using boats, some cloaked, as they travel across the water, to come and go. I haven't seen any women near the dock leaving."

Arius turned and looked at Victor. "Their barrier prevents porting."

Victor rubbed his hand along the bridge of his nose. "So it would seem. That is a huge oversight on their magic makers' part. It is good for us though, we'll know who is coming and going." He picked up his phone and glanced to Emil. "I'll send two guards back with you. Enlist the help of your sons. We need any movement recorded, as well as a count of any you see that remain." He tapped the screen on his phone. "I'll send them to the landing room."

Emil nodded. "Let me know when a plan is being formed. I want in on it." He walked out of the room quickly.

Chase rubbed a hand over his jaw. "This has been in the works for years, maybe longer."

Alona looked at Bethany. "Is the data still printing?"

Beth nodded. "I left Mac and Sith there loading paper and skimming the files to select only those important to finding locations." She pushed the hair back from her face. "I needed a break from staring at the screen."

Daxx nodded. "My eyes dried out a few hours ago."

Alona looked at me. "Paisley and I can take a turn while you rest."

Michael motioned to Arius. "After practice, I need to nap. While you're pacing around, you can coordinate between the locations the girls find, and the teams going to check them out."

Arius gave an abrupt nod. "I've no plans for sleep any time soon." His eyes moved over my face briefly.

"That's what I thought." Michael said with a smirk. He shrugged. "We've found four so far." He grinned at Alona. "Guards are on standby to go to the new safe house when it's confirmed."

She nodded. "I'll know about that later. Liza and I have been scouring the city for fast closings with minimal strings."

"Let us know if there's anything we can do." Troy offered. "We have a few Alterealm residents living on that side who can assist, without raising suspicion."

Alona smiled. "Chase told me. Thank you, but so far there have been no hitches."

I frowned. "You're not only rescuing these girls…"

"And kids." Crissy nodded.

I looked at Arius, he nodded confirming children had been involved. "And kids, but you give them a home afterward?" I finished.

Arius sighed, his brow furrowed as his eyes moved over my face.

I took a shaky breath. "That's incredible."

"Many wouldn't be in this situation, or be sought by Hubert's men, if we had a better system over the past centuries." Victor said quietly.

"What do you mean?" I glanced around at the others.

Arius stopped the restless movement and put his hands on his hips. His grey eyes held my look. "The women being taken are for one reason or another from an Alterealm blood line." His eyes flicked to my mouth for a second. "It may be several generations removed, as you are, but they still are."

My mouth hung open as I looked around. "I thought my situation was unusual."

Chase pointed at me. "You are, in many more gratifying ways."

Alona patted his arm, so he'd stop talking. "Their hopes are to breed a new, stronger generation of Alterealm—or that's the impression we have."

I leaned on the table, covering my mouth with both hands. My heart was in my throat. I dropped my hands and looked at her. "I didn't realize it was this big. I thought it was just us on the island."

"It's widespread." Arius said quietly watching me. "Even outside of the city, if they found Emil's daughter."

I looked at Bethany. "How soon can we go through the data?"

She sighed. "We've been trying to sort it as it prints. In an hour we should be able to start organizing the teams. The four we found earlier were a long shot, guessing more than knowing."

I nodded. "I'll help."

"I don't know about you guys, but I'm ready for practice to burn off some anger, so I can grab a nap." Quinton got up. "Who volunteers to get beat on first?"

Rafael snorted. "In your dreams, old man." He stood up and motioned to the door. "I'll give you a head start."

Quinton sneered at him then bolted out the door.

The dishes on the table rattled as Rafael ran past the table, cutting the corner tight.

"Mitz catches them racing in the halls, she'll string them up." Leone said with a smirk.

"My money is on Raf." Michael got up.

"Please." Troy pushed back from the table. "Quinton has more endurance than Raf, by a long shot."

Victor held out his hand to Crissy. "Only way to know is to be there." He stood up and hugged her then they vanished.

"Cheater." Michael hissed then he vanished as well.

I gave Daxx a wide-eyed look, she shrugged. "We have to know." She stood up and leaned into her mate then they were gone.

Chase looked at Alona.

She bit her lip. "If I take us to the mall again, don't get cross."

He stood up, "don't think about the mall and we won't end up at there."

She got up. "Now I can't help but think about it—you said it." She took a deep breath and closed her eyes.

"Practice room. Practice room." She whispered, then they vanished.

Leone winked at me then he and Bethany were gone.

I looked at the empty chairs then to Arius. "I think I'll walk."

He nodded. "I'll go with you, so you don't get lost."

"We need more arrows." I told him as I got up.

He smirked. "I'll see what can be done."

We walked together, each on either side of the hall. I had to respect that he was giving me space. I glanced at him. "My heart just freezes when I think about all those women."

His watched me as I spoke.

"I was lucky. I got away before anything—bad happened to me." I stopped and held my hand over my chest. "What about those that aren't?"

He took a step toward me, then stopped. His jaw was tense, eyes reflected pain. "We will find them, Paisley, you have my word. Those responsible will be brought to justice."

I closed my eyes for a second.

"Hey," he touched my chin.

I opened my eyes to see he had moved closer.

His eyes held a soft and sincere look. "We will find them, and do everything possible to help them."

I nodded.

He dropped his hand away then motioned down the hall, so I would start walking again.

"I didn't know you had safe houses set up for them. What happens then?"

Crossing his arms over his chest, he kept walking with a slow stride. "We'll help them overcome trauma—counselling, whatever they need. Once we stop Willis and his group, they're free to live their lives." He shrugged. "Whether on this side or that one."

"Won't they have to wear devices if they live here?"

He nodded slowly. "Most will."

"But I don't have to because—"

He glanced to me briefly. "Because you're my mate. Fate wasn't taking any chances that you couldn't be here."

"Were you planning on explaining that at some point?" I watched his face, waiting for him to answer.

He sighed. "I was." Pausing in step, he looked down at me, then started walking again. "It's like hearing a fairy tale for over two hundred years, you think at some point there may have been some facts that lead to the story," he rubbed his hand down his face, "but, over the years the information has been misconstrued—altered—then all at once you know it's all true, and not a fairy tale at all." He took a deep breath, then exhaled slowly. "Once I knew you were real, I didn't want to take a chance that you would vanish, like some mythical fairy tale."

I looked up at him. "You've put some thought into this conversation."

"The last twelve hours, I've rehearsed it a thousand times, trying to express why I did what I did."

"How's this working out compared to your rehearsals?

His lips quirked. "Not as well as I'd hoped."

I took a deep breath, not knowing if we'd get a quiet moment alone like this again. "The attraction between us—is it this mating pull?"

Stopping he looked down at me. "No. It may contribute to how heated it gets without warning, but I was interested before we ever spoke."

I gave him a blank look, what he said made no sense.

"I stood on that shore and watched a woman leap off a cliff into the unknown. I watched her fight to swim and get away. I was taken by your strength and courage, even after you tried to kick me in the head to get away from me."

I stood there lost in his words, his eyes confirmed each one he spoke.

Hesitating, he motioned down the hall. "It's just around the corner."

I nodded and started walking.

"At least you don't hate me, as I feared you might."

"You can feel that through the blood bond?"

He stopped at the double doors. "No. The blood bond is mostly worn off now. I know that because you're wearing the lipstick." His eyes moved over my mouth. "And now I'm plagued with wondering if purple tastes the same on your lips as the other shade did." He smiled and went into the practice room.

I walked in.

"One foot. You won by one foot. If you hadn't shoved me into the wall, I would have won by at least ten." Rafael said pointing at Quinton.

Quinton shrugged. "A win is a win, little brother."

You couldn't help but smile, the way they were with each other. You'd never know how old they were by the way they acted.

"Cristy." Victor looked up to a beam with the ropes hanging from it. "You need practice on the ground. Not in the air."

I watched Crissy swing her leg over the beam and use some sort of pulley on her belt to drop to the floor. She retracted it, then turned and went over to him. "I'm a little tired, but I'll try." She nodded.

"Tired, little sister?" Arius smirked. "I've never seen you tired enough to stop."

She grinned. "I do. When I'm sleeping or reading."

Victor huffed out a breath and shook his head. "No, heart, you do not."

"Oh." She put her hands on her hips and looked at the brothers. "So are we doing it like always?"

Leone nodded. "No pulley, no clamp, no rubber ball. You need to practice for when you have nowhere to climb or hide."

Unclipping the belt, she nodded. "Okay. But I like being high. It's better." She set the belt down and walked toward the door.

I went over and stood beside Bethany as the men and Daxx lined up down the length of the large mat. "What are they doing?"

Alona came over and stood with us. "If they catch or stop her, she loses." She said quietly as she turned to watch.

My eyebrows went up. "That's like an ant trying to escape a giant."

Beth nodded. "She's good at it, but I still don't see why. We're never out there on our own."

I glanced at her then to Alona.

Alona's lips quirked. "You ladies could practice that tag team move you used at that office. I know I'll feel safer if you're both beside me."

Bethany looked at me. "We need to be closer or I'll knock the guys flying."

"Don't try with Daxx," Alona warned, "she's immune to abilities being used on her."

Nodding we went over and stood by the mat.

"You aiming for feet or bodies?" Beth whispered.

"Feet, then if you hit them, they'll topple."

She chuckled. "Too bad we can't get Alona to record it."

I grinned. "That would give away the surprise."

"Two feet around them, right?" Crissy looked to Victor.

He nodded and motioned so she'd begin.

Crissy nodded again. "Okay. I got it."

She took off running toward Rafael.

I lifted my hand. "One, two," I whispered then looked at his feet just as Crissy would have been within his reach.

"Three, release." Beth said and flicked her hand toward him.

He stumbled but didn't fall.

"What the…" He turned and looked at us.

Daxx was next, so we watched.

"Send on the four count." I said watching Crissy approach Michael. I raised my hand. "One, freeze." I stopped his feet.

"Three, blast." She flipped her hand and he fell back, but caught his balance and glared at us.

"Timing is still off." I said softly.

"Yeah," she agreed.

Arius was next, he leaned forward preparing to lunge.

"One, stop." His arms flailed.

"Three," she flicked her wrist and he fell forward, landing on his hands and knees.

Alona laughed behind us.

Leone was focused on Crissy, he took a step. I stopped his foot, then he fell and landed on his butt.

"Beautiful." Daxx called out.

Quinton growled, "I got her."

I stopped both of his feet and Beth pushed his side and he fell over. Crissy ran past him.

"Cheaters." He called out.

Troy laughed and hunched to grab Crissy.

"Chest," I said quickly freezing him.

"Chest," Beth repeated, and Troy was knocked on his back.

"Tag team nightmare." Rafael called out laughing.

Chase glared at us, then prepared to make a move toward Crissy.

"Whole body." I said as I stopped him.

"Foot shot," Beth said laughing.

Chase toppled to the mat.

Crissy laughed and launched herself at Victor.

We both dropped our hands down as he caught her in the air and hugged her.

He looked over at Beth and me. "That isn't quite how I pictured Cristy succeeding." He looked around at his siblings with a smirk. "But practicing on working together is just as important."

"Easy for you to say, big brother, you weren't knocked over like a domino." Troy said hugging Daxx to him.

Bethany shrugged when Leone gave her a playful scowl. "Getting the timing right is hard." She motioned to Rafael and Michael. "We failed the first few times."

Michael rubbed the back of his neck with a smirk on his face. "It didn't feel like a fail on my end." He glanced from Bethany to me. "It was frightening to have a body part just stop."

Chase snorted. "Try your *whole* body."

I glanced at Arius, he was looking at me, I couldn't be sure, but it looked like pride in his eyes. He glanced at my mouth quickly, then around at his brothers. "If you combine the women as a team, they're—"

"Lethal." Michael said with a grin.

"Scary as hell." Quinton nodded.

"Able to look after themselves." Daxx added. She pointed to Alona, "get her in there with those long legs and num-chuks and you men do not have to babysit us in the field anymore."

There was a lot of grumbling from the men.

Daxx put her hands on her hips. "I'm serious. Leaving us behind or telling us to run and hide has got to stop." She scowled at her mate. "What was it Elder Drusla said?"

Troy gave her a blank look.

"Oh." Crissy jumped down from Victor's arm. She closed her eyes. "To Elder Moire? About the prophecy?" She looked at Daxx who nodded and smirked at Troy. "Elder Moire, do you really believe the prophecy would have spoken of meek women that needed coddling as the mates to the royal brothers?" Crissy nodded and grinned. "That's what she said."

"That." Daxx pointed to Crissy, then motioned to all of us women. "Are we not the mates to the royal brothers?"

Chase held up his hand. "Okay. Okay, we get it. Please stop before cutie recites the whole damn history of Alterealm."

"I don't know *all* of it." She shrugged, "yet."

Chase gave her a dumbfounded look. "I'm sure you will at some point. What I meant was we do acknowledge all of you beautiful ladies are a force to be reckoned with." He looked to see his brothers nodding. Chase placed his hand over his chest, his expression changing to a somber one. "You have to see if from our point of view—we brothers have been waiting hundreds of years to have you by our sides." He nodded, a heartfelt expression on his face. "The very idea that something could happen to our cherished, long-awaited mate would destroy us."

"Really?" Alona looked at him then to the other men. "You're playing *that* card?"

Chase gave her a hesitant look. "Is it working?"

There were a few snickers in the room.

Alona looked to me, then Beth.

Glancing at each other, we both turned and raised our hands at Chase. He sprinted and stood behind Alona.

She started laughing.

Even Victor was laughing.

We dropped out hands.

I looked at Daxx. "I don't *belong* to anyone, to be told what I can and cannot do. So I'm going to help find these women, then help find the insane people taking them and stop this." I nodded.

Daxx glanced over at Arius quickly, then motioned to the door. "Let's go get the addresses for the teams."

I looked to see Arius watching me, his expression hard, almost determined. We were almost to the door when Troy called out.

"Daxx."

She stopped.

"Don't forget the gown fitting later, wouldn't want you to distress Mitz." He grinned.

"Troy, don't make me cut out your tattoo and divorce you."

"Oh." Rafael exclaimed.

"Ouch." Quinton winced.

Daxx gave her mate a smile that was more baring her teeth, then turned and went through the door.

Chapter Eleven

We worked for hours in the girl cave. Sorting, searching and marking a map. We'd snack, and a few took a short nap, Arius or one of the personal guards checked in often to get new locations to send the teams to.

Alona hung up her phone. "Two more on the way to a safe house, unharmed." She clapped her hands.

Crissy jumped up and went over to the map and placed two more green pins on it. She set the pages on the table then went and sat back down.

I set my phone down and went over and picked up the pages with the addresses highlighted. I glanced over my shoulder to her. "If we could all read at the speed you do, this," I motioned to the stacks of papers on the table, "would be all done by now."

Crissy shrugged. "Reading is the only way to get out of my head."

I paused, not sure what that meant.

"We're making a dent, at least." Daxx said pointing to the large pile on the floor at the end of the table.

I huffed out a breath. "Still feels like we're not doing enough."

"Do anymore and our teams are going to collapse from exhaustion."

I turned to see Arius standing in the doorway. A large man with short black hair and eyes as pale as Welsley's stood beside him.

Arius motioned to him as he stepped into the room. "This is Felix. He'll be your personal guard whenever you are outside the royal chambers."

I raised my eyebrows and looked over at Alona, she shrugged.

"Sith is a great help."

Biting my lip, I looked back at Arius. The look in his eyes told me there was no wiggle room with this. I turned to the man. "Felix." He nodded. "What's your favorite band?"

His eyebrows rose, he looked at Arius, then back to me, a blank look on his face.

I grinned. "Excellent a clean slate. I can work with that. If you'd been a thrash or screamo fan, it would have been a deal breaker."

He looked at Arius again. "I don't know what that is."

I gave him a thumb up.

Arius shook his head and motioned to the door. "You can go out with the next team."

"Oh." I turned and went to the table, grabbing the next addresses. In the process I cut my finger on the edge of the paper. Sticking it in my mouth, I went over and handed Arius the pages. Turning he handed them to Felix. With a nod the man walked back out the door.

Arius pulled my hand away from my mouth. Holding it, he looked down as the blood filled the cut again. Leaning down, he put it in his mouth, rolling his tongue over it.

I stood there, holding my breath looking up into his red eyes.

He lifted his head slowly, pulling my finger across his fangs.

I shuddered, heat moving through me.

He backed away, releasing my hand. Turning he walked out.

"Did the temperature in here just get hotter?" Daxx asked.

"I think it did," Bethany said softly.

"I don't know how you resist him." Crissy said.

Alona fanned her face. "I'm going to go find Chase and cut my finger."

"Chase doesn't have healing saliva." Daxx stated.

Alona rolled her eyes. "Who cares?" She pointed to me. "I want what she just got."

My cheeks heated. I put my hands over them. "Is it true the blood bond has worn off?

Daxx looked to Alona. "When were we in that office?"

Alona sighed, "It's been more than long enough."

I huffed out a breath and dropped my hands. "So he's not cheating, and knowing what I feel?"

Alona shook her head. "No, that's all Arius magic now." She smirked.

"I'm sunk, aren't I?" I looked from one to the next.

"I don't know how you've resisted this long," Bethany whispered as she stood up and stretched. "Only thing that delayed Leone and I was I fell out of a building and broke—" she looked down her body, "everything."

Alona nodded. "Resisting Chase was like denying my body its breath."

Daxx snorted. "As you know, there was no resisting from me." She went over and looked at what was left on the tray of snacks.

"I just don't know—" I said leaning against the back of the couch. "We've known each other for less than a week."

"We should get her gloves." Crissy got up and went and added more pages to the pile at the end of the table.

"Gloves?" I gave Alona a wide-eyed look.

Alona nodded. "If your left palms can't touch, the mark can't happen."

Beth groaned. "That tip would have saved some tense moments after my accidentally agreeing to be marked."

Daxx shrugged. "Next female that ends up in our lives, I think we should just hand her gloves."

Alona laughed. "We'll make an introductory package, tell them what's really going on."

"Why does that sound like it would be bad for us?"

We turned to see Chase leaning in the doorway.

"We were discussing gloves." I said.

He raised an eyebrow and zeroed in on Alona. "I'm quite fond of gloves."

Alona blushed. "Behave, I'm working."

"I know. It's been non-stop commotion and fighting for hours now." He sighed, "Except the trap, it was a bust. So we still don't have a group we can trust."

"Fighting?" I straightened away from the couch.

"Mmm," he moved toward the map. "Not all our searches have been abandoned by team bad's goons."

"Oh." I hugged my waist. "Is everyone all right?"

He leaned closer to the map and nodded. "Our teams are fine, Arius has new residents in his *maze,* so all are happy." He shrugged and turned around. "Well, except the new residents." He glanced to Alona. "I've come to tell you that we now have the rat scientist in custody as well, and," He smiled, "to see if I can steal my mate away for a break."

Daxx nodded. "I was going to suggest we all take a break." She motioned to the papers. "After the near miss with Paisley's hand, we don't want to chance more of that happening again."

Bethany and Alona laughed. Crissy jumped up and grabbed her pack. "I'm going to go find Victor." She ran out of the room.

"What have I missed?" Chase looked from Alona laughing behind her hand to Bethany.

Alona waved her hand at him. "It's complicated."

He frowned. "I can do complicated."

Daxx was texting on her phone. "I'm going to go see if I can find my king."

Bethany grabbed her phone. "Can I lead you anywhere? I know where most of the hallways lead."

I nodded. "I'd like to go see if I recognize any of the men being brought in. I can't stop thinking about those women taken off the island."

She nodded. "Okay, I know how to get to the cells."

"Dress fitting in two hours." Daxx called out. "Don't make me do that alone."

I stood in front of the monitors, looking from one to the next, trying to see if any of the men in the cells looked familiar. Each time Arius was on one of the monitors, I was distracted. The way he held himself, the confidence he exuded was striking. I blew out a breath. This wasn't a blood bond, or something created by being his mate, this was just the fact that he was an attractive, confident, sexy man.

He finished talking to a guard, then walked out of view of the camera.

I felt him come in, before I heard him. I turned, he stood there looking at me. "I wanted to see if any of the men brought in were the ones that left with those girls." I hugged my waist. "I can't stop thinking about them."

He motioned to the monitors. "Are any of these them? There's more in the cells without the cameras."

I turned back to them. "I can't really see them clearly."

He stepped over and reached around me. "These buttons select the corresponding monitor."

I watched him punch one of the buttons.

"You use this to zoom in or out." He ran his hand over a track ball next to the buttons.

I looked up to see the man's face much clearer on the monitor. "That's much better."

"Take your time, they're not going anywhere."

I could feel his breath on my neck as he spoke. I hit the next button and watched the screen as he zoomed in. I shook my head and went to the next.

Arius continued to stand close enough that our bodies brushed against one another as we went through all the screens.

"I don't have the rest in the files yet, the guards are still processing them."

Turning, I looked up at him.

His eyes held mine. "I can take you to see the rest."

I nodded, unsure if my voice would work. Being this close to him was causing reactions inside me that made me wish I was here for other reasons.

"We'll go now," he said looking at my mouth, "before I get myself into more trouble." He stepped back.

I followed him, he stopped, swore softly and spun around. He cupped the side of my face and kissed me. Before I could react, he lifted his head and let go of me.

"I'm starving for you." He said, then backed away and held his hand toward the door.

I stood there for a moment with my mouth open. What does a girl say to that, I wondered, then realized he hadn't waited for me. I went out and rushed down the hall to where he stood.

"They won't be able to see you." He waited until I acknowledged I'd heard, then started down a hallway lined with clear walls.

We moved along, one cell after the other, stopping so I could look at the man inside.

"There's so many." I whispered after going by a dozen or more.

"We've had a huge increase lately with everything Hubert has been doing." He stood and waited for me to study the next man.

I looked down a hall of more clear walls to our left. "What happens if you run out of room?"

He smirked, "those with lesser crimes," he took a few steps to the next one, "are transferred to work farms to rehabilitate. None associated with Hubert will ever see outside of these walls."

I crossed my arms and looked at the man standing in the middle of his small cell, staring off into space. I didn't know the first thing about him, but he had an expression on his face that clearly said he regretted decisions that landed him here. "He's having a serious discussion inside his head." I said quietly.

Arius chuckled, "most do. The ones that don't are the ones that are harder to contain." We stepped to the next cell, he motioned to the man inside. "Like him."

I turned to see the man pacing frantically, then smacking the wall each time he met it.

He placed his hand on my back. "Step back for a moment, so he can't see you."

I nodded and watched while he did something on a panel.

Arius knocked on the wall. The man stopped and glared at him. Crossing his arms, Arius just stood there looking at him. The man's brow furrowed. He shook his head, then stepped back and sat down. Arius tapped the panel.

"Did you do something?" I stepped back beside him.

He shook his head. "I have to be touching someone to get in their mind." He motioned to the man. "He's not wearing a device, so he's from this side." He shrugged, "most know me—and what I can do, so just my presence settles them down."

"You like being," I waved my hand around, "scary?"

He smirked. "Not necessarily, but it is helpful to make life in here easier."

We stepped to the next cell. "What if they're wearing a device?"

He crossed his arms. "Then they're usually so shell-shocked they're manageable."

I shook my head, so we'd move to the next one. "And when they're zapped here, or whatever—what if they need a device and don't have one?"

Glancing down at me, his eyes moved over my face for a moment. "I won't lie and say none have died, but we do have intake cells prepped that can act like a giant device." His jaw clenched, "sometimes it doesn't register on the initial scan for one reason or another, so as soon as we take them out…" He gave me a quick look but didn't say anymore.

I looked from him slowly to the man in the cell. There was something familiar about him. I looked at his arm to see he had no device, or cuff. "Can you get him to look up?"

Arius cocked his head and looked down at me, then he nodded and hit a button. "Stand on the line." The man's head snapped up, he looked around like he was expecting someone to be in there with him. Getting up, he moved over to a white line on the floor and stared at the wall we were looking through.

"He's one of them. He left with a tiny blonde woman." I nodded and hugged my waist. "Was she…" I swallowed, not sure if I wanted to ask.

"I can find out." He picked up his phone. "Michael, you have the women catalogued?" He shook his head. "Paisley recognizes one of the men who left the island with one of them." Nodding, his eyes stayed on my face the whole time. "Grab Troy and get him down here too, I want to know what's in his head." He smirked. "I don't care what he's doing." Shaking his head, he hung up. "Michael has photos of the women."

I nodded.

Turning, he motioned to one of the guards at the end of the hall. "Do you want to wait in the office?"

I looked back at the man. "I'll wait here if that's okay."

His grey eyes moved over my face slowly. "You may not want to…"

I shook my head. "I'll wait here."

"As you wish." The guard came over. Arius motioned to the man I'd identified. "Did he come in alone?' The guard shook his head. Motioning to a cell on the corner, "move the other one to that cell." The guard nodded and went in the other direction.

I heard footsteps echoing and turned to see Victor striding toward us, Michael right behind him. Victor gave Arius a curious look.

Arius motioned to the man still standing on the white line. "Paisley recognized him as one of the men that left the island with a woman."

Michael glanced up and then tapped the tablet he held.

I looked up to see a number at the top of the cell.

He looked up from the tablet to Victor then to Arius. His jaw muscles clenched.

"She had short choppy blonde hair." I added for clarification sake. "She would cover for me as I searched for a way off." I said quietly.

Victor gave the man inside the kind of look I'd never want to be on the other end of.

Michael handed the tablet to Arius.

He looked down at it, then to me and heaved a heavy sigh. Holding it out, he placed his hand on my shoulder. "Is this her?"

I looked at the tablet to see a photo of the woman I remembered, the one side of her face was bruised and swollen. I covered my mouth and nodded quickly.

Arius handed the tablet back to Michael and turned.

"Arius." Victor said in a firm tone.

Stopping, Arius looked at him.

Victor shook his head. "We'll let Troy look, first." He motioned to the cell the man stood in. "If you go in there, his mind will be clouded with pain."

Arius stopped and crossed his arms over his chest.

A commotion at the end of the hall, had him spinning around. The guard was back with a man, he was pushing him in our direction.

Victor grasped my shoulders lightly and moved me, so I'd step back.

The man wore a blue cuff on his arm.

As they reached the corner the man turned and grabbed for the guard, his eyes were bright green.

Arius bolted toward them and used his forearm to knock the man back. He made a low growling sound when the man glared at him. "Try it."

A shiver went down my spine from the lethal tone in his voice.

Arius, shoved him toward the open cell. Then hit the panel beside it. He turned to the guard. "What class is he?"

The guard looked at the floor, then to Michael briefly. "Class five."

Arius jolted like he'd smacked him. "And you didn't bind his hands and cover them to move him?"

The guard stared at the floor. "He's been complacent the entire time."

Arius made a sound of frustration. "So is a wild animal, *until* you open the gate." He motioned down the hall. "Go review the regulations, so you remember *all* of them."

The guard nodded, turned and hurried down the hall.

Arius huffed out a breath and glared at the man he'd just shoved in the cell.

I looked up at Victor. "Class five?"

Victor nodded, without looking away from his agitated sibling. "A ranking system in place to categorize the level of danger associated with certain types of feeders."

Eyes wide I gawked at him. "And class five is?"

"The highest level." He said quietly. "With a touch he can drain the life from you."

I blinked and looked at the man in the cell.

Arius heaved a loud sigh and came over. He motioned to the man he'd pushed in the cell. "Is he familiar at all?"

I took a deep breath and looked at the man sneering at the wall. "He looks similar to the man that left with the women, but I can't be sure. I only recognized the other one because he kept looking at me and giving me a creepy smile."

Arius growled and turned to Michael.

Michael nodded, "I'm looking."

"What did the other woman look like, Paisley?" Victor asked in a calmer tone.

"Uh," I closed my eyes for a second and tried to calm down. Opening them I looked at Michael. "She had shoulder length brown hair," I bit my lip, "and a beauty mark beside her mouth."

Michael tapped the screen. "Yes, she's here." His eyes flicked to Arius briefly.

I looked at the man with the blue cuff. "What about the girl he was with? Did he…"

Michael looked up from the tablet. "We've had each one seen by a doctor, I don't see anything to indicate he fed from her."

I nodded and held my hand over my fast beating heart. "That's good."

Troy came walking quickly down the hall, his hair wasn't neatly secured behind his head. "What's going on? I was," he paused and looked at me, "busy."

Victor smirked and motioned to the two cells. "Paisley has identified two males that left the island with women."

Daxx came down the hall quickly. "This better be important."

Troy looked at her for a moment then to Michael. "And the women?"

Michael held the tablet out and scrolled between two screens.

Daxx hissed out a breath and turned to look at the men. "I can go in and stick my raptor in his…"

All the men turned to look at her.

Troy groaned and leaned to look at her back. He pulled a leather case with small curved handle sticking out of it. "You know you're not supposed to bring weapons into the cells."

She shrugged. "Let one of them try to get it off me." She snarled at the man in the cell.

Sighing, Troy handed the blade to Victor. He bent down and shoved it into his boot.

Michael motioned to the cuffed man, "he's a level five, so it's going to get tricky."

Troy looked at the other man. "Which one was with the blonde?"

Arius motioned to the first prisoner.

Troy nodded. "We'll start there." Reaching into his pocket, he pulled out a leather cord and quickly pulled his hair back to secure it.

With an abrupt nod, Arius did something on the panel beside the door to that cell.

Troy, Arius and Victor stepped in and the door closed.

Daxx leaned closer. "He turned off the blocker for abilities, so Troy can use his."

I nodded, not taking my eyes off the men inside.

The man backed away as Troy walked over to him. There was no emotion visible on Troy's face as he stopped and just stood there, looking at him.

I waited to see what he did, but he just continued to stand there. I looked at Daxx. "Is he in that man's head?"

She bobbed her head. "Yep."

Troy straightened and glanced at the wall we were looking through then turned to look at Arius and Victor. He shook his head. Victor's expression hardened. Arius' went from distaste to fury. He stepped past his brother and grabbed the man by the throat.

Troy spun and pulled at his brother's arm until Arius released him. The man slumped to the floor, his chest heaving.

Jerking his arm from Troy, Arius went over and hit the pad by the door and stepped out. Troy and Victor followed him.

Daxx gave me a startled look, then she turned to her mate. "Troy, what did you see?"

Cold hazel eyes looked at her for a moment, then he gave an abrupt shake of his head.

I took a step toward Arius, he stood there his chest rising and falling quickly. Seeing him that upset bothered me. I placed my hand on his arm and looked up at him.

Looking down at me, he took a few deep breaths, not looking away from me. When he was calmer, he touched my hand and gave it a gentle squeeze.

"Do we want to know with this one?" Troy motioned to the cell the man with the cuff was in.

Michael motioned down the hall. "I can go get our leather jackets."

I looked from him to Daxx, then realized they wanted to cover their skin, so he couldn't touch any of them. "I can help."

Arius frowned down at me and shook his head.

I motioned to the door. "I can stand at the door and stop him from moving." I turned and looked at Troy, "you don't need to touch him, right?"

Troy gave a slight shake of his head, his eyes moving to Arius'.

"No." Arius shook his head.

"I can hold him immobile for a minute or so," I glanced to Victor, "I don't know how much internal damage it would do to hold him longer."

Victor raised an eyebrow and looked over my head to Arius. "We can stand on either side of her." He motioned to Michael.

Turning back, I looked up at Arius, touching his arm lightly again. "I want to help. We need to know, so those women can be properly treated."

The nerve in his jaw twitched as he looked down at me. His eyes flicked to his brothers and then back down at me.

"Please, Arius. Why was I given this ability if I don't use it for good reasons?" I whispered.

He inhaled slowly and then let it out. Lifting his head, he looked at Troy. "You have thirty seconds, brother, so dig quickly."

Troy gave him an abrupt nod.

Glancing to me once more, Arius searched my face, then reached over and did something on the panel beside the door.

He stepped into the cell and slowly walked toward the man. He stepped back a few feet.

When Troy went in the man sneered. "Your highness."

Victor and Michael went in and stood on opposite sides of the door, the man's expression became guarded.

I stood between the two large men.

"Well, well." The man looked at me a lewd expression on his face. "Hello, pretty. I know you." His eyes moved over me. "I should have selected you."

Arius growled.

"Do it now, sister." Michael whispered.

Raising my hands, I focused on him and his expression changed. "Don't step in front of me. I have to be able to see him." I said quietly.

Troy moved closer.

My heart was racing in my chest as I waited for them to tell me to stop.

"Let him go." Troy said. As I did, he swung and punched the man in the face, he slumped to the floor. "I just saved your worthless life." He growled.

Turning, he motioned to the door, making sure Arius went in front of him.

I stepped back out into the hall.

No one spoke until Arius closed the door again.

The nerve in Troy's jaw twitched. He looked at Daxx for a moment, then turned to Michael. "He didn't feed off her," his eyes flicked to me briefly, "it may have been better for her if he had."

Daxx covered her mouth.

I took a ragged breath and looked at Arius. "Can you make someone forget something like that?"

He gave me a pained look, then shook his head. "No. Not with that kind of physical trauma."

I held my hand over my chest, trying to not shake. "There's a—" I couldn't say it out loud, "crisis center for women downtown," I glanced to Daxx, "on our side."

"We have to be careful who knows the location of the safe houses." Michael said quietly.

Victor cleared his throat. "I'll get in touch with our medical staff and see if we have anyone qualified, or if they know of someone on the other side."

Troy nodded slowly.

"Can we round up some more telepaths, males only, and have them help Troy with every man brought in on these raids?" Arius was watching me as he spoke. "So we can help any women involved."

Michael nodded. "I'll get on it."

Victor turned. "I'll go talk to the doctor and send more guards down here to help."

I put my shaking hand over my stomach. "I don't feel well," I said breathlessly, "that—that could have been me if I hadn't jumped off the cliff." I leaned over my knees.

"Get her out of here." Troy said in a soft tone.

Arius came over and scooped me up into his arms. I wrapped my arms around his neck and squeezed as I pushed my face into his throat. I was trying not to cry but the reality of what could have happened, what *had* happened to others washed over me. My breath caught in my throat and the tears started to fall.

Arius leaned his cheek to rest against mine as he walked. "Babe, don't cry."

I did what everyone does when someone tells you not to cry. I started crying harder.

I heard doors open, then close, behind us.

"Arius is my twin hiding…" Chase stopped speaking.

"Paisley?" Alona's voice reflected my pain.

"Talk to Michael." Arius said and started walking again.

"Daxx?" Alona sounded like she was crying.

"I can't right now, Alona, I'm sorry." Daxx said.

"What the hell is going on?" Chase sounded angry.

Arius held me tighter, "My room is just around the corner."

I nodded and squeezed his neck tighter. "I'm sorry…"

"Don't be." I heard a door close then he sat down. Shifting, he gently pulled my head, so I would look at him.

We were sitting in a large armed chair. I looked in his eyes, so full of pain and compassion, I started crying again.

Gently cupping my face, he wiped the tears from my cheeks with his thumbs. "We will do everything inhumanly and humanly possible to help those women." He leaned forward and gently kissed my quivering lips. "We have an entire realm of abilities, we'll find something to help them." His eyes searched my face. "Each man involved will be punished and pay for their involvement in this."

I tried to slow my breathing, to calm down. I squeezed my eyes shut. "Those poor women."

He hugged me against his chest, his hand gently stroking my hair. "Thanks to you, we're finding each one of them."

"We're too late for some." I started sobbing again.

He rocked me gently in his arms. "It's killing me to see you like this." His breath was warm against my ear. "I need to help you." He kissed my cheek. "Let me help you, babe, let me soothe your pain."

I looked at him. "You want to get in my head and tell me to not feel it?"

He leaned his forehead against mine. "No. I don't want to change a thing inside this beautiful mind."

I wiped my eye roughly. "I don't understand."

Lifting his head, his large hands surrounding my face. "With my blood, through that connection."

I hiccupped. "How? I thought that…"

He kissed my mouth softly. "I didn't project to you before, just monitored how you were feeling," His eyes searched mine, a look of vulnerability in them. "Not to spy on you, or use against you, just to know your reaction—to me."

I felt dumb in that moment. I'd assumed he was being a creeper like Martin had been. I took a shaky breath. "So-so you can project feelings to me?"

He nodded. "Mates do it through their connection. I have something similar with my brothers…"

"And you want to be connected to me too? That's a lot of connections." I frowned.

His mouth quirked, "I can compartmentalize. Trust me I only share with my brothers when it's absolutely necessary."

I blew out a shaky breath, holding my hand over my stomach. "I still feel sick."

"That's delayed shock." He brushed the hair back from my face, "most would have felt that right after being hauled out of the water and being ported to another realm."

I glanced to his eyes again. "I'm different."

He smiled. "I know. In a perfect way." He kissed my mouth softly. "Let me help you. Give you some peace, and keep you steady, so you can help us find all those women."

Inhaling through my nose, I blew it out trying to shake the churning in my stomach. I was cradled in his lap, the last thing I wanted to do was throw up on him. "Arius, we barely know each other." I looked into his eyes as I spoke, he returned my look without hesitation. "I feel some kind of connection to you, but—" I sighed, "I don't want to jump into this mating thing," I frowned, "I have horrible taste in men. Look at Martin."

He raised an eyebrow. "You're comparing me to that scum?"

I shook my head, "No. I was just saying I tend to misread signals and ignore all the signs that I should be reading."

He studied me silently for a moment. "A connection through blood wears out of your system if it's not renewed frequently. This will not tie you to me irrevocably." His tone was quiet, guarded.

I felt lower than slime. He was trying to help me, and I was comparing him to someone who used me, drugged me and then left me on an island with insane people. "Can it go both ways?"

His brow creased. "A blood bond?"

I nodded.

"It can," he said slowly, "if we exchange each other's."

I nodded again. "Then we'll do that. It's only fair that I lurk about in your emotions if you're doing it to me."

He gave me a surprised look. "You want a full blood bond?"

I didn't know if I did, but I nodded once more anyway. The idea was intriguing and definitely something I could say I'd never done before. "I'd feel better about it then."

Leaning forward, he kissed my mouth softly. "Then we'll do that." Shifting, he let go of me and pulled his shirt over his head in one fast, smooth move.

I looked at his chest for a moment, as traumatic moments went, that wasn't a bad way to distract me from the turmoil inside me.

"Paisley," he said softly.

My eyes jumped to look back to his.

He raised an eyebrow, "looking at me like that isn't going to help me behave and earn your trust."

My cheeks heated. "Sorry. I'm used to meeker, unmuscular humans."

He chuckled, then jerked his chin to the right. "Reach down and pull the blade from my ankle."

I turned and reached down, pulling his pant leg up, I took the handle sticking up out of a case. "I thought weapons in the cells were a no-no." I held it out to him.

Grinning, he looked at me for a moment. "My cells, my rules."

"Uh huh." I watched the playfulness leave his eyes and a softer, more serious look replaced it.

He inhaled slowly, his eyes holding mine. "You completely undo me when you hold my gaze and don't look away." His voice was so quiet when he said it.

I touched his face gently. "There's no reason to look away."

Grasping the back of my head, he shifted and slid down in the chair a bit. He didn't look away from me as he cut into his chest. I leaned forward at the same time he moved my head closer. Licking the blood trailing down his chest, I closed my mouth over the slice in his flesh and sucked on it.

He took a ragged breath when it sealed, and I lifted my head. His eyes were red, his fangs visible as he took deep breaths. "I don't think I can cut you." He said softly.

I leaned back. "Then use these." I touched the sharp teeth in his mouth.

I heard the knife hit the floor, then he moved so I was lying across his lap. Supporting my head and upper body with one hand, he leaned me back. My own breathing became as uneven as his gaze traveled over me.

Leaning forward, he pulled my hip tight against his body. He licked over my neck, making me suck in my breath. When his fangs punctured my flesh, the breath escaped all at once. A heat filled me when he lifted his head and looked down at me. I could feel the blood running over my skin from the open marks.

With a soft growl, he leaned down and sucked on my neck. It was the most erotic thing I'd ever felt. Licking the wounds, he lifted his head and looked down at me again. His breathing was heavier.

The hand holding me shook slightly as he bent down to place a soft kiss on my mouth. Shifting again, he cradled me in his arms, so my cheek rested against his chest. Part of me was disappointed he'd stopped, the other part respected that he had been able to stop, despite my hormones wishing for more.

I closed my eyes and listened to his heart beating, the soft rhythm of his breathing. My stomach settled and the feelings of mourning inside me eased. It was the first time since I'd woke up on that island that I'd felt like I might come out on the other side of this. "Are you doing that?"

"Mmm," he kissed the top of my head, "just relax and go with it for a while."

Curling my arms into my chest, I snuggled my face into his neck and sighed. It felt good.

I don't know how long we stayed like that, I felt like I was drifting in and out of a dream state.

I heard a soft knock on the door but didn't move.

"I brought some tea." It was Bethany.

"Thank you." Arius said quietly.

"How's she doing?" Leone whispered.

Arius' chest rose and fell with a deep breath. "She's exhausted and emotionally drained. She agreed to a bond so I can help her rest."

"Good." Beth whispered. "You need to rest too, Arius. I don't think you've slept since you saw her jump off that cliff."

He inhaled a deep breath. "I'll be fine."

Leone made a hissing noise. "Stretch out with her for a few hours. I'm heading to the cells to help, so is Raf. Quinton is leading the teams going out. Troy is wrangling Daxx right now, she wants to go kill anything that moves."

"She doesn't do emotion well." Beth whispered. "Alona, Crissy and I are going to drag her in to help go through the files and find more to rescue."

"We've got it covered for a few hours, brother. Ensure you and your mate rest. We're going to need you both at full strength when we breach the island." Leone said, his voice moving away.

"We'll see you later." Beth said quietly, then a door closed.

"I know you're awake." Arius said quietly.

I leaned back. "Through the bond?"

He shook his head, "no, your breathing." Taking a deep breath, he stood up, taking me with him. "They're right, a short rest wouldn't hurt either of us." He walked over and stopped at the bed. "Or would you rather go lay in your bed?"

I shook my head. "No. Alone is bad right now."

With a quick nod, he knelt on the bed and lay me on top of it. "Do you want some tea?"

"No. Not right now." Even in the low light, I could see the hesitation on his face. Reaching up, I tugged on his hand. "Rest."

He lay down slowly, then pulled me against his warm body. Reaching behind me, he pulled the cover and draped it over me. I wiggled so I was cuddled into his chest. He huffed out a breath. "I feel like an awkward teenager right now." He said with emotion in his voice. "I've never lain in bed with a woman before."

I rolled back, so I could look at him. "If you tell me you're a virgin I'm going to call you a liar."

He grinned. "No. I didn't say I'd never had sex before." With a soft touch, he brushed the hair out of my eyes. "I said I'd never lain in bed like this before." His gaze caressed my face. "Women I've been with won't even look me in the eye, so cuddles afterward are definitely not on the menu."

I took a moment to decide if I was shocked or just angry by that. Both perhaps.

Arius studied me. "I can feel your anger." He sounded surprised.

"I am angry. That's cold and awful." I cuddled against him again. "If we are confessing things, I've never lain in bed with such a sweet, irresistible inhuman man before."

It was his turn to lean back and look down at me. "You caught that earlier?"

I nodded. "Is that what your people are classified as?"

His brows furrowed, "I don't know that it is or isn't. We're not human, or not *just* human at least. Troy likes to say we're demons, but that doesn't fit either and Chase…"

"Is his own specie."

He chuckled. "That he is." He took a deep breath. "I don't know what I am or aren't, right now I'm just happy I'm with you." Pulling me tight against his body again, he kissed the top of my head. "Rest. The next few days are going to be very trying."

"Arius—thank you." I closed my eyes and pressed my ear against his chest, so I could listen to his heart beat.

Chapter Twelve

I woke up with a start, not knowing where I was. A warm arm wrapped around my waist and pulled me tight against a hard body.

"If you wake up running, I'm going to be grumpy." Arius mumbled from behind me.

I relaxed again. "No. I hate mornings, at any time of the day." I wiggled in his hold until I was on my back, so I could look at him. "How long have we been sleeping?"

He pulled me tight against him again. "No idea. Don't care."

I grinned. "Where did that fierce warden guy go?"

He groaned and buried his face in my neck. "He's dormant until after coffee." Sighing, he lifted his head. "It's going to take an hour to get the tangles out of my hair. I never sleep with it loose."

"It can't be that bad." I sat up and looked down at him.

"Your expression says otherwise." Rolling to his back, he lifted his hips and pulled his phone out of his pocket and looked at it. Turning it toward me, he grimaced. "Twenty-five messages."

"I'm sure if it was important they would have come and got you."

He dropped his hand to the bed and looked at me. "I can't believe we slept."

I gave him a wide-eyed look. "Wasn't that the point?"

"Yeah, just—" He sat up, shifting so he could flip his hair back. "I didn't even feel my phone vibrate."

"That's a good thing." I started sliding toward the end of the bed.

He grabbed me by the waist and pulled me on his lap. "Not so fast." Leaning back, he pulled me down with him. Propped on his elbow, he searched my eyes and must have found what he was looking for when his mouth covered mine. He kissed me in a slow exploratory way, teasing and gentle.

Lifting his head, he rested his forehead against mine. "Thank you for trusting me enough to help you." He kissed me softly. "I'm fighting the impulse to mark you and force things, but this connection will help me as much as it will you."

Grasping his face, I smiled, "less talk, more sleepy kisses."

He grinned. "As you wish." He brushed his lips over mine, then both of us froze as his phone vibrated on the bed. "Good morning, reality." He whispered, reaching over me. He picked it up and looked at it. Then put it to his ear. "Barely." His gaze moved over my face. "She is." He stared at my mouth. "We'll be there shortly." He clicked the button and tossed the phone behind me again. "That was Daxx—the fitting was postponed last night, it's in an hour. Breakfast is waiting for us." He rolled, so we were both sitting up.

I wiggled off his lap and stood up. "Where's your brush? I'll help with your hair."

He gave me a surprised look, then pointed to the dresser on the other side of the room.

I went over. "I used to have really long hair, so I know what mornings are like." I stopped. "Is it even morning or is it this night-morning thing? The two kings, different times is confusing."

Moving, he stood up and stretched. "It's actual, daylight morning. We slept for six hours."

I paused and watched muscles extend and flex as he moved.

Arius growled and closed the distance between us. Grabbing me by the waist, he lifted me up so our faces were level. "Stop inviting me to do what I want to."

I bit my lip. "Stop looking so damn good."

Laughing, he kissed me hard on the mouth, then set me on my feet.

I motioned to the bed. "Sit."

Alona glanced up from watching the seamstress pin the hem of her dress. "I can't believe he just laid there and held you all night." She adjusted the red sash across her shoulder. "I love the red on black."

Bethany turned and looked at herself in the mirror. "Royal blue is going to look so good on Leone." She turned and looked at me. "I'd like to say Leone was that sweet, but I was broken when we did that, so I don't think it counts."

Crissy walked in. Her gown was black with a deep emerald green waist sash. She turned slowly. "It's so pretty. I've never had a dress like this before."

"You look lovely." Alona told her.

I lifted my arm, so the seamstress could adjust the side of my gown. I was still in shock. When they'd said I was wearing a gown, I would never have pictured a full fairy tale, Cinderella goes to the ball, gown.

"That deep purple is almost the shade of the lipstick you have." Bethany said, smiling as I blushed.

"Imagine that, Arius knowing the exact shade my gown would be trimmed with." I said smirking.

"Mmm, he's got subtle down." Alona nodded.

"I feel like a cake ornament." Daxx walked in, her gown swaying as she came in.

"You look wonderful." Bethany told her.

Daxx's gown was black with red trim as the other queen's was.

She turned around and looked in the mirror. "Do we have to keep the big bow on my ass?"

I covered my mouth and laughed. "We all have one." I turned so she could see mine.

"Why can't we put a bow on the men's asses for a change?" She mumbled.

Alona got down off the platform. "At least they made you one without a tight bodice."

Daxx sighed. "That is something."

Mitz came in looking completely energized, carrying a box.

Daxx pasted a smile on her face, but no one was fooled.

Putting the box down on the table, she turned and looked at each one of us. Covering her mouth, she shook her head. "You are all so beautiful." Her eyes teared up.

Daxx lunged toward her. "What's in the box?" She said loudly, while giving Mitz a wary look.

"Oh." Mitz opened it. She glanced to Alona, "this was your mate's suggestion."

Daxx frowned, "Suggestions are allowed?"

Smiling Mitz nodded. "Especially from one of the kings."

Daxx rolled her eyes. "Of course, they get to wear pants."

Mitz pulled a pair of black ankle boots out and looked at them. "These are yours." She handed them to Alona.

She held them up and looked at them. "Oh, that sweet man." Leaning down, she lifted the hem of her dress carefully and put her foot in the first boot. "Oh, they're comfy." Putting on the other, she stood up and went to the mirror. Grinning, she lifted the hem and looked. "They're flirty."

Mitz clapped her hands once, then turned and pulled out the next pair and handed them to Bethany.

When she handed me a pair, I wasted no time putting them on, then went over to the mirror and looked. "They're great. Barely any heel so we can dance." I looked at Mitz. "I love the boots." An idea hit me. "Boots." I ran over and picked up my phone and started scrolling through songs. I nodded, then looked at Bethany. "It's an old song, but sassy, I could pump up the base and add some techno," My jaw dropped, and I turned to Alona, "we could do a sassy little line dance for those brothers." I nodded again and started flipping through songs I could mix it with.

"A line dance?" Daxx looked at me.

I nodded, my whole body vibrating with the excitement of it. "Not a prissy line dance, one with attitude."

Her expression changed slightly, but I still wasn't sure if we'd convince her.

"Like fighting moves, to a beat."

Her eyebrows went up.

"I love it." Bethany nodded.

Alona laughed. "You had me at boots."

Mitz wiped a tear off her cheek. "It's been a long wait for my boys' mates—you all, each one of you, light up this entire realm." She nodded, patted my cheek and walked out of the room.

Daxx with her eyes huge looked around at us. "Not a single tear. Seriously, all this crying and emotional—stuff, is killing me."

The phone ringing in my hand startled me and I almost dropped it. "Hello?"

"How is the fitting going? Has Daxx stabbed anyone yet?" Arius asked.

I smiled and looked at her. "Not yet, but it's been close a few times."

Alona grinned at me. "She's blushing, I wonder who is on the other end of that phone."

"Hmm, that's a hard one." Bethany said with a smirk.

I waved them off and walked to the other side of the room.

"Women harassing you?"

I sighed, "Yeah, apparently there were bets placed on whether we'd walk in this morning sporting new tattoos."

He laughed. "Yes, I heard that too." He cleared his throat. "I just sensed a high spike of energy and wondered for a moment if something was wrong."

I pouted, even though he couldn't see me. "Does this bond thing come with instructions? I haven't picked up anything on your end."

He chuckled, "I've had a few hundred years to master it."

"That's cheating. I was talking about music."

"That would explain it." He made a sound of annoyance, "my brothers are banging on the door to get in, I had better let you go. See you shortly."

"Okay." I hung up and turned.

"He picked up on how excited you got?" Bethany was taking her boots off.

I nodded. "I haven't sensed anything."

Daxx impatiently watched the seamstress undo her gown. "They're cold as ice unless they want us to sense something."

I held up my arms when she came over to get me out of the gown. I was still afraid I'd rip it if I moved. "How is that fair?" I frowned, "and how are we supposed to keep this a secret?"

Crissy turned one last time and looked in the mirror before standing still to get the gown unzipped. "We could say we're working out together—which by all technical points that define working out, we will be." She looked up from what the woman was doing and nodded.

Alona looked from her to the rest of us. "It could work."

Holding the gown up as Daxx walked to the other room, she shook her head. "They'll want to watch."

"Oh." Alona sighed, "She's right."

Bethany shrugged. "We have large guards for a reason."

Crissy laughed, "Vic is not going to like it." She stopped moving completely and looked at me. "I like it."

"Okay. We'll figure out practice time later. Keep the moves simple. I'll figure out the mix later and see if you like it." I looked one more time at myself in the mirror. I was in another realm, wearing a ball gown. Life was full of surprises.

"Leone just messaged, meeting in Victor's office as soon as possible." Bethany called out as she walked into the changing room.

"No, we turn here." Daxx looked back the way we'd gone.

Alona peeked around the corner. "I'm hopelessly lost."

I scrolled through another few songs. "I know how to find our cave, that's it."

"Don't look at me, I just message Leone to come find me." Bethany waved her phone.

Crissy giggled. "Can I help now?"

Daxx sighed. "Fine, yes miss map, which way do we go to get to Victor's office?

She turned and pointed in the direction we'd come from. "The hall back there."

Throwing her hands in the air, Daxx turned around and went back.

When we saw the pink arrows, we all knew where we were.

"You need to make us a map we can put in our phones." Alona told Crissy.

Crissy nodded. "I can do that."

They all stopped walking, I bumped into Alona and looked up from my phone.

"That's not lipstick." Daxx said with a grin.

I looked to see we were outside my room. In front of the door was a large wrapped box that went up to my hip.

"Definitely not lipstick." Alona agreed.

Tucking my phone in my pocket, I dropped down and opened the paper on the top and peeked in. I squealed and ripped it off. It was a sound system. "It's got a subwoofer and mixing board," I tore the rest of the paper off, "and two monitor speakers." I hugged the box.

"Damn he's good, she's a puddle right now." Alona said quietly.

"You're going to have to make love to it later, Paize, the guys will be waiting."

I nodded. Standing up, I opened the door and pushed the box inside. I stood there looking at it. "I've never had a real mixing board before."

Beth laughed. "I don't know what that is, but I guess changing that song will be easier now?

I nodded and closed the door. "Yes. Oh my god, it's going to rock." I was half-skipping down the hall.

As we rounded the corner that lead to the practice room and Victor's office, Arius was leaning against the wall. His expression gave nothing away. I continued to walk the same pace as the women until he raised one eyebrow slightly. I squealed and ran toward him, unable to play it cool a second longer. I launched myself at him when I was a few feet away, he caught me without pause. I wrapped my legs around his waist and grabbed his face, kissing all over it.

He laughed.

"Gods, I thought we were under attack." Chase stood outside Victor's office with his hand over his heart.

"Why don't you catch me like that?" Alona asked.

Chase looked from her to Arius and I. "You don't throw yourself at me with a battle cry?"

Alona grinned. "Fine. Be accurate, and pedantic."

Michael stood there with his eyes huge, he glanced to Leone, who shrugged.

"He got her a subwoofer, mixing something-or-other and speakers." Daxx said as Troy stood there with his arms crossed over his chest.

"Little brother is making you old guys look bad." Rafael gave Arius a thumb up.

Chase looked at Alona, "I buy you shelves of boots and endless rivers of wine."

She smiled at him. "You do, I'll throw myself at you later."

He rubbed his chest and nodded. "Damn right you will."

Victor stood hugging Crissy against his side.

Quinton, lifted his hands and started waving them toward the door. "Let's give them a minute, so we can get back to having this meeting."

We watched them go in and close the door. I grabbed his face again. "You knew the second I opened it didn't you?"

He laughed. "I almost had a heart attack. My brothers' thought I was."

I kissed his mouth hard. "Thank you. I love it."

His grey eyes held mine. "I just want you to be happy."

"I've never had a real mixing board before."

He smirked, "I had no idea what I was telling them to buy, just told them make it portable so I wasn't lugging it all over the realm." He sighed, his expression changing. Shifting, he grasped the back of my head and kissed me, slow.

When he lifted his head, I sighed. "This isn't a meeting we can just skip, is it?"

He shook his head. "It's about the island."

I rested my head on his shoulder. "That's like a cold shower on my giddiness."

"Sorry, babe." He lowered me to the floor. "You have that system to play with when it's over." Dropping a light kiss on my mouth, he patted my hip and straightened from the wall. "Did the lab guy find you at the seamstress' for the blood test?"

I nodded.

"I thought you'd want to get that done as soon as possible."

"Thank you."

He opened the door and motioned for me to go in.

Chapter Thirteen

I looked up from the page in front of me. I was looking for more confirmed addresses. The next time I told someone to copy entire hard drives, I was going to explain how to dump the cache and useless files first. Some of our printouts were a mess of garble.

Leaning back, I held my fingers over my eyes. We'd been at it for six hours. The others had needed to get up and move around, so they'd gone to get coffee and food.

Dropping my hands, I looked over at the map. There were a lot of pins in it now. Many had been changed to red, meaning the team had been there. I sighed, we'd found twelve women so far, so it was worth every stiff muscle in my body from sitting here.

Moving forward, I rested my head on the desk. Just a few minutes, I thought.

"You *can* take breaks."

I looked up to see Arius standing in the door, a concerned expression on his face. "I know. I just—the more time we let pass, the fewer we'll find. We know they're moving them, or the teams would find more."

He came over and leaned on the edge of the desk. "The teams are on a constant rotation, we can't move any faster than we are."

I looked up at him. "I know, we're only human." I smirked, "well, some of us."

With a grin, he knelt beside me, spinning the chair, he pulled it toward him. "I'm okay with being a sweet irresistible inhuman."

I grinned. "It's true, you are."

Reaching, he pulled me to the edge of the chair and rested his forehead against mine. "You are the only one that thinks that."

"I'm the only one that matters then."

"You are." His gaze caressed over my face, a tender light in his eyes. "I came here for a reason."

"Oh, what reason?"

He looked at my mouth. "I can't remember."

I bit my lip. "Maybe you should kiss me instead."

He grinned. "I think I should."

Rising, he put his arm around me and cupped the back of my head. Brushing his mouth over mine, he paused and looked at me, his eyes were turning red as I watched.

Weaving my hands into his hair, I pulled his head closer.

"I want to share how you make me feel, through the bond."

"Okay." I dipped my tongue into his mouth and touched it against his fangs. He closed his eyes and sucked in a breath.

A heat edged with anticipation flooded into me. My breath caught in my throat.

With a soft noise, his hand flexed against the back of my head, then his mouth covered mine.

Our tongues moved against each other. The kiss deepened, became rougher, almost desperate to consume one another.

I didn't know where my desire ended, and his dizzying need began.

He growled low in the back of his throat and then his mouth claimed mine with what I could only think of as primal need.

"I thought we established no sex in the girl cave." Alona said loudly.

Arius broke the kiss and dropped his forehead to rest on my shoulder.

I tried to catch my breath and looked over to see Daxx, Alona and Bethany standing near the door holding trays. "It was just a kiss."

Daxx snorted. "What your mouths were just doing to each other was a lot more than a kiss."

Arius chuckled against my throat.

"I've never seen Arius out of his cells this much." Bethany said. "Then again, I haven't been here long, so I could be wrong."

Daxx shook her head and walked to the table near the couches. "You're not."

Lifting his head, he gave me a heated look, then turned to look at them. "I actually came here to give you ladies an update, then Paisley distracted me." He shrugged, "and I think my brothers wanted me out of the cells, so they could sit down and take a break."

"Update?" Daxx put the tray on the table.

He stood up. "Last trap yielded a rat."

I looked up at him. "You know who's been leaking information?"

He nodded. "For this last one we only told three men, all in positions of leadership. We narrowed it down to two, by the third's reaction to the false information when they arrived at the location."

"So it's two men?" Beth asked.

"We're not positive just yet, but it's at least one of them."

Alona moved over and set the tray down. "So what do you do now?"

He rubbed the back of his neck. "With the island breach tomorrow, nothing—we'll give them some menial assignment, keep them away from anything important until we have time to sort out what's next."

Daxx crossed her arms and nodded. "We'll have a full team tomorrow?"

He nodded. "We cleared ten more guards today using Paisley's idea."

"Oh, good." Alona sat down. "I feel much better with more. That's a huge area to cover."

"With that being said, I'm here to steal my mate for a break."

"Mate?" I stood up.

"Unofficially," he smiled.

Daxx laughed. "From what we just saw—it won't be unofficial for much longer."

"I don't know how she resists." Bethany said quietly, sitting at her desk.

Arius grinned. "Neither do I." he looked from one to the other. "Any and all tips are welcome—unlike my brothers, you ladies might have useful ones."

Alona laughed. "You're doing just fine on your own."

Daxx nodded. "I can't believe you're even related to your caveman brother."

Arius ran his hand over his jaw. "I've had to be much more disciplined than my brothers, the curse of my ability."

"I think you have the most challenging job, too." I said.

He looked down at me. "I chose that position." He watched my face with a guarded look. "There was a time when even I was afraid of what I could do. So, I thought better to be surrounded by criminals than innocents."

"Whatever the reason," Daxx said, "no one could manage it the way you do. Troy has said that a hundred times."

Arius turned and inclined his head to her. Holding out his hand to me, he gave me a soft look. "Now if you'll excuse us, I'd like a demonstration of what the confusing devices I bought her can do."

I covered my mouth. "I forgot all about that. How could I forget about the best gift I've ever gotten?"

I looked over my shoulder at Arius. "Ready?"

He opened his arms. "Show me."

I pressed play, then backed up so I could hear how good the sound was.

The song was soft, not heavy, an instrumental opening that would put the speakers through the various chords. I used it whenever I was testing a sound system. I looked at him. "It sounds good." Lifting my chin, I glanced to the ceiling, "I wasn't sure how the acoustics would be in here. What do you think?" I closed my eyes and listened.

"I think you could be playing anything right now and I wouldn't notice because I'm too busy seeing the joy on your face."

I opened my eyes and turned to look at him. "I am very happy right now. Music is my escape, the way I express—everything. It's always been my go-to.

He studied my face for a moment, then walked toward me. "I hope someday to be your go-to for everything." He stopped in front of me. "But I'm willing to share you with your first love." His grey eyes reflected sincerity and hope.

I tapped my head. "You've helped me so much in other ways. Several times today I had some shaky moments going through those files."

He held my look in a steady gaze. "I know. I felt it."

"Each time a calming warmth surrounded me, like a hug. I don't know how you did it with everything going on with your maze and coordinating the teams…

Reaching out, he caressed my cheek with the back of his hand. "You have priority, above everything else going on around here. That's how mates are. We may not be marked, but the instinct is there. The need to protect and care for each other. It's there. It's the only thing giving me the strength to not mark you."

"I don't feel it. This instinct."

He gave me a soft smile. "Maybe not, but it's there. The way you tore into those guards, the way you watch me, assessing if I'm all right, when you come to me if I'm upset. You can't feel it, but you're doing it."

I bit my lip. It was true. I'd step into anything to protect him, regardless of his size and strength, I would. "It is." I admitted softly. "I didn't even notice."

His eyes started to swirl like they did when we kissed or before he bit me. He closed them for a second.

"That's the only sign I see of you struggling. Your eyes."

He looked at me again. "Then I'm much better at hiding it than I thought."

"What do you mean?"

"My eyes, are always on you, stalking you like prey. The urge to mark you is almost animal like."

"What's it like?"

Cupping the side of my face, his gaze rested on my mouth. "The constant need to taste you. Your mouth. Your essence. Your desire. Every time I kiss you or touch you it's like a beast inside me screams for his mate, demanding that I mark you. That I claim you for the whole world to see, for them to know that if they cross you—they answer to me."

I was breathless from his words. A side of me I'd never known wanted this. "And now? What do you feel right now?"

"Right now?" He searched my face, "rage. Right now, if anyone were to come between us, I could crush their throat with my bare hands. There's nothing but rage inside me, Paisley. A rage born of the seclusion of having to cut myself off from others to carry my burden and protect them from me. I didn't ask to control minds with a mere thought." His eyes were red again. "But you—you touch me without hesitation, you hold my gaze with no fear like no other has, and you make the rage fade."

My heart was beating so fast listening to the emotion in his voice.

"Right now." He continued. "I want to lay you on the bed and make you mine. I want to feel your mind so consumed with me, your body tremble beneath me—I want to put my mark on you more than I want my next breath." He inhaled slowly, "I can lay with you and hold you and feed other needs long denied, but I know my limits and that you're not ready."

I felt mesmerized by his words, I couldn't have moved or spoke if I'd wanted to.

He stared at my mouth. "I can barely feed now. When I bite into another and they don't taste like you, I want to tear their throat out."

I didn't even know how often he should feed.

"Tomorrow, I don't want you to go. But I can't stop you from going. I know you need to be there—that you need to have a hand in stopping this. In freeing those women so you can find peace again." He touched my lip softly with his thumb. "Just know that if anything happens to you, the man you see now will become the beast everyone fears. Living so long on the idea of you was one thing. Having seen and held you, and know that your real and then to lose you—" His jaw tensed as his eyes went a brighter red.

I reached up and touched his face. "Nothing will happen to me. I'm not there to fight men, I'm there to find those women and get them to safety. I'll leave the fighting to you brutes." I stood on my toes and kissed his mouth. "I want to exchange blood again. I may not be able to work this damn bond, but I can feel your presence in me fading and it's a lonely feeling."

His red eyes held mine.

"And I think that's why you're struggling more right now—because you're losing that tether telling you I'm right here and I'm all right."

He took a deep breath and exhaled slowly. "That's part of it."

I waited for him to tell me the rest, but he didn't say anything? "How often do you have to feed?"

"Varies," he whispered, "depending on how much energy I use, how often I use my ability…"

"Okay, so a guesstimate since the first time you fed from me."

"Not as often as I should."

I gave him a stern look. "Why didn't you say something?"

He sighed, "Because I'm trying not to push you."

"You haven't been."

"No, but I have hit more prisoners since meeting you then in the last twenty years."

I shrugged. "The ones I saw you manhandle deserved it."

Shaking his head, he went over and sat on the big chair. "Feeding from you—and by the way you taste like fucking heaven and my favorite dessert I never knew existed all rolled into one," he turned and looked at me, "it's too hard to stop at just that."

I smirked. "Your favorite dessert? What do others taste like?"

He made a sound of exasperation. "Don't ask."

"I don't know much about this, but I get the impression that it's not something you can go on a diet with."

"It's not." He leaned his head back and looked at the ceiling.

"Arius, I'm okay with you feeding from me. I know I said it was vampy—but now I know what it's like and I won't object." I walked over and leaned over his face, looking down at him. "You've been inside my mind when you fed from me, you *know* how it makes me feel."

He looked at me. "Yes, and it doesn't help in preventing me from pushing you before you are ready." He pointed to the bed.

"I feel like this disagreement is backwards." Moving around to the front of the chair, I bent down, pulled up his cuff and got his knife. Straightening, I pointed it at him and waved it around a few times. "Here's the deal. We exchange blood, you feed—when needed—we keep our clothes on and you don't touch my hands."

He raised an eyebrow. "Been getting some coaching?" His eyes moved from my face to the knife in my hand.

"No, they just told me what I need to know." Stepping closer, I climbed on the chair and straddled him. "Deal?"

"I don't want to lose control and possibly hurt you."

"Then don't" I held the knife blade toward him. "Take off your shirt."

He gave me a heated look for a moment, then leaned forward.

I moved the knife.

He pulled his shirt over his head and tossed it to the floor, then looked at the knife again. "Blood, I feed from you, the rest of the clothes stay on and I don't hold your hands?"

I nodded.

"Deal." He said barely above a whisper.

I held out the knife.

He shook his head. "You keep it, in case you need to use it. I have to feed *now* or I won't be in anyway controlled."

I looked at the way his chest rose and fell, he was fighting the urge. I set the knife on the arm of the chair. "After what you told me, I feel like I'm torturing you by not just saying *let's go for it, mark me.* Am I being terrible?"

He shook his head and closed his eyes for a second. "No. I understand. I saw what Troy and Daxx went through, I honestly wasn't sure they were going to make it. I've seen forced mating's that didn't work out because lines were crossed." His gaze moved over my throat. "I'll wait ten years if I have to, so it's right for us." His expression sobered, his eyes flicking back to mine. "Please don't make me wait ten years. I'm not that strong."

I shook my head. "Sometimes I don't think I can wait ten minutes."

He grinned. "Okay. I can work with that—not the ten minutes, but that you're not denying me completely."

I looked down at our laps. "I'm sitting on you, telling you to bite me and asking for a blood bond—I am so far from any form of denying you that it's insane." I held his look.

"That right there. That's what will get me through this."

With a quick move, he grasped the back of my head and pulled me closer. His hand was so large, he was able to tilt my jaw up and expose my throat to his mouth before I could take a breath. His hold gentled, his breath brushing over my skin, then he bit into me.

I clung to his head, encouraging him to continue, to sate himself properly. In moments like this I wanted to be joined to him in all ways, I just didn't know if I could live with it after. "Arius, don't take my blood yet." I whispered.

With a soft growl, he lifted his head and licked over the mark. Then he pulled me back, so he could look at me. Even with his eyes red, I could see the doubt on his face.

I touched his mouth. "I said yet." Leaning forward, I kissed his fanged mouth. "I have a sexy idea." My stomach filled with heat from the very notion of it.

He looked at my mouth then back to my eyes. "What idea?" There was no mistaking the lust in his rough voice.

Leaning forward, I rubbed my face into his bare throat, he tipped his head back giving me access. Kissing his skin softly, I whispered, "what if you took blood from somewhere else, somewhere only you and I would know about and you left a temporary mark—would that appease the beast?" I nipped the muscle in his neck, he growled. I wished for a startling moment that I had fangs to bite him with. I lifted my head and looked at him.

His eyes locked on mine, his brows moving as he tried to puzzle out what I was saying.

"When you sucked on my neck last time, you left a small bruise…"

"I tried to be gentle."

I covered his mouth. "You were. I'm not complaining, and I don't want to hide what we did—before you even think that." I took a deep breath, my nerves starting to question what I was thinking. *Where had this woman come from*, I thought. "I just want something private, that's just for us."

He took a shaky breath. "What are you asking me to do?" He shook his head, "I'm drowning in lust for you right now and I can't think straight."

I smiled at his confession. "It's mutual. I want you to take blood from another bite, and not heal it completely, so it's there and only we'll know. Is that possible?"

He sat there breathing slowly, just looking at me. I couldn't read the emotions going through his eyes. "I've only ever fed—women in my past only wanted to fuck the beast for bragging rights, they never…"

I put my hand over his mouth again. "I'm not them. I'm not embarrassed by you, and I don't see you as a beast." I bit my lip feeling nervous, "will it help your struggle, knowing you've marked me in that way? Knowing that I am with you and yours, even if it's not the mate mark?"

His eyes caressed my face slowly, "Yes. I think it might." His voice was gravelly. "Where?"

I hadn't thought that far ahead in this hormone-driven plan. Straightening, I looked down my body, then lifting my gaze back to his I touched the side of my breast.

His nostrils flared. "And how are we managing that without taking clothes off?" His voice was strained.

Inhaling a sharp breath, I reached behind me and undid my bra through my shirt. Pulling the straps over my arms through the sleeves, I pulled it out the neck of my top and dropped it to the floor.

His gaze left my face and moved over the front of me. His hands moved to grip the arms of the chair. "That is not enforcing the clothes-on rule." He said in a choppy tone.

"My deal. My rules." I mimicked what he'd said to me about his cells and weapons.

"You take my blood first, or my mark will heal immediately." His red eyes moved to my face again. "You're inviting the beast to come out and play."

I picked up the knife. "It's your choice, if you want to do it or not."

He took the knife and cut into his chest, not once by two slices one above the other. Dropping it to the floor, he looked at me. "I can't touch you right now." He gripped the chair again.

I looked at the blood running down his skin and leaned over, cleaning it with my tongue. He hissed in a breath. Closing my mouth over the wounds, I sucked harder than I had before. He growled in his throat. My body responded to the sensual sound. When the marks closed, I sat up and looked at him.

His jaw was clenched, his eyes locked on my face. He shook his head slightly.

It was the first time I'd ever witnessed the battle going on inside him. "You're not a beast." I whispered. "You're my mate. You won't hurt me." It was the first time I believed that this connection was some ancient, fated match. "Arius." I whispered.

His red eyes flicked to my face. With shaking hands, he released the chair and put one hand behind me, pulling me closer to him. Inhaling a deep breath, he leaned into me and rubbed his face along my chest. I could feel how tense his whole body was. His other hand gripped my waist, clenching with indecision as he lifted his head.

Reaching between us, I pulled the hem of my top up slowly revealing skin. I held his eyes with mine as I moved, so he would see I had no fear of him.

Sucking in a breath, his hand released my waist and slid up my ribs to rest just under my breast. Pushing the shirt out of the way, he leaned closer and hesitantly licked over my nipple. I sucked in a breath, then he bit into the flesh beside it.

A soft moan escaped my mouth when he lifted his head and closed his lips around the mark and sucked on it gently. When his mouth released my flesh, I could feel his breath against my skin. "Don't heal it," I reminded him.

With a groan, he pulled his head away and grasped mine to pull my mouth down to his. His kiss was hard and brutal. Jerking his head up, he lifted his hands from me. "You have to get off me." He squeezed his eyes shut. "Babe," he implored in an unsteady voice.

With my own legs shaking, I slowly got off him and stood in front of the chair. My breathing was uneven, and I had my own inner battle taking place. I wanted to climb back on his lap. His head was resting against the back of the chair, his muscled neck and chest on display…

"Don't look at me like that." He warned.

I moved my eyes to his.

Leaning forward, he grasped my hips and stood up, pushing me back. He dropped his hands away. "I have to go, now or I won't." His gaze moved to my chest, he nodded. "Yeah I have to go." He started for the door.

I bent down and picked up his things. "Arius."

He stopped and turned, I held up his knife and shirt.

With a growl, he came over and took them from me.

"Go command your inmates to heel to your demands." I smirked.

He pulled his shirt on and then looked at me. Leaning down, he kissed me quickly. "You are incredible." He went back to the door, then looked at me with his hand on the handle. "I have to go."

When the door shut, I picked up my bra and worked it on, pausing to look at the punctures and red mark on my breast. Just knowing it was there, sent heat through me. Who knew I was into something like that, I thought as I adjusted it to put my arms back in the straps.

Huffing out a breath I went over and picked up my phone and tucked it into my pocket. I should get back to help search. I stopped and looked at the system sitting there, my hard drive beside it with thousands of songs on it. One song.

Quickly scrolling through the screen on the console, I selected one that had always been my victory song. My sound for when I'd had a moment where I prevailed against all odds. I hit play and adjusted the balance, then turned up the volume.

With a smile, I closed my eyes, raised my hands to the ceiling and started dancing.

Chapter Fourteen

My stomach lurched, I stopped and opened my eyes. It was complete darkness. The music had stopped. "Someone forgot to pay the electricity," I joked and pulled out my phone to turn on the flashlight. When I did, I froze. Where the hell was I? This wasn't my room. My heart began to pound in my chest. The floor was covered in scattered garbage and layers of dust. I turned and shone the flashlight around, there was old furniture stacked and long forgotten. I looked back at the floor, the garbage was covered in dust and cobwebs. Moving carefully, I walked toward a wall and held the light, so I could see it. It was a boarded up, window. No light shone through.

Lowering the phone, I opened my contacts and tapped Arius' name. I held the phone to my ear, my hand shaking.

"Second thoughts, beautiful?"

"Arius," I almost cried, "I don't know where I am."

"What? You were just in your room a minute ago."

I shook my head. "I'm not. It's dark and dirty and I don't know where I am." Tears threatened to fall.

"Paisley, listen carefully. I want you to hang up and open the app on your phone marked team. There's only one group on it, dial that, it will call all of us." His tone was so even.

I nodded.

"You got it?"

I nodded again. "Yes. Yes."

"Okay, do it now." The line went dead.

Shaking, I held the phone, so I could read the screen and opened the menu. I'd seen it and thought it was some preinstalled thing that came with the phone. I opened it and hit the only group listed 'good team'. I put the phone to my ear.

"I'm here." Arius said quickly. "Do you have your earbuds with you?"

I nodded then remembered he couldn't see me. "Yes. Hang on." I reached in my pocket and pulled them out, one fell to the floor. Clasping the other one in my palm, I lowered the phone and pushed the side of the earbud, so it would connect. It took two tries to get it in my ear properly. "Okay." I said.

"What's going on?" Victor's voice was in my ear.

"Paisley has somehow ported herself somewhere." Arius said sounding like he was running.

"How is that possible?" Chase asked.

"I didn't think it was without the full mating bond." Troy said, "Except in the instance of the huntress others cannot do that."

"So how did she do that then?" Chase said sounding serious.

"Can we fucking analyze this later?" Arius barked into the phone.

"Paize?" It was Daxx.

"Yeah?"

"What do you see?" she sounded calm.

I turned the flashlight back on my phone. And turned. "It's completely dark. Dirty, furniture and garbage stacked all over," I moved back toward the window, "It's boarded up."

"She's on your side, Daxx." Quinton said.

"Yeah that's what I'm figuring." Daxx replied.

"What were you thinking about just before it happened?" Alona asked.

I closed my eyes, remembering Arius and I, but wasn't going to say that. "I-nothing. I put a song on and was going to listen to it then come back to the cave." I took a deep breath, trying to stay calm.

"What was the song about?" Crissy asked sounding more serious then I'd ever heard her. "Did the words make you think of somewhere? That happens sometimes, small cues trigger memories."

I opened my mouth, then closed it and thought about the song. "The words hadn't even begun, I was just feeling good." I looked around the musky space I was in. "Where I am does not make me feel good."

"Can you feel her through the bond, Arius?" Leone asked.

"Barely. Because she's on the other fucking side and I'm not." He bit out. "I don't even know where to port to start and try to get a reading on her." He growled.

I heard a grunt.

"Arius," Michael hissed, "killing guards that get in your way is not going to find her."

"Paize, what do you smell?" Rafael asked.

I closed my eyes and inhaled slowly. I grimaced. "Dirt, mold and that mildew smell and something that smells like—" I inhaled again trying to place it, "I don't know but it gives me that metal taste in my mouth."

"Old factory district?" Quinton asked.

"Could be." Daxx said. "There's new factories over by the older neighborhoods though, so we need more. It could take hours to search both."

I turned, flashing the light all around me. "I can-can look around more."

"Be careful." Arius said, sounding more level headed.

I moved slowly, flashing the light at my feet, then checking ahead so I could take a few more steps. "There's a door. I don't think it leads outside though."

"Try it, maybe there's another way out." Beth suggested.

I nodded. "Okay." I shone the light around the door, then moved closer. I didn't want to touch the door, it was dirty, but I didn't want to stay here either. There was no handle, so I leaned against it and pushed with my shoulder and hip. It didn't move at all. "I think it's nailed shut."

"What about windows? Can you see out of any of them, give us some landmarks to go by?" Daxx asked.

Turning around, I shone the light along the wall. "I don't see any space around the boards." I looked around for something I could use to pry them away. "Just a second." I went over to some chairs that looked like they'd been tossed in a corner. "I'm going to need to be disinfected after this," I mumbled to no one in particular. "I'm going to try to break a leg off a chair and see if I can loosen a board to see out."

"Do what you need to, some of us are going to port to Alona's apartment so we're on that side. We'll reconnect to the call when we get there." Michael told me.

"Okay." I looked for good place to prop my phone, so I had light.

"One of us will remain on the call the whole time, Paisley." Victor informed me.

"You are not alone." Beth said softly.

I nodded. "Good, when we find me, we'll have a party here."

Someone chuckled.

"It's been work, run, run for days—we needed this rousing game of hide and seek." Chase said not sounding as amused as the words would imply.

I set the phone down propped against an empty bottle on the floor, shining the light on the chairs. If anything scurried out when I moved them, I was going to scream. "I do try to entertain." I said quietly.

"Don't encourage him, Paisley." Alona said in a monotone voice.

Going to the pile, I tried to make out which one I could move without all of them crashing on me. "If I scream, it's nothing, okay."

"Scream?" Arius said briskly.

Grabbing the leg of an upside-down chair, I tested the weight of it. "Yeah, I'm pretty sure rodents are the only inhabitants here."

"And you all wonder why I wear boots." Alona said, now sounding out of breath.

A few chairs shifted as I moved the top one. Slowly I picked it up high enough to free it from the pile. "I'd be happy with a baseball bat right now." Setting the chair down on the floor on its side I went over and picked up my phone. "I think I can break this chair. It's pretty old." I raised my foot and brought it down on the leg. It didn't budge. "What I wouldn't give for your ability right now, Beth." Stepping up onto the edge of the seat, I put my hands out to balance myself as it wobbled.

"Just ran down the alleys near the new metal plant," Quinton said sounding out of breath, "nothing boarded up here."

"I'm checking the next block." Rafael said.

"Are you able to sense her Arius?" Troy asked.

There was a quiet sound of annoyance. "Not enough to get a direction."

I wobbled again. "Can I do anything to help that?"

"When I get closer, I'm sure I'll feel your fear." He said quietly, sounding distracted.

I nodded. "Yes, there's plenty of that. If you could bring some hand sanitizer with you too, that would be great." I took a deep breath and jumped onto the leg of the chair. It cracked, and I found myself sitting on the filth on the floor.

"Did you break it?" Leone asked.

I looked to see the leg lying on the floor. "I did, and my butt too I think." I got up, trying not to touch the floor with my hands. Picking up the leg, I aimed the light and tried to look for a space in the boards. Something moved on the floor and I froze, slowly lowering the light, trying to see what it was and where it went. "Did you sense paralyzing fear, Arius?"

"No." He huffed out a breath like he was running. "What's wrong?"

I moved toward the wall. "Oh, just things scurrying around in here." I whispered.

"Anything in there should be very scared, sarg," Chase sounded like he was running, "I've seen you in action. My moneys on you." He huffed out a breath.

"We're covering the city sister, one street at a time." Rafael said, his voice sounded like he was running.

I stopped and stared at my phone. They were literally running through the city looking for me. "Thank you." I took a deep breath and exhaled slowly. "I'm going to try to pry a board loose."

I heard banging through the headset.

"Let us know if you hear any banging against the boards." Crissy said. "We found some buildings boarded up, so Victor is kicking them."

"Oh, trust me if you're close I'll let you know." I nodded.

"Okay." She said again.

I moved the light around the one board, looking for the best spot to try. There was a small space at the bottom. I kicked it with my foot and the board moved. Going back over, I picked up the grimy bottle to set the phone down against it.

I tried to wedge the chair leg under the board. It wouldn't fit. Turning the leg around, I jammed the broken end in and pulled up. It didn't move. Stopping, I huffed out a breath, then picked up my phone to shine it around the room.

"How are you doing?" Alona asked me.

"I could use a crowbar." I said, walking around to see if there was anything I could use for leverage or pry with. "A hot shower."

"Checked the lower south side." Michael reported. "None of the abandoned buildings are boarded up.

There was nothing the right size to use. I went back over and put the phone down.

"My question," Chase said sounding out of breath, "is why none of you have given her a device that will take her back to the landing room."

"Why haven't you given her one?" Quinton asked.

"Me? I'm a king, I can't be expected to remember everything." Chase replied.

Placing my foot on the leg sticking out of the board, I put my hand against the wall to balance myself. "Device? I thought I didn't need one." Slowly I moved my other foot and wobbled on top of the leg.

"Different device." Daxx said breathlessly. "This one brings you back to Alterealm."

I closed my eyes. "That would be handy right now."

"I didn't think to give you one because you had no way to leave on your own," Arius sounded stressed.

"Can we give me one that stops this from ever happening again?" I bent my knees to prepare to jump.

"Could it have something to do with her ability with time?" Troy asked.

I stopped moving. "If you tell me I've transported through time, I'm going to cry."

"No. No, I didn't mean that. To my knowledge and our scholars, that *is* impossible." Troy said.

"Caveman. Stop talking." Daxx said abruptly.

Someone snorted.

"Now you know how it feels, brother." Chase said.

It was comforting to listen to them, to know that I wasn't alone. I don't think I'd be as calm as I was in here without them chattering in my ear. "When I get out of where ever here is, someone needs to tell me how to never transport again." Bracing myself, I jumped and dropped both feet down onto the leg. I heard cracking, but didn't fall, so I tried it again. This time there was cracking, the leg broke and I stumbled across the floor to keep from falling on it.

"Paisley?" Arius said cautiously.

"I'm okay." I looked down to see some light shining in. "I broke part of the board off." I went over and grabbed the board and pulled on it. It wasn't coming off. Squatting down, I bent and looked to see what was on the other side. "I can't get it all the way off." Kneeling, I leaned down further. "I can see buildings."

"What kind of buildings?" Daxx asked quickly.

I looked again, trying to fit my head out. "Nothing that stands out." I turned the other way.

"Take pictures." Crissy said. "Up high ones and I will know where you are."

I sat back on my feet.

"I see where she's going. Aim the camera up and take the pictures of the height of the buildings and anything else you think will help."

I turned and picked up my phone. "Okay. Then just send them to Crissy?"

"You can send them over this app." Rafael informed me.

"We can send pictures?" Chase asked.

"You cannot." Alona told him.

"Ruin all my fun." Chase sighed.

"If you open the screen we're on, there's a settings icon in the top right corner, Paisley, open that and it will have send photo option." Michael said, then huffed out a breath.

"Give us a direction." Arius said patiently.

"Okay, hang on." I opened the app and did as Michael instructed. When the camera option came up, I leaned back down to the hole and aimed the phone up. I clicked it then turned the phone to make sure I got a picture of something. I sent it and then did six more, from every direction I could.

"I don't know buildings like that." Rafael said.

"They look familiar, but I can't place them." Leone told us.

"Criss, any of it look like somewhere you've been?" Daxx asked.

I turned and leaned back against the wall beside the hole. Listening, hoping.

"It makes me think of the old part, Daxx, after that bridge that fell down." Crissy said slowly like she was picturing it.

"Yes, they do. The city expanded but the original main hub was over there." Daxx blew out a breath. "Just give me a second, I have to get it right to get us there."

There was no talking for a few minutes. They felt like hours.

"Okay, meet at the building we used when Criss ran us across the supports of the old tracks, I can get us all to the old side from there." Daxx said.

"I'll stay on with Paisley. Let me know when you're back on." Arius told them.

I smiled, he knew not to leave me alone.

"We'll figure it out." He said quietly. "Find out how you did this, so it doesn't happen again."

"I know you will." I closed my eyes and pictured his face. My phone sounded the low battery warning. "Arius, my battery is dying."

"How much is left?"

I turned off the flashlight and checked. "Five percent. The flashlight must have drained it."

"We have the pictures now. I will find you." His voice was strained.

"Please hurry I don't want to be here in the dark alone." I pulled my legs closer and looked at the bit of light coming through. At least it wasn't dark outside. If it had been I wouldn't have been able to take the pictures.

"Okay, Arius, we're all here. Get your butt here." Daxx said.

"Her battery is almost dead." He said quickly. "I'll be there soon, Paisley."

My phone beeped again then powered down. I clasped it in my hand. It was completely silent now. No breathing, talking or background noise coming through the ear piece. I looked at the hole beside me again, making sure there was still daylight on the other side. I didn't even have enough light to see to get up and move around.

I listened, waiting to hear footsteps or someone calling my name. A shiver went through me and I didn't know if it was the damp air or fear. I tried not to think about rats or mice, but the more I tried to think of something else, the more I thought about rats and mice.

I closed my eyes, determined to push it from my mind and find something else to focus on. Reaching behind me, I jammed the phone in my pocket and hugged my arms around my waist. As I did my arm bumped Arius' mark. It was tender, but not in a bad way. I smiled to myself. I still didn't know where the idea had come from, or that I'd been bold enough to suggest it. I didn't regret it though. Arius, his family—this whole other realm, it was different in so many ways, but in others it was the same as anywhere else.

"Please find me Arius." I whispered. I rubbed my hands up and down my arms, trying to distract myself enough that I wouldn't freak out. If it hadn't been so dark, I could have paced. Sitting still always made time pass slowly. Sitting in the dark and silence made it feel like time stood still.

I thought I heard something outside. Dropping down, I looked out, listening.

"I'll take the alley."

It was Rafael.

Getting up I picked up the broken leg and hit the board. "I'm here." I screamed. I hit the board several more times, as hard as I could then stopped and listened.

"Paisley." Arius shouted.

I dropped down to the hole. "Arius, I'm here."

"Stand back."

I jumped up and stood to the side. The boards crunched, then broke with the next hit.

Light filled the dark space and Arius stood in it, his red eyes glowing. I launched myself at him into his arms.

"I've got you." He said against my ear, hugging me tight.

I didn't let go as he walked out into the light. The others stood near the corner of the building. They looked out of breath, anxious. I still couldn't believe they ran around the city, literally, looking for me.

"Thank the gods." Troy said.

"I don't need exercise for a week." Quinton sighed.

Arius stopped walking and set me on my feet. Leaning back, he cupped my face, searching it. "Are you all right?"

I nodded. "In desperate need of a shower, but okay otherwise." I rested my forehead against his chest.

"Do you recognize where we are?" Victor asked.

Lifting my head, I looked around.

"Wait." Alona rushed toward me, taking a device off her wrist. "Put this on. It will either land you in my apartment or the landing room."

Arius took it and lifted my arm.

While he did it up, I looked at the building I'd been stuck in. There was something familiar. "I have been here." I pointed to the corner. "There was a street dance. It was the first time I'd seen a professional deejay and knew that's what I wanted to do."

"But you weren't thinking about here when you ported?" Troy asked.

I shook my head. "No, I was just happy." I looked up at Arius, his eyes locked with mine.

"What were you doing right before that? Before you turned the music on?" Michael crossed his arms, looking concerned.

I felt my cheeks heat and looked back up at Arius.

He glanced at his brother. "We'd renewed the blood bond."

"No more happy thoughts for you." Chase said. "Ever." He motioned up and down Arius. "We need to find out why the pretty one's blood can do that to a woman." He smirked.

"I doubt it was the blood, but we have to know if she can do it again." Victor glanced to Arius.

He nodded and looked down at me. "I'll be with you, and you have a device now."

I looked down at my wrist and placed my hand over it and squeezed. "What do I do?"

He wrapped his arms around me. "Close your eyes, focus on one place, picture it."

I nodded and closed my eyes. Resting my head against him, I thought of his room. I pictured it in my mind.

After a few moments, I opened my eyes and looked around. We were still here with the others.

"That's very curious." Victor said.

"Could it be another ability that's been dormant?" Quinton's brow furrowed.

"I don't know what it could be at this point." Victor said quietly. "The royal blood is what allows us to transport without programmed devices, but others not born to it can only do it with a full bond," he motioned to my arm, "and only when marked." He looked to Arius again. "Have Clairee take a look when we get back, see what she senses."

Arius nodded.

"You should have her room checked too." Leone said, hugging Bethany against his chest. "Just to be on the safe side, after the spies we've discovered have had access inside the chambers."

"I agree, we can't afford to not be certain. Their attempt to get Marcus freed failed once, what's to stop them from trying another way?" Michael looked to Troy then Chase, both nodded.

"You think they were going to use her?" Arius asked, a low rumble in his chest.

"I would put nothing past them." Bethany said. "They've got to be desperate now."

Daxx nodded, "You spent the night before in Arius' room that was the first time you were back in yours for long enough to grab something, right?"

I nodded and glanced up at Arius. "They did something to my room?"

He hugged me against his chest. "We'll find out."

"Get Clairee and Romulus here to check this building as well, see if they can sense magic." Troy said in a hard tone.

"I think we should get back, and let Paisley take a shower." Alona said softly.

I turned in Arius' arms and looked at them. "Thank you. For looking for me." I felt my eyes tear up. No one had ever done something like that before.

Chase pointed at me. "Don't even think it." He grabbed Alona and they vanished.

"Oh, I am not doing this again." Daxx turned and grabbed Troy's arm and they both disappeared.

Beth gave me a soft smile. "They don't do emotions well." She nodded then leaned into Leone. Smiling down at her, then they were both gone.

Arius looked down at me, "my shower will have to do, you're not stepping in that room until it's cleared."

"They better not touch my sound equipment." I leaned against him and wrapped my arms around his chest.

Chapter Fifteen

I turned off the music and turned around, Daxx dropped down onto the mat and lay there on her back. "That looked great."

She lifted her head and looked at me, "easy for you to say, you're not doing all the moves."

I shrugged, "I would if I thought the guy doing the music would get it right."

To take our minds off the fact we were going to the island, we'd spent the last two hours coming up with our surprise performance for the ball. Finding moves all of us could do, that would be noticeable wearing floor length gowns and went with the music had been a challenge. With such a short time to the ball, we had to keep it simple.

Alona picked up her water bottle. "The way you do it is perfect." She grinned, "And you need to record the expression on the guys' faces, so you can't be down with us."

Bethany nodded and sat down beside Daxx. "Who knew dancing could be so—"

"Vigorous," Alona sat down wiped her brow.

I was running over the songs in my head. "The mix will be better with the big speakers, I'll get the timing right on that last part." I went over and sat down with them and grinned. "It looked amazing."

Crissy bound over and dropped down on the mat. "That was so much fun." She bit her lip. "I'll have to remember to hold my dress out of the way though."

"Has anyone else wondered what the guests are going to think?" Bethany asked quietly. "I mean, we're mates to the royals and we're doing this."

Daxx lifted her head, "Fate chose us, she had to know we weren't going to just smile pretty."

Alona huffed out a breath. "Even if it's not perfect, it will still be a defining moment."

Daxx rolled her head to the side and looked at me, "I don't dance, but this is more…"

Felix stuck his head in the door, "are we supposed to stop the kings from entering as well? Because both are coming this way with the Justice, warden and enforcer."

I looked to Daxx.

She smirked, "probably picked up the high energy through the bonds."

I looked at Felix, "buy me a few more minutes so I can pack this up." I pointed to the system as I scrambled to my feet.

He nodded and went back out.

"They're not going to like being blocked by five guards." Alona said with a grin.

Crissy giggled. "Victor doesn't take orders well."

Bethany got up and came over to help me unhook it. Setting it quickly all together on the floor, we went back over and sat down.

"Shh." Daxx pointed to the door.

"Let me get this straight," Chase said loudly, "we are not *allowed* to enter our own practice room until one of the women say you can let us in?"

The answer was too quiet to make out.

"I know you know who we are." Troy's voice came through the door.

"Why would they do this?" Leone asked.

"Perhaps one of their guards would be so kind as to ask if we're allowed to enter our practice room yet." Victor didn't sound pleased.

"Felix." Arius growled, "You have about thirty seconds until I get pissed off."

Alona looked at me, her mouth an O. "I think we'd better let them in."

The door opened, and Felix gave me a curious look. I nodded.

Both doors opened with a bang. Serious looking men came in with long strides, testosterone pouring off them. They stopped and looked at us sprawled on the mat.

"Daxx what is going on?" Troy demanded.

She turned her head and looked at him. "Workout."

He raised one eyebrow. "Workout? Since when do you work out?"

She snorted, "If you'd seen my ass in that gown, you'd understand."

Leone came over and looked down at Beth. "Workout?"

She nodded.

Alona wiped her brow. "A vigorous one."

Chase raised an eyebrow and came over. "I picked up on the exertion and couldn't imagine what you could be doing."

"Sweating mostly." She motioned to me. "Paisley is a serious task master."

Arius looked over to see my system stacked and turned grey eyes to move slowly over me.

Crissy jumped up and ran over to Victor, she launched herself at him. "It was fun." She smiled.

He smiled back at her. "Perhaps next time let me know prior to doing something like this, so I know not to worry when I pick up odd things. Your level of energy is always high, that was—concerning."

She nodded.

"You ladies could have invited…"

Alona held out her hand to Chase, "not a chance."

"That's why the guards were at the door. We don't need to be ogled." Daxx said sitting up.

Troy went over and pulled her to her feet.

She huffed out a breath. "All the final details hammered out?"

He nodded.

"Good." She looked around at us. "We have enough time to grab a shower and eat, then we get to go kick ass." She smiled.

"Do we need to know more than we were told earlier?" Alona leaned against Chase's side.

"I don't believe so." He kissed the top of her head.

"I'm still not convinced of some of the placements," Victor looked at the woman in his arms, "but I understand the need for it."

Crissy hugged his neck. "I'll be okay."

"I don't understand this cloaking." I said crossing my arms over my chest.

"Oh." Beth turned to Leone, "I've been practicing. I can't do it for as long as Clairee, but I can manage a few seconds." She closed her eyes, took a deep breath, then opened them.

As she moved her hand down over Leone, he disappeared. Not a poof, vanish, but gradually faded. Moving her hand back up he reappeared. "That is so cool." I whispered.

She grinned at me then hugged Leone. "There will be twelve from the temple going and they'll each ride in a boat and cloak it all the way there, so no one sees us."

"That's just crazy." I grinned.

"Four mages will be working on taking down the barrier as soon as our feet are on the island." Troy said, giving Leone a wary look.

He rubbed the back of his neck, "Romulus better have it down in case any of the girls need to port off."

Chase nodded, "yes, I don't see any of them willing to jump off the cliff to get off either."

I shook my head. "No. Once was more than enough."

"With half of the guard's garrison going, no one should be able to get near the women." Arius crossed his arms over his chest, "their personal guards better be their shadows with every step they take."

"Are Emil's sons coming?" Daxx asked.

Chase shook his head, "not on the island. They're staying with the boats. Their fighting skills need some serious improvement before they can step into the battle."

"Emil is coming on the island?" Alona asked him.

"Try to stop him. Rena is there, so no force on earth could stop him." He said giving Troy a quick look.

"I've seen him practice at the guards' training yard." Leone shrugged, "he's good. Could take you down." He grinned at Troy.

Troy turned his head slowly and gave him a hard look, "we'll invite him to practice when this is over."

Arius grinned. "I'm in. One more brother to beat on."

Chase smirked, "you're just not happy that you're not the only pretty one now."

I lifted my hand as I went to say something, and Chase ducked behind Alona. I stopped and gaped at him, turning slowly I pointed to my system. "I was going to say I need to take that back and grab a shower."

There were several snickers.

Chase cleared his throat. "I knew that."

Alona covered the smile on her mouth and nodded. "Of course, you did."

He winked at me, then grabbed her and they vanished.

"I think he's a bit wary of you, sister." Leone nodded. "I like it." He hugged Bethany. "See you shortly."

"Let's go shower." Crissy said to Victor.

He smiled. "As you wish." They were gone in a blink.

Daxx sighed and looked at Troy. "That leaves us to help carry back her system."

Troy opened his mouth, then closed it and inclined his head.

They went over and picked it up.

Arius looked down at me, his eyes searching mine. "I don't know what you're up to, but I'm not buying the workout bit." He whispered.

I gave him a wide-eyed look. "Maybe it's a surprise." I glanced over at Daxx and Troy quickly.

He tilted his head. "Good or bad?"

I shrugged, "a good one."

"Mmm," he glanced at my mouth, "we'll see." Leaning down he kissed me, then turned to my equipment.

Daxx looked at me quickly, then smirked.

After the last two hours, I should have been exhausted, but I wasn't. I knew the plan and the backup plans, but no matter how carefully plotted, things could go wrong. I watched Daxx and Troy walk ahead of us. I cared about these people. I was terrified something would happen to them.

My part was relatively easy, find the women, and get them to safety. I knew the layout of the building. Had thought of three possible locations to take them. The part I couldn't get past was the men and what they could be facing. This wasn't some office building, this was an entire island.

"It will be fine." Arius said quietly.

His voice jolted me out of my head. I glanced up at him. "I hope so."

His pale eyes gave me a concerned look, there was something he was thinking but didn't want to voice.

"Don't say it." I warned quietly.

"Say what?"

"That I don't have to go." We turned the last corner before my room. "I would never be able to live with myself if anything happens to one of you and I'm sitting here."

We were at my room. Daxx and Troy set the units on the table, then vanished.

Arius set the mixer down. "I'm still not sure why you needed the whole unit to work out."

I grinned, "Gotta be able to *feel* the beat." I didn't want to talk about what we had been doing in the practice room. I couldn't continue to avoid answering his subtle inquires. "I need a shower."

His gaze moved down over me.

I blushed. "I'm pretty sure inviting you to join me would be breaking the clothes on rule."

He laughed. "Oh, I see, it's okay for you to bend the rules when you want, but I'm not allowed."

Walking over, I gave him a heated look. "That would be smashing the rules, not just bending, and then we'd be late to meet the others at the boats."

The muscle in his jaw pulsed. "You're right. It's a hell of a spot to be in—being naked with you in the shower or fighting with my brothers."

"It will help your rage issues."

"Showering with you?"

I smirked, "no, I meant fighting."

He laughed. "Both would help in completely different ways."

Stretching up, I kissed him softly. "I'm almost there, not quite, but close."

He growled quietly and grasped the back of my head. "I'll be back in ten minutes, so you better shower fast." He kissed me, then let go. Backing toward the door, he smiled, "you don't have to be all dressed when I get back."

I blushed, "clothes rule."

He growled again then spun on his heel and walked out.

I blew out a breath and looked at the door for a moment. I needed to figure this out. What was I waiting for? I still didn't know.

Turning, I went into the bathroom.

I'd never felt the way I did with him—with anyone else before. I knew it was the bond, but seriously, if normal folks had that, there would never be another divorce. Being in synch with someone in that way was the ultimate guide to understanding your partner. So what was I doing?

Shaking my head, I pulled off my shirt and made fast work getting out of my bra. As long as there was the slightest hesitation, I couldn't.

Stripping off the rest of my clothes, I stepped into the shower.

Fate sure messed up choosing me. I jumped into nothing without thought.

Chapter Sixteen

I stood in the middle of my room looking around slowly. The level of comfort I had in this room was gone. Now I was afraid to move anywhere I hadn't stepped since they'd told me.

Someone knocked on the door.

"It's open." I called out.

Arius came in and closed the door. He stopped and looked at me. "They removed it. Warded it. You are completely safe in here."

I gave him a blank look.

He shrugged. "I can feel how uncomfortable you are."

I waved my hand, motioning to the room. "They had a—magical trap in here." I frowned. "Anyone could have stepped in it. What if it was," I looked around, "whoever cleans this room and they had no one to call?"

His brows furrowed, "you're mad because someone else could have tripped it?"

I nodded. "Yeah. Well, I'm not happy it was me, but I had you to call—and the entirety of *good team.*"

He grinned. "Raf's doing, naming our chat call that." He sobered, "what happened in ten minutes? You were okay when I left."

"I was left alone with my head."

He grinned. "I'll have to remember that."

I stopped, just noticing he was in all black leather, his hair braided and weapons all over his body. I put my hand to my chest. We were going to the island soon. "I'm nervous." I admitted. "You look good like that, I didn't tell you last time because we were on a roof."

With long strides he came toward me.

My brain was saying 'wow' as I watched him. So much confidence in that stride, not to mention he looked so hot.

As he reached me, one eyebrow went up. "Don't be thinking like that right now. I have to focus."

I gave him a 'huh' look.

He chuckled, "I can feel hormonal urges as well as I can sense anxiety or fear."

I pouted, "It's not fair! I can't work this bond stuff and I've told you before not to look so damn good."

With a smirk, he shrugged, "it is better you don't feel everything I do." He tapped his forehead, "it's a mess of rage up here more often than not." His eyes moved slowly over me. "You look sexy in that. Mitz chose well for you."

I turned and looked in the mirror. Mitz had brought me a short leather jacket with some sort of ribbing made into it to protect me. The sleeves were loose all the way to the cuff, it emphasized my hands, which I'm sure she planned. "I like it." I looked at him in the mirror.

"I've brought you three things." He said, his eyes still locked on my reflection.

"Oh?"

He nodded and stepped up behind me. Reaching around, he held out a device. "This one is programmed for the girl's cave. So if anything happens today, you hit that button and get out of there." I held up my arm and he put it on. Straightening, he held up a small knife in a black case.

I cringed. "I've never really used a knife." I held my hands up. "I have these."

He nodded. "I know, but just make a paranoid man happy and agree to carry it."

I nodded. "Okay."

"Right or left leg?" He asked.

I looked down at my feet. "Right."

He knelt beside my leg and lifted my pant leg and wrapped a strap around my ankle, then adjusted it so it wouldn't interfere with my movement.

I lifted my foot and looked at it. "If I stab the wrong person, I'm blaming you."

Standing up he grinned. "Try to miss all of my brothers please, I don't need to hear *that* for hundreds of years," he rolled his eyes, "remember that time your mate stabbed me."

I laughed. "Okay I'll try not to."

The smile on his face faded, a nervous look appeared on his face.

I went to turn to ask what the problem was when he placed his hands on my shoulders and looked at me in the mirror instead.

"I don't know if you remember when we went to the Elder's chamber, when Elder Roan wanted to know why a royal medallion didn't adorn your neck—"

I nodded.

"I know it's not official," he ran his hand down my left arm, "But I'd like you to wear mine today."

His grey eyes held mine in the reflection, a hesitant and vulnerable look in them.

I nodded.

His stance visibly relaxed.

He reached into his pocket. "I had them add something to it. On the back. The front is the same as mine." He held up a chain with a pendant on the end. He opened it, reaching around me, and put it around my neck. When he clasped it, he leaned over my shoulder and held it up.

I held it in my palm and looked down at it. It was the same as what he wore, just smaller. A symbol of scales the center a sword pointing down, a sun on one side and moon on the other. I turned it over to see the face of a small clock had been etched into the back. Turning my head, I met his hesitant look. "I love it, thank you."

Reaching around me, he hugged me against his body, kissing the side of my neck as he did. I watched how he looked at me in the mirror. He had that look often, when he looked at me. It made me feel cherished and special. A feeling I hadn't felt often in my life.

He moved his hand to touch where his bite mark was hidden. "Is it sore?"

I shook my head, "not in a bad way." I met his eyes in the mirror again. "It's a constant reminder, in a good way." My cheeks heated.

With a soft growl, he turned me into his arms. "We can't keep doing that."

I wrapped my arms around his neck and looked up at him. "Why?"

"Because my control has been pushed to its limit both times—and knowing there's a mark on your body bothers me, even if I put it there." He leaned down and lightly kissed my mouth.

"I like it. Maybe someday we can use a different part of my body."

He gave me a heated look. "You are killing me." Grasping the back of my head, he pulled until I was on my toes and attacked my mouth.

A knock on the door startled both of us. Huffing out a breath, I moved back from him a few inches. "It's open." I called out.

The door opened, and Elder Roan stepped in. "If this is a bad time, I can return later."

I shook my head. "No, it's fine. We'll be going shortly."

He clasped his hands in front of him and stood very stiffly. I had to wonder if he was always so tense and formal. "I've just come from the lab and wanted to share the results with you in person."

I leaned into Arius, not sure how I felt about that. The idea that I may have a relative from another realm…"

"What were the results?" Arius asked.

He could probably sense my apprehension.

Elder Roan gave a small smile. "It seems," he cleared his throat, "that we are, in fact, related."

I put my hands over my mouth.

"It appears—that I am your great-great-grandfather. That you are my great-great-granddaughter." He smiled. "My son was the only member of my family to go to the other side—he never mated here." He cleared his throat. "Your age fits when you consider the average human life span, then adjust for when he disappeared, it is great-great."

I dropped my hands, but still didn't know what to say. I had family.

He cleared his throat. "You have many, many cousins and aunts, uncles—quite a large family here." He glanced to Arius, then back to me. "I can introduce you at the ball." He nodded abruptly.

"Yes, please." I turned and looked up at Arius. "I have family."

He smiled down at me.

I turned and rushed toward my great-great-grandfather, then stopped right before I reached him. I nodded. "I would like that."

His smile was genuine, and it changed his hard appearance, the only one I'd seen him have. He glanced at the pendant hanging over my jacket, his eyes flicked to Arius, then his eyes reflected his emotions. "It's a great honor for us to have one of our princes join the family."

Arius snorted as he walked over. "I'm sure that's not what they'll say when you tell them which prince."

Elder Roan shook his head, "you have always held honor in this realm, warden. No one will speak otherwise from my family line."

Arius inclined his head slightly. "We need to get going shortly."

The aged brown eyes moved over him, then he turned to me. "Paisley is going with you?"

Arius put his arm around me. "She is just as much a warrior, able to protect the realms as I am."

I glanced up at him, a little surprised.

Elder Roan inclined his head. "As you say." He straightened and gave a polite smile. "I will leave you to make your preparations and wish you much success." He bowed formally, then stepped back several steps before turning and going back out the door.

Arius blew out a breath. "Chase is going to try to spin this to earn favors, or forgiveness, from the Elders."

I smirked, "I was thinking the same thing. After his initial reaction to meeting me."

Arius laughed. "That scene is etched in my mind forever." He looked down at me. "Ready? We decided to get over there and organized earlier. There are a lot of guards to take over. We have to meet the others at the armory."

I looked up and down at the weapons already on his person. "You can't possibly carry any more."

He chuckled. "No, that's just where we port from."

I took a deep breath. "I'm nervous, but let's go get those women."

Chapter Seventeen

I stood at the bottom of the rocks and looked up at the men. Several of them were spread out between the bottom and top the jagged rocks. Bethany stood beside me. We had been dubbed the tag team, and both of us were okay sticking beside each other.

There were mages in a cloaked boat by the shore. To me it looked like they were doing some sort of dance, waving their hands around. Daxx assured me they were working on taking the barrier down.

"How are you doing, Leone?" Troy's voice came through the ear piece.

"Getting there. Slow going with ten of us." His breathing was heavy.

I still couldn't believe they were climbing the cliff I'd jumped off.

"Cristy?" Victor said.

"I'm okay." She answered quickly.

"We have her anchored to both Leone and I." Rafael informed him.

"I must have been mad to agree to that." Victor complained.

"She's actually making our best climbers look bad, brother." Leone said sounding amused.

"I have no doubt of that." Victor said sounding distracted.

I looked up to see him pointing for Arius to look down the beach.

"Crissy, you can't pass Raf and I, or the anchor rope would pull us off if you slip."

"Then hurry up." She said not sounding as winded as Leone did. "I can see the top."

"Don't go any closer, little sister—I have to check it—with the crystal." Rafael said in a choppy way.

We'd been afraid after my escape they may have put a barrier on the cliff side of the island.

"I remember. I never forget things." Crissy sounded bored.

"On your call, Leone." Quinton said.

Beth nudged me with her arm. I turned to see her motion up the rock. Daxx and Alona were working their way up. Now I understood why the men were spread out in that way. We would never be out of reach from one or the other as we climbed.

Beth went before me, she made it look easy.

I glanced up to Arius. He knew how I felt about heights. He gave me a quick nod, then a warm feeling surrounded me. Crissy was scaling a hundred-foot cliff, without guide ropes—I could manage twenty-five feet.

I grabbed the first rock and stepped up.

"Romulus says they are almost there." Michael reported.

"Checking for barrier now." Raf said sounding winded.

"It's clear." Leone said. "First climbers on the ground. Pulling up our gear."

"Wimps." Quinton joked.

"You know what to do, Cristy." Victor reminded. He turned and held his hand down to me.

"Climbing that in leather was challenge enough, brother. You do it with all your gear on." Leone dared him.

The men were practically throwing us four women up the rock facing. I clasped Victor's wrist and was lifted up to the next flat surface.

"Getting in the tree now, Vic." Crissy said quickly.

There was a snort.

"Pretty sure it's the tallest one on the island. She will be able to see anywhere and everywhere." Rafael told us.

"I am no longer shocked." Was Victor's monotone response.

Arius clasped my wrist and pulled me up. When my feet touched the ledge beside him, he leaned down and touched his forehead to mine for a moment.

I gave him a serious look, my voiceless way of telling him to be safe. Turning, I climbed up to the next spot where Troy would pull me to the top.

"We're just behind the building now." Rafael said in a hushed voice.

"Four guards at the back." Crissy reported. "Three more that I can see in the upstairs window. They are not paying attention to the outside."

Grabbing the rope, I turned and started down the other side of the rock. Hitting the bottom, I pulled off the gloves and tucked them in my pocket.

Bethany was doing the same. We were probably the only ones in this fight today that had to have our hands unprotected.

We followed Chase as he led us up into a stand of trees. Staying out of sight until the last moment was important.

"Oh, can we drive up on the golf carts?" Daxx asked.

I checked behind us to see a steady line of men right behind me.

"Waiting on the go." Leone said.

"Three guards west side." Crissy said quickly. "I don't see any on your side, Vic." She paused. "Which is silly with the stairs there."

"Barrier down. On my way up." Michael said hurriedly.

"They aren't reacting." Crissy told the men. "They don't know it's down."

"Romulus got it right." Quinton sounded surprised.

I was too nervous to even feel tired as we kept moving.

"Building visible." Troy said quietly.

"Give us thirty seconds for the rest to get here and breach." Chase said, his tone harder then I'd ever heard it.

"So many fucking stairs." Michael panted out. "How did I get mage sitting duty?"

"Quinton volunteered you." Raf whispered.

"Bastard." Michael huffed out a breath. "At the carts."

"So fast?" Alona said quietly. "You are to be commended, Michael."

"Yeah if I don't have a heart attack first." He replied. "I need lighter swords."

"I've been born into a family of crazy people." Emil said into the mic. "It's an honor."

"Breach in fifteen. Fight well brothers—and sisters." Leone said.

"Our sisters will make us all look bad." Rafael chuckled.

I couldn't believe they were joking, then realized this was their way, their lives.

"Anyone makes you look bad, Raf." Quinton chuckled.

"Fight well, brother king." Troy said.

"You as well, twin king." Chase responded.

"In eight." Leone whispered.

I looked down the line of men to the one that never left my thoughts. "Arius?" I said quietly.

He turned and glanced at me.

I winked at him.

"Yeah, babe?" He watched me.

"Show them my beast."

"In Three." Leone announced.

Arius grinned. "My pleasure."

"Ready." Leone said.

"Outdone." Chase said.

"Let's party." Daxx growled out.

Chapter Eighteen

Bodies filed out of the trees in a long line, moving silently toward the building.

I was leading the women, our guards flanking us. Arius and Quinton would be right behind us, but I focused on where I was going.

I knew the lower door held only one guard, so we were going in that way. Bethany was close to my side, we were short enough, it enabled us to stay low and out of sight. I paused as we reached the door and stood to one side. I knew there would be a guard on the other side. Turning, I glanced to Arius, he gave an abrupt nod and pulled a sword off his back.

"Contact in three." Quinton said softly into the mics.

"Confirmed." Leone replied.

"Ready to engage." Troy answered.

We were all a second from our presence being known.

I put my hand on the handle of the door. Beth nodded and raised her hands, the colorful arc moving between them. Turning the handle, I pushed the door and stepped back.

Arius went through the door. That first clang of metal against metal had me cringing.

Daxx went through, box in one hand and thin sword in the other.

I rushed in behind her, my hands raised. Huddled in the corner were four of the women I'd left behind.

"You're alive." One said, her eyes huge with surprise and fear.

I nodded and turned to see the guard vanish as Daxx used her zapper box.

"We're here to get you out." I said softly going toward them. Their eyes moved to where our guards came in the door. "They're with me." I nodded. "Four women on the lower level." I reported for the others.

Alona motioned with her hand, so the women would come out of the corner.

"Two on the second floor." Troy said.

"Three, one is our informant." Victor added.

I glanced to Arius. "We need to get to the room we slept in."

"Go." Daxx said. "We've got this." She motioned to the first woman to step outside with Tim.

Emil came through the door. He had blood across his neck and shoulder.

Arius gave him a once over.

"Not mine." Emil said quickly.

"Lead the way." Arius told me.

Felix moved to walk beside me, Arius right behind. Alona and Sith came with us.

I moved down the hall, pausing to glance into the bathroom. It was empty. I pointed to the corner. The bedroom was right after it. Felix nodded and moved quietly toward it, with Arius right behind him.

As I reached the corner I heard the clash of swords and paused. I looked to see Alona beside me and Emil watching behind us. I went around the corner to see Arius and Felix fighting with the huge guard I used to avoid being near. He was the largest man I'd ever seen, and always stood closest to the larger groups of women here.

Felix stumbled back, and Arius stepped in to take the brunt of the next swing. He blocked it, then kicked the giant in the chest barely making him move, but it unblocked the door.

"Go." Alona hissed beside me.

I crouched down and headed for the door, the guard saw me and turned. Raising my hands, I caught his sword as it aimed for my head. It stopped. The guard howled in rage as he tried to move it. Alona touched my side to help me step closer to the door and out of the range of the swing, so I could keep my eyes on it and hold it still.

"I've got it." Arius growled and stepped between us, in the way of my line of sight to the guard.

As we went into the room I heard the sound of a sword clattering to the floor.

"Dad." The woman I knew to be Emil's daughter came flying across the floor and into his arms.

"I've got you." He said holding her.

Alona motioned to Sith, "take them to the apartment."

Emil frowned, "I should…"

"Go, brother. Take your child to safety." Victor's tone came over the ear piece.

Emil nodded. Hugging his daughter with one hand he reached for Sith. "We'll go to the beach and get my sons." The three of them vanished.

I turned and made a quick count of the frightened faces of the women. "Eight more women in the bedroom." I did the math quickly, that was fifteen in total.

"Can we get a—porter—here?" Arius grunted.

I glanced back out the door to see Arius down to one sword, still fighting the large guard. Felix was now fighting someone else. I looked at Alona, she stood ready with her num-chuks in hands.

"Trying," Michael grunted, "bastards are like ants coming out of everywhere."

"I can…"

"Daxx stay—with the women." Troy growled.

"I can't get there, Arius." Leone sounded out of breath, "Keep him busy."

Arius lunged for the guard, his expression cold and lethal.

"I'm going—" there was a loud crash, "to need a moment." Victor said into the mic.

I turned to Alona, then motioned to the women. "Stay close together."

Alona went out the door. "Heading to you Daxx." I informed them then I stood watching the commotion, my hands raised. Checking quickly out of the corner of my eye, I saw the last one going around the corner.

As I turned to follow I caught the glint of something out of the corner of my eye. Then Arius was there his blade blocking the swing intended for my head.

"Get clear," he barked, then kicked the guard back. "Like stopping a fucking—" he hit the sword, knocking it from the guard's hand. It clanged to the floor. "bulldozer," he growled to his brothers.

I went to the corner and watched down the hall as Daxx ushered the women outside.

"Anthony and Liza are on the way with a big boat." Crissy reported. "Can I…"

"No. Keep watch." Victor said, his tone leaving no room for questions.

Turning back, I saw the guard running out the side door with Arius following. I motioned for Daxx to go, then turned to follow them.

Outside, I paused to see which way they went. Rafael ran past, chasing down two guards heading around the corner. Leone, right behind him. I saw the flash of a long braid flying out behind someone disappearing into the trees.

I went racing after them. I held my hand over my ear, so I wouldn't lose the piece. "Arius, you're running toward the cliff." I warned and ran faster.

"Bastard isn't getting away," he huffed as he ran, "swung at you twice."

I cleared the shrubs and slid to a stop.

Arius had no weapon, neither did the guard. They were hitting each other with their fists. I looked to see that the ground dropped off five feet from where they were fighting. I didn't dare warn or interrupt him right now.

He kicked the man in the chest, he stumbled back and fell to his knees. Wiping the blood off his mouth, Arius stepped toward him, vengeance pouring off him.

The guard stood up and swung a large broken branch at Arius' head. The sound of the hit echoed through the ear piece. Arius was knocked back a few feet but regained his balance.

Victor ran past me, kicked the guard's feet out from under him then zapped him with the box.

I heaved a sigh of relief.

Arius stood there, trying to catch his breath. He wiped at the blood running down his face, then stumbled back a few steps.

It happened so fast, but was in slow motion at the same time. He fell backwards over the edge.

"Arius." I screamed and ran to the edge and fell on my stomach. Holding my hands out I stopped his fall as soon as I was able to see him.

"Paisley." Victor was beside me grabbing my waist to stop me from falling over the edge.

"I can't look away, Victor, is he over water?" I swallowed, trying to focus on Arius alone.

I felt Victor move to look, his hold keeping me in place. "No." he said in a hoarse voice. "Hold him there."

"Okay." I whispered. "What do we do? I can't look away from him or he'll fall." My heart was beating so fast.

"We're on our way." Beth's voice shouted in my ear.

"Rafael." Victor barked, "Get to a boat and to the north side. Now."

"On it." Raf answered.

"Go." Daxx said. "We've got this."

"Coming with you." Troy said quickly.

"Kinsley," Victor said moving slightly.

"Can you hold a man's weight?" Michael asked

I heard footsteps. "I don't know. Let me try." A woman said.

I felt someone on the other side of me. "I can't, he's too far for me."

"Cristy, we need your belt for Bethany." Victor said in a brusque way.

"I'm here." She answered.

"Leone, climb down with Beth and keep her steady." Michael said from the other side of me.

I focused on Arius, my breathing frantic. I would not blink or look away from him.

"Hold on, Paize, we're almost level with him." Beth said.

"Hurry. I can't hold him too long. I don't know what it will do to his body." I was trying not to cry. Tears in my eyes would break the connection.

"Almost there." Rafael said loudly over a motor.

"Okay, Paize, I'm there. On three. One. Two. Three."

I dropped my hands and watched Arius fall a short bit, then Bethany hit him, and he flew out over the water and splashed into it.

Victor pulled me back from the edge. I didn't take my eyes off the water. "Where is he?" I kicked off my shoes and stepped back and threw myself over the edge.

I felt something hit me in the air and knew Beth was making sure I hit the water too. I looked as I fell, trying to see him.

I dropped into the water and kicked to the surface. "Arius." I screamed as soon as the air hit my face.

I turned and saw something in the water. Diving under, I grabbed for it and felt leather in my hand. I kicked as hard as I could to pull him high enough. My head broke the surface again.

"Paisley." It was Troy.

I heard a splash, then Arius was pulled above the surface.

"Arius." I coughed.

"Paisley, take my hand." I turned to see Rafael hanging over the edge of the boat. I reached, and he grabbed my wrist and lifted me into the boat.

I clung to the side and watched as Troy held Arius and Raf pulled him out of the water. Going over I grabbed the strap across his back and lifted as much as I could.

Troy pulled himself in and dragged the rest of Arius into the boat. They lay him down on his back and started pressing on his chest.

"Paisley," Troy said between compressions, "talk to him. Bring him back—you can do that through the bond."

I dropped down beside Arius' head. "Arius. You need to wake up." I said next to his ear. "I jumped off a cliff for you." I told him. I touched his face, then leaned over and rested my forehead against his. I couldn't lose him. "Arius, let me see those eyes." I whispered.

His body jerked, and he coughed. Rolling onto his side he coughed again, spitting out water.

"Oh. Fuck. Scared the hell out of me." Raf said and slid to the floor of the boat. "We got him." He informed the rest.

I lay down with Arius and wrapped my arm around him. He pulled me closer, his breathing still ragged.

Rafael got up slowly. "We're coming back to the dock. Is everyone all right?"

I lifted my head to see him give Troy an odd look. I didn't know what it meant.

Troy rested his hand on Arius' shoulder and leaned back closing his eyes for a moment.

"No sign of Willis or any of his men." Raf reported.

Arius was shaking, the shock finally hitting him. "Did you really jump off the cliff after me?"

"Yes. And for the record it's not safe to swim in that much leather."

He grinned.

Troy opened his eyes. "She's not kidding. I almost sank to the bottom when I jumped in."

Arius turned his head to look at his brother. "Did you jump off the cliff too?"

Troy shook his head. "Hell no. I took a boat." Getting to his knees, he sat up on the seat. "You need to feed, brother, we almost didn't get you back."

Arius nodded slowly. "I feel it."

I propped up on my elbow and leaned closer, placing my throat by his mouth.

"You're sure? Right here?" He asked.

I nodded. "Yes, because I can't lift you out of this boat, so you need your strength."

I heard Troy chuckle.

Arius kissed my cheek, then grasped the back of my head. His mouth was cold and his bite harder than normal, making me realized how close I had come to losing him. I reached and stroked my hand over his head after he healed his bite.

The boat stopped.

Troy stood over us. "Let's get you up, so we can check out that missing chunk of your head."

He helped him sit up.

"Always said you had a hard head." Rafael joked as he helped pull him to his feet. "He'll need blood to replace the river of red pouring out of him."

Arius swayed. "Just not Raf's blood, okay? Any kind of bond with him creeps me out—all those urges and women."

Rafael grabbed his arm when he swayed again. "Asshole. Next time I'm rowing there and not using the motor."

I gave him a hard look, releasing his arm so the men could help him. "There will be no next time. Period."

Chase stepped into the boat and helped get Arius off it. "Sarg is giving orders again."

I rolled my eyes at him.

Arius stopped and held his head, wincing. Squinting at me, he checked I was all right. "We always end up swimming together."

I rubbed my hands over my arms trying to warm up. "Can we make it in hot water next time?"

He grinned slightly. "Deal."

Chapter Nineteen

I held the cloak tight around me and looked around. Arius was sitting on a rock, a few of his brothers beside him. Victor had given him blood and his head wasn't bleeding anymore, but he was still cold and looked shaky. I was still processing the fact that they could only replenish blood loss from ingesting royal blood, but that didn't heal them, only feeding would. They were literally a whole species of their own. When Rafael had said he'd need blood, I thought needle and vein. I had so much to learn, and I wanted to learn it.

I watched the boat carrying the women get smaller as they moved further away. We'd done it. We'd gotten them off this island to safety.

"They're done coddling him," Alona motioned to Arius.

With a smile, I walked over and stopped in front of him. His eyes searched my face, then he wrapped his arms around me.

Michael came over and said something quietly to Troy.

Troy put his hands on his hips and stared at the sand for a moment, then lifted his head and looked over at Chase. He gave a brief shake of his head.

"What's going on?" I asked Arius quietly.

"We can't find one of the guards." He said softly and looked toward the stairs. "The rest are searching the trees and growth.

"I can go help." I started to drop the cloak.

His arms tightened around me. "I need you close."

I looked back to him and touched his face. "You're still pale." I titled his head to check the cut, it still wasn't completely healed up.

He gave his head a slight shake. "I'll be fine. Just need some food and a hot shower."

I kissed his forehead. "I almost lost you."

"From Victor's account, we almost lost you too." He leaned back, "he said if he hadn't grabbed you, you would have slid right off after me."

"I didn't have time lay down slowly." I said quietly. "Remind me to hug Mitz when we go back though, her leather and ribbing saved my skin, literally."

He pushed me back, his brow creased and opened the cloak. He paused and moved my sleeve to see the gouges on my arm. Seriously unhappy eyes flicked to mine briefly, then he unzipped my jacket. I pulled the cloak around his shoulders, I was only wearing a bra underneath. With a sound of pain, he touched my waist that hadn't fared as well as my arms when I'd landed on the ragged edge of the rock at the cliff. He moved to undo his vest.

I stopped his hand. "Put your beast away." He looked at me. "I'll live until you're stronger."

The muscle in his jaw clenched a few times. "As soon as we get back." He said in a tone that told me that was the most compromise I would receive.

I nodded, knowing the inner battle taking place inside him right now. I was injured and visibly so. "Okay. Now do up my clothes." I whispered.

His lips twitched as he opened the jacket all the way and stared at me. With a sigh, his big fingers fumbled to get the zipper latched and then did it up. "Just my luck, we're surrounded by dozens of people."

Everyone walked by us, all were looking at the stairs. I turned to see several men carrying someone down. Quinton and Victor were at the front of the eight men with the body resting on their shoulders. I didn't need to be part of the family connection to know it wasn't good.

"Help me stay on my feet." Arius said as he pushed me back slightly and stood up.

As he wrapped his arm around my shoulders, I wondered how I would do that if he stumbled. We'd both hit the ground.

We walked over to wait with the others.

"Who is it?" Arius asked Troy.

Troy shook his head. "Not sure yet, we just knew we were down one." He motioned with his head to the man following them down the stairs. "Ira will know."

I heard Alona sniffle and looked to see her shaking her head at something Chase said. Empath or not, she was not going to be whisked away at a moment like this.

When they reached the last step, Arius took a deep breath and straightened. He released my shoulder and walked over with the rest of his brothers. Victor knelt beside the guard and unzipped his jacket. I wasn't sure what they were doing, I thought perhaps trying to find the injury that had killed him. There was blood everywhere, and a deep ugly cut over the man's heart. It wasn't until Victor pulled the shoulder of the jacket down to reveal part of a tattoo that I understood. He glanced up to Ira.

With a nod, he pulled out his phone. "I'll call Mitz, so the women can get to her."

My eyes teared up when I realized they were talking about the man's mate. I took a shaky breath, Arius turned around and looked at me, then held out his hand. I rushed over to him and stood there.

I'd seen these people fight and laugh together and realized that this, right now, was also a part of their lives. It was their purpose to keep the balance from one realm to another. It was a heavy burden and it wasn't fair that they had to bear it. Yet they did for long centuries without hesitation.

"Arius." Michael said abruptly.

I looked up to see Arius' eyes glowing red.

"Go back and recover." Quinton told him.

"Troy?" Arius growled.

"Brother?" Troy stepped closer.

"You look and find who did this." Arius said in a low tone. "I will make his mind torment him for a thousand years."

A shiver went down my spine. Anyone would be frightened by his words. I leaned closer to him and reached up and touched his face. His red eyes looked down at me. "Take me home." I whispered.

"I'll go with." Rafael said and came over and stood on the other side of Arius, his hand on his shoulder.

"Go, brother, we'll be there shortly." Victor said getting up and motioning for Crissy to come to him.

I sat wrapped up in Arius' robe. He wouldn't even remove his jacket until I was out of my wet clothes and dry.

Rafael came out of Arius' bathroom and threw his hands up. "It's like talking to a deaf man in there. I think that blow to his head scrambled his brains."

I got up off the chair, I had to bunch it up the robe to be able to move easily. "What's wrong?"

He waved his hand at the door. "I can't even get the stubborn ass— who's shivering so hard it's like he's being electrocuted, to soak in the tub until he's healed *your* injuries." He put his hands on his hips and looked me up and down. "Are you injured?"

I wasn't about to flash him my stomach, so I shoved at the sleeve of the robe and held up my arm.

He winced.

"Both arms and my stomach." I said softly.

"Well, fuck. Why didn't he just tell me that?" He motioned to the bathroom. "He shouldn't be bleeding for anything right now, but the mate instinct overrides everything, including common sense apparently. He's really shaky and needs more blood to replenish, to warm up, to feed—" He held up his hand as I reached the door. "I'll be right outside the door." He glanced at it. "He's walking a fine line right now with healing and—" he waved his hand, "everything."

I nodded. "He won't hurt me."

"I don't think so either, but I've never seen him like this before." He huffed out a breath and then leaned in front of me to open the door. "Look after your mate, then get your ass in the tub." Rafael barked.

Arius growled at him.

"Don't make me call, Mitz." Rafael said then closed the door behind me.

I stood inside the door and looked at the leather strewn around on the floor. Arius stood by the counter, in just his leather pants. His whole body was vibrating. His eyes were red, and they were locked on me. "You should give him a break." I said quietly walking toward him. "You weren't breathing when we got you on the boat." I stopped in front of him. His eyes watched me, but he didn't speak. "Internal war with the beast?" I asked quietly.

His chest expanded slowly, his eyes assessing me from the bottom of his robe then back up to my face. He dropped to his knees and pulled me by the robe to stand closer.

I put my hand on his cool shoulders, I could feel how much he was shaking.

He pulled open the robe.

When his cool touch grasped my hips, I gasped. Before I could say a word, he bent his head down and ran his tongue softly over the scrapes along my waist. I clutched his head. It stung but was so intimate and tender I wasn't going to complain.

When he finished licking over each mark, he pushed the sleeve up and looked at my arm. With a soft growl, he reached behind him and pulled the knife out of the back of his pants. I grasped his hand and he looked at me.

"You're shaking so much, let me do it."

He released the knife and pulled me down to straddle his legs.

I swallowed and looked at his bare chest. My hand was shaking as I raised the blade. I didn't know if I could cut him. Reaching, he put his hand lightly over mine and guided it. The knife left a trail of red in its wake. I flicked it to the floor and leaned forward, catching the dripping blood with my tongue. His large hand covered the entire back of my head holding me close as I sucked on the wound.

When it healed, he pulled my head back and attacked my mouth in a savage kiss.

Someone banged on the bathroom door. "Arius." It was Victor.

Lifting his head, his breathing frantic, he turned and looked at the door.

"They're just worried." I said touching his face. "Let them in while I go get dressed."

He turned, his red eyes noting my lack of dress. He nodded and grasped my waist and lifted me to my feet. Standing up, he stepped back, his jaw clenched and motioned to the door with his head.

I gave him a soft smile, clutched the robe closed and went to the door and opened it.

Victor stepped in and gave me a quick once over then inclined his head. "We'll meet you at the dining room shortly." He stepped further away from me.

I looked to Arius, he gave a quick nod, but still didn't speak. I walked out of the room and the door closed.

Rafael stood there.

A loud bang sounded through the door, I startled and spun around.

Rafael stopped me before I could open it. "He'll be fine." He looked at the door. "In a weakened state, the emotional upset of losing one of our guards and being—" he looked at me for a second, "close to his mate, but not," he shrugged, "it's riding him hard right now." He motioned to the door after a second loud sound. "I better go help." He gave me a soft look. "He'll be fine. We'll see you at the dining room." He quickly went into the bathroom.

I stood there hugging the robe to me, staring at the door, listening to the sounds and hushed voices on the other side. Taking a ragged breath, I turned to go back to my room.

I was hoping I was taking the right halls when I saw Daxx and Troy come around a corner. She looked at me, concern on her face.

"What's going on?" Troy asked immediately.

I motioned down the hall I'd just come down. "Arius isn't doing well. Victor and Rafael are with him."

Troy looked down the hall. "He's mostly healed." He glanced back to me. "More blood and feeding and he'll…"

I shook my head, "he's not being very cooperative."

His expression went blank. "I see." He cleared his throat and looked down at Daxx. "I'll go see if I can help."

She nodded, then watched as he walked quickly down the hall. Turning to me, she looked at me in the large robe. "Damn giants." She motioned with her head, "come on I'll keep you company while you rinse off and get dressed."

I nodded. "Thanks." I waited for her to start walking so I was sure of the direction. "He's so full of rage right now."

She tucked her hands in her pockets and nodded. "I know. Troy as well. It's not often they lose a man in battle—" she stopped and opened the door to my room, "add that to the fact that we didn't get a single one of Hubert's top lunatics, and Arius almost dying, along with you…" She closed the door after I went through it. "They handle emotion worse than I do."

I sighed. "Rafael hinted that some of it is being close to me but because we're…"

"Not fully mated." She nodded. "Yeah they're more animal then man then." She snorted, "Trust me, Troy was out of control. Arius has been doing great compared to that."

Going over to the closet, I flipped on the light and walked in. "I just feel like I'm to blame, well, part of the reason he's like this right now is because of me."

She leaned against the door and watched me grab clothes off hangers. "Don't let him hear you speak like that—" she waved her hand, "it will prompt his protectiveness to come out and it turns into a vicious cycle. Trust me." She grinned.

I checked to make sure the jeans had a pocket then stopped. "I drowned my phone."

She chuckled, "phone killing is a favorite pastime around here. Honestly if they don't own stock in a cell phone company, they should." She shrugged, "Troy killed his too."

"We need life-proof cases. Aren't they supposed to be waterproof?" I walked out of the closet.

"Maybe, but are they sword and battle axe proof? Because that is part of life here." She came out and sat on the bed.

I paused in the bathroom door, "not that I'm complaining, but why—" I motioned to the air around me, "do they fight like that when they have all this technology?"

Daxx bobbed her head, "I've asked Troy the same. I mean, I'm glad we're not dodging bullets—and I've done my fair share of that hunting down bounties, but his answer is consistent with the whole thread that holds this realm together."

"Which is?"

"No honor. Only a coward would stand a hundred feet away and fire a bullet into someone. It takes courage and honor to be close enough to your opponent to see the color of his eyes and fight." She shrugged.

"Wow." I reached in and turned on the light in the bathroom. "It makes sense when you think of it that way."

She sighed, "It does." She grinned, "Not to mention they look hot when they're all decked out to do battle."

I smirked, "I had noticed that."

She motioned to the bathroom. "You better hurry. I figure you have about fifteen minutes before Arius comes looking for you."

Daxx hadn't been wrong. When we opened the door of my room, Troy and Arius stood there. She smiled at Troy. "Did you have to block the door?"

Troy gave her a half shrug. "He managed to hang on to it and just stand here," he looked at his brother, "mostly." He put his arm around her. "We'll see you in the dining room."

We both watched them walk away. I looked up at him, relief filled me to see his grey eyes hesitantly watching me. "Beast on lockdown?"

He nodded. "Yes." Taking a deep breath, he exhaled slowly. "I'm sorry about earlier."

I shook my head and went over and rested my head on his chest. "Don't be. It's been quite the day, night." I looked up at him. "I have no idea what time it is. I drowned my phone."

He grinned. "Troy and I did too, Michael's got smashed and Quinton thinks his got transported with a prisoner, and they're probably ordering pizza with it right now."

"Wow, do we buy them in bulk?" I put my head against his chest again and listened to his heart beat.

He hugged me to him. "I think we have stock in a few companies, so it evens out."

Tilting my head back I smirked, "you guys really have been around forever, haven't you?"

"That's what I'm told." Leaning down he kissed my mouth softly. "I want to scold you for putting yourself at risk and coming into that bathroom with me like that, but at the same time I needed you at that point."

"I don't understand it completely, but I knew I had to be with you."

His gaze moved gently over my face, "you realize all that this mating is lacking is the marks on our arms, right?"

I nodded slowly, "I'm starting to."

He kissed me again, his lips lingering over mine. "Thank you for saving me."

"Mmm, don't make me do it again." I smiled.

"Get a room. We have several dozen down here somewhere." Rafael walked by.

"Maybe they're trying to keep it fresh and try new places." Quinton said looking over his shoulder as he walked by.

Arius rested his forehead on mine. "Sometimes having so many brothers is…"

"The best thing in the world because they save your ass." Michael said.

We turned to see him leaning against the wall a few feet away.

"Sorry to interrupt this hallway interlude, but I thought I'd give you a quick update before we reach the food."

Arius straightened up and put his arm around me instead. "With what?"

Michael shrugged and started walking, "Oh, those cells that you're in charge of." He grinned.

Arius snorted, "Yeah, because I forgot that I've been in charge of them for the last two hundred years."

"Just checking. You were pretty out of it. I had to pop a vein for Raf's face."

We walked slowly.

Arius glanced at him over my head. "Maybe I knew what I was doing at that point and decided he needed a good punch in the face."

Michael paused and then nodded and started walking. "I can see that." He cleared his throat. "Forty-five new residents await your menacing stare, brother."

"That many?" He motioned in the air, "I was so occupied fighting that god-damned bulldozer I didn't get to see any of the action."

Michael's eyes went wide. "I popped down to check him out, seriously where the hell is he from? You're lucky you have a head left."

I stopped and looked at Michael.

His expression sobered. "Sorry."

Arius smirked. "I can still feel the vibration in my bones from blocking his swings. It was like it was my first hit blocking a sword all over again."

"No doubt."

We stopped outside the dining room. Michael patted him on the shoulder. "You took on a tank today and won." He went in.

I looked up at Arius, then hugged him tight.

"I'm okay, it's over with." He glanced in the door, then to me and whispered. "I need you to sit beside me, please." He exhaled slowly, "it's just too fresh right now."

I nodded, "for me too."

He kissed my forehead and we walked in.

Chase started clapping. "Seen your bulldozer, brother. Thank the gods it was you and not me taking that on."

I remembered Felix. "Is Felix all right?" I hadn't seen him on the beach.

Arius shook his head. "Wow, short lived concern for your mate. He's fine." He gave me a playful glare.

I smacked him on the chest lightly. "I had to check. Everything got a little crazy for me after you decided to chase him down." I sat down in the chair he pulled out. "You do realize that if you'd just let him run, he would have hit the rocks below, where you fell." I looked around the table. "I, at least jumped off where there was water below me."

He sat down and looked at me for a second, then glanced to Victor. "What fun would it be to see him broken on the rocks, he's like a trophy in that cell. I plan on selling tickets to show people what I fought."

Victor grinned. "Leaving off the fact I came to your aid at the end, of course."

Arius gave him a quick glance as he heaped food on his plate. "Of course, or I wouldn't sell any tickets."

"Arius?" I said softly.

He looked at me.

"You should just put that food in your mouth now." I smiled.

He grinned. "Yeah, babe, shutting up now."

Chase wasn't the only one to chuckle.

Chapter Twenty

Alona came into my room. "Daxx is having a meltdown." She stopped and grinned at me.

I nodded, then checked my lipstick. "I know I got the text." I paused to look at her in the gown. "You look amazing. I'm jealous, your hair just curls and looks fabulous all pulled up."

She laughed, "Fighting every step of the way. I just threaten to shave it off if it doesn't sit pretty at the end."

I inhaled sharply and put the lipstick into the little clutch Mitz had given me. "I still can't believe the family of that guard told them not to postpone this."

"They're a proud culture, and they revere the royal family." Alona came over and checked her hair in the mirror again.

Crissy raced in and spun around. "I can't believe how I look."

I smiled at her. "I didn't recognize you with your hair done up like that, or wouldn't have if you hadn't run in and bounced like that."

She smiled. "I'm so excited. I've never—even with all I see, have seen me doing this."

I blew out a nervous breath, "I understand that."

Bethany came in, she looked like she was gliding as the skirts of her gown floated with her. "Did Daxx message anyone else?"

Everyone nodded.

She laughed, "Running into an army of men wielding weapons doesn't scare her but…"

"This is serious heart-stopping terror." Daxx finished as she walked in fidgeting with the sash across her shoulder.

I stopped and gaped at her.

"What?" She asked her eyes wide. "I told them my hair looked ridiculous."

I shook my head, "No it looks wonderful. You just-just…"

"*Look* like a queen right now." Bethany finished for me.

"Yeah." I nodded.

Daxx snorted, "Yeah until we…"

"Gods."

We turned to see Chase standing in the doorway.

He looked at all of us. "I was looking for these five women that kick ass, have any of you seen them?"

Alona laughed and walked toward him. "I'm torn now, I don't know if you look sexier in your leathers or that tux."

He straightened and adjusted the sash he wore. "I look good all the time, my beloved." He gave her a lecherous look. "You on the other hand—" he motioned to her gown. "I have many plans for *that* gorgeous piece of cloth later on."

Alona chuckled. "If you can find the way out, you're welcome to."

"Does anyone know where…"

Troy stopped a foot in the door and stared at Daxx.

"Close your mouth brother, you'll drool on my shoes." Chase told him.

Daxx actually blushed and then walked toward her mate. "It's not too much?"

He shook his head quickly.

"As you can see, ladies, we may look alike, but I got all the charm." Chase drawled.

Troy turned and scowled at him, and then smiled at Daxx. He went over and walked around her, then stopped to stand behind her.

Chase came into the room, Alona turned and showed her bow on the back of the gown.

"Oh," he went over and wiggled it, "does it come off, I have plans for that later."

Daxx turned to Troy, "not a word."

He shook his head, "no it just leads thoughts elsewhere, not in bad way."

Daxx gave him a heated look.

Leone came in adjusting his cuffs, then looked up and stopped. "Fuck me." He whispered.

Chase turned to Troy. "I take it back, at least you said that inside your head."

Leone gave him a bored look, then went over to Bethany. He held out his hand and she took it, he spun her in a slow circle. "You look amazing." He whispered and leaned down and kissed her bare shoulder softly.

"Okay, he's trainable." Chase admitted.

"Speaking of charm," Alona lifted the hem of her skirt and wiggled her booted foot, "I absolutely adore these, my charming mate."

Chase grinned. "Are they comfortable? I insisted they be comfortable, so I could dance with you for every song." He looked to me. "There will be dancing, right?"

I smirked, "Like you've never seen before."

Crissy giggled.

We turned to see Victor standing in the door. His eyes glued on her.

"I feel like Cinderella." She told him.

He shook his head slowly as he walked toward her. "Cinderella doesn't stand a chance beside you, my heart." He lifted her hand and kissed it, lingering for a moment.

"Quinton is bitching again, that…" Arius stopped in the doorway and stood there, his eyes looking nowhere but at me.

"Is bitching?" Chase inquired.

Arius blinked and looked at him. "That he has to go." He walked to me slowly.

Leone huffed out a breath, "he got out of *how* many formal events?"

"Too many." Arius said, still looking at me. He stopped and then glanced to the dresser beside me. Coming over, he picked up my chain and pendant.

"I was just going to put it on when everyone started wandering in." I said quietly.

He stepped behind me and put it on, then leaned down and kissed the side of my neck gently.

"Arius," Troy said in a firm tone, "are we going to have to take turns watching you?"

I turned and looked up to see his eyes were red.

He shrugged, "I seem to recall two kings whose eyes changed in front of all of Alterealm when the Huntress was walking toward them at the last ball."

Leone snorted. "Oh man—that was something to see."

Chase cleared his throat. "We won't bring up the lot of you keeping us from dancing with Daxx then."

Alona turned to look at Victor, "oh, I'd like to hear that story sometime."

Victor smirked, then glanced to Arius.

"I will be fine. As long as no one tries to come between Paisley and I—" he shrugged, "it's under control."

"Noted." Troy said, then held out his hand to Daxx. "We're running behind, so unless you want Mitz to storm in here, we must go."

She nodded. "What is this announcement thing she was talking about?"

Troy glanced briefly at Chase as they walked out. "It's a formal tradition. As we walk through to the platform, they will announce us."

We filed out as couples and followed them.

"What do you mean?" She asked.

Chase chuckled. "Presenting, our Night King, Troy and The Huntress Queen, Damariss."

Daxx stopped walking.

Chase and Alona almost walked into her.

She shook her head. "No."

Troy shrugged, "I'm afraid so, even I can't change that."

"Seriously? What good is it being a king then?"

Leone looked at Arius, "at least she found out *before* she stopped the procession."

Arius smirked. "I say we run down the carpet, so they have to say it so fast no one can understand it."

Leone shrugged, "at least yours sounds like a title. The Enforcer, Prince Leone and Princess Bethany sounds like I'm her bodyguard."

Bethany smiled. "You guard my body, very well."

He smiled down at her. "Yes, I do."

I glanced up at Arius.

His eyes searched my face, "yes when we start walking they will say, The Warden of Justice, Prince Arius and Princess Paisley."

I cringed. "I sound like a doll."

"Oh, no. No that is fine." Alona gave me a wide-eyed look, "Try this on for size, the Day King, Chase and the Queen of Light, Alona. I sound like a troll doll."

I turned and looked at Victor and Crissy.

She grinned up at him then looked at me. "*The* Justice, Prince Victor and Seer of Truth, Princess Cristy."

I shook my head, "If I were you two," I looked at Chase and Troy, "*Kings*, the first order of business would be to get some reasonable handles for your folk. Those are just..." I shuddered. "Horrible."

"I'm wearing my leathers next year and glaring at people." Arius said with a smirk.

"Can we?" Daxx looked excited.

Troy shook his head. "It would break Mitz's heart—speaking of which, we are even more tardy now."

Daxx sighed loudly. "Fine."

"You should have gone for points, brother, told her we refused to wear the crowns this year." Chase said.

Troy glanced over his shoulder and glared at his twin. "I *was* saving that for a time when I needed it."

Chapter Twenty-One

Arius spun us away from Elder Roan. "If he interrupts again to introduce you to your third cousin, twice removed on his mothers' sisters' side, I'm going to *suggest* he go for a long walk—for ten years."

I looked up at him, trying not to laugh. "At least he's proud that I'm related."

"Mmm, who wouldn't be?" He smiled, "And his great-great-granddaughter is mated to the Warden of Justice, Prince Arius. Did you notice he adds the *prince* in there every damn time? Like they don't know who I am. I've never smiled so much in my life."

Reaching up, I touched his face gently. "At least he doesn't think what most of the residents do."

He grinned down at me. "I think you've dared more with a look then I have today."

I shrugged, "Maybe. Now shush and dance with me and stop grumbling. This is the last slow dance for a few songs."

He gave me a wary look. "Do I have to dance the fast ones? Because I have to warn you I'm smooth with a sword, but it's a scary thing, me trying to move to a beat."

I laughed, picturing Daxx the first few times we'd tried to teach her how to move. "No, the beast can watch me dance."

He leaned down and nipped the side of my neck. "That I can do."

Alona and Chase whirled past us, she gave me a look then glanced to the stage.

I looked over, the deejay nodded at me. I stopped moving. "I'm spinning the next song."

"Oh." He looked pleased. "I get to see what you do, I've been hoping." He nodded and followed me as I worked my way toward the stage. People noticed as we passed and bowed their heads, moving out of the way.

Bethany and Leone met us there.

Leone leaned over, "she said we have to show our support." He smiled at me.

I gave her a look and tried not to laugh. "How sweet." Stretching up, I kissed Arius and ran up the stairs. I motioned with my hand for the deejay to let the song play out.

Turning, I checked to see a nervous, but excited looking Daxx working her way toward us. Crissy was practically dragging Victor. Looking to the other end I saw Rafael point and say something to Michael. Good, I thought, all the brothers will move this way. Of course, as they did, the crowd moved out of the way. Standing, not too far away, was Mitz and her mate, Ira. Mitz was beaming. She knew what was coming.

Lady-like or not, I reached down and pulled the hem on the side of my skirt up, so I wouldn't trip over it. I glanced to Arius as I did, he was grinning, so he was okay with it.

As the dancers on the floor started to slow to a stop when the song wound down, I stepped over behind the table and cued the soft, non-revealing chords. Picking up the headphones, I placed them around my neck, so I wouldn't miss a cue during the mix.

Flipping the mic closer to my mouth, I smiled down at the nervous women looking up at me. "How's everyone doing today?" The entire crowd turned to look at me. "I'm so happy to see everyone here, to share this special day with us."

I glanced at Arius, he placed his hand over his heart and inclined his head to me.

I smiled. "This next song is for our royal brothers." The men all looked at one another then smiled. They had no clue, I thought. "As you know they've had a long reign of bachelorhood." The crowd was smiling. "Well, now as that is slowly becoming a thing of the past, the royal sisters have chosen this song for them."

Daxx looked like she might faint.

I looked back at Arius and winked, then brought up the song and adjusted the volume. I'd left the beginning of the song as the old version. There was no person in any realm that wouldn't recognize the intro to this song. That drop in the guitar cords. How many songs were about boots, sung by a woman? As soon as the singer sang the first words, the men's expression changed. I laughed.

I couldn't do the turns, but my boots were stomping in time to the girls down below. I glanced down and made sure I had the heavier bass I was mixing in set up. I held my hand on the slide, so I could adjust the vocals to be heard. When the beat changed to electric guitars and bass, my fist was in the air pumping in time to the beat.

Mitz and several other women were lined up watching the steps their queens and princesses were doing. The line of women in front of the stage just kept growing.

The royal brothers' expressions were a mix of awe, laughing and just plain shock, but all in a good way.

Fist jamming to the beat, I glanced at Arius. He was grinning so wide I could see the light in his eyes from here.

I remembered the pictures and picked up my phone the deejay had sitting beside the table for me. I lifted it and snapped pictures in all directions. The entire crowd, old and new was loving this. Setting the phone down, I put the one side of the headset to my ear. I kept an instrumental rhythm going and backed the main song up to play through the main chorus again. Timing it, I cranked it and let it start over.

Daxx was actually laughing, Troy's head was bopping to the beat.

I looked around, then did a slow double-take. Standing out in the crowd like a neon light were three men, they were not moving a single muscle to the beat. The look on their faces screamed retribution. I glanced to Arius, still pumping my fist in the air. His smile faded.

I nodded, to the deejay and pulled the headphones off, then danced my way down the steps.

I looked at Beth, and then to the crowd and held up my hands.

She frowned, but kept dancing, only her hands were no longer moving.

Arius stomped in time beside me, watching my every move and not to learn the dance. He looked to Victor, then Troy. Michael had even come over. The family mental hotline was fully activated.

Beth and I moved closer, and started dancing our way forward. I tried not to make it obvious that I was looking for those men. I glanced over to see a few of the brothers and guards had split up and were going down the outer side of the crowd.

The song was winding down, we had to move or might lose them. I leaned closer to Beth. "There's three men."

She nodded and raised her hands, the arc forming above her head.

The crowd was cheering, their expressions in awe and parted for us.

I looked quickly and saw the man I'd first noticed, he was reaching inside his jacket. As soon as the light glinted off the metal, I lifted my hands, stopping him.

"Got him." Beth said.

I dropped my hands and he hit the ground.

The two with him weren't even smart enough to disappear into the crowd. I didn't wait for either to reach into his pocket. "Left one." I said and stopped his entire body.

"Left." She said. Then the man toppled beside his friend.

The third one turned to run. I stopped his feet. "Feet." I told her. I lowered my hands.

"Head." She hissed. And he fell face first and hit the ground.

Michael, Ira and Quinton were there now. They pulled a dart gun from one man's jacket and a small collection of knives from the third.

My heart was racing as the guards started to close around us.

"Your royal princesses, ladies and gentlemen. Our realm has never been safer."

I spun around and looked at the deejay. He grinned down at me. The crowd clapped, as the men flanked us, watching all around us.

I could feel the rage inside Arius through our bond. Turning, I touched his hand. He grasped mine and gave a squeeze. I looked up to see his eyes were red as he scanned the crowd. Now was not a good time to tell him to dampen the scary. After what could have happened, if there were any more in the crowd slinking away, I wanted them to know what they were up against.

Beth looked at me and blew out a breath. "They ruined our dance."

I grinned and looked around for Daxx. She was right behind us. "Better for us to deal with them than Daxx."

People were trying to move closer to us, but the guards were now all around us. I nudged Arius and motioned for us to go back up to the platform where our tables were, rather than stand in the middle of the crowd. He gave me a skeptical look. "It will be easier to see into the crowd." I told him. He nodded slightly, then tapped Ira on the shoulder and spoke to him.

Ira nodded and started to lead the way up. The crowd parted, so the trip there was much faster. Once we were on the platform, all the brothers were scanning the crowd.

I glanced to the deejay and motioned for him to get some music going again in the background and keep the volume down. When it started playing, Arius looked at me. "It will help with the tension in the crowd. Easier to see those not here for the celebration."

He leaned down. "Is that how you spotted them?"

I nodded. "They were the only bodies in that entire crowd that weren't moving something to that beat."

He smirked. "That's the first time we've caught criminals because they don't dance."

"My mix was sweet, there's no way not to jam to it."

Kissing me quickly, he straightened. "I agree. You're amazing up there."

Troy came over and gave me an odd look. "That was your doing. No one else could have come up with that song."

I shrugged. "It's a skill."

He nodded. "So the workout was learning that?"

"Yeah."

He shook his head. Then sobered as Ira came up on the platform. He walked right to Troy.

"I don't know how they got in. Security is tight."

"Not tight enough." Arius said.

"So what do we do?" Troy looked over at the other brothers and motioned with his head.

"I don't have the skill our princess does, but this song needs a repeat."

I turned and looked at the deejay. He grinned and faded in the song we'd danced to. The crowd loved it. I looked at Arius. "Now watch. Anyone not moving some body part to this doesn't belong here."

He looked at Ira and motioned to the crowd. Nodding, Ira went to the edge of the stage and said something to the guard standing there. He nodded and moved on to the next guard.

I looked at Daxx, she had that look. The same one as when she grabs her blade and says, let's party. I nodded. Looking up at Arius, I gave him a pleading look. "Better tell the guards we're on the move." I danced down the steps. Glancing behind me I saw the other women following. Our mates, looking very unhappy, were walking alongside us, then guards.

I put my fist in the air, jamming the beat. The crowd parted and let us bounce through to the beat. All the bodies we passed were bopping along with us.

Daxx caught up to me. "First time I've hunted to a beat." She raised her hand and did a fist pump too.

We paused and did it in one spot for a minute, eyes scanning the crowd.

Troy looked to Arius. "Control your mate."

Arius raised an eyebrow and looked at Daxx. "After you."

"Listen to the words, boys, I think you're missing the point." Daxx said and bounced through the crowd in the other direction.

Chase and Leone were bouncing and fist pumping right along with us. I glanced over to Arius, he scowled, that was a no to the bounce for him. I laughed.

I leaned closer to Daxx. "We need to bounce toward the gate. I don't think our boots are a threat to them now."

She nodded and changed direction.

The deejay cued another song with similar beat. The crowd kept moving. I noticed even a few in the Elder robes were dancing.

As we reached the gate, Felix came over and handed me my clutch and phone. He had a big grin on his face too.

Victor wrapped his arm around Crissy, inclined his head and disappeared.

"I'm with him. No carriage rides out." Daxx said.

Arius didn't even ask, just grabbed me around the waist and then we were standing in the hall outside the dining room.

As the others appeared, I looked in and grinned. "I know food is a big thing, but you do realize we left Mitz back there dancing, right?"

A few of them glanced at each other, disappointment on their faces.

Rafael's head was still bobbing to non-existent music. He stepped up to me and held his hand up for a high five. "Best ball ever."

I tapped his hand and grinned.

He motioned to Arius. "Before those jokers ruined it, I think he was moving a bit."

I laughed. "He was with me in spirit."

Alona smirked. "Even Elder Drusla was dancing."

Bethany nodded. "I think at one point everyone was, that's how Paisley spotted those guys."

Quinton leaned against the wall. "So maybe we'll switch up our methods and flush out the bad guys with tunes." He smirked at me, then winked.

"Why would they bring a dart gun?" I asked.

"They what?" Daxx was no longer smiling. She looked at Troy. "You find out if they planned to shoot me in the ass again. I'll beat them into…"

Troy grabbed her. "With the size of that bow, no dart could get near your ass."

She smacked him.

Chase bowed formally to me, then straightened up. "That was the most entertainment at one of those balls I've ever seen." He looked around. "And we've seen a lot of them."

Even Victor nodded.

"I'm glad you guys liked it." I hugged the clutch to my chest.

"We're doing more dancing around here." Rafael said, then saluted me and started walking down the hall.

"I'm in." Bethany said.

Leone nodded. "Private parties, family and friends instead of all of Alterealm works for me." He bowed his head. "Now if you'll excuse me, I have to go figure out how they got my mate into all that material." He grinned. They walked away hand in hand.

Quinton went into the dining room. "I'm going to forage in Mitz's kitchen.

Crissy grabbed Victor's hand. "Let's go dance."

He grinned at her and scooped her up and started walking down the hall.

Chase watched for a moment then turned around. "I'm not sure they're both thinking the same thing."

Alona laughed. "Well, I want to actually dance." She held out her hand.

"For you, anything." He took her hand and they danced down the hall and around the corner.

Shaking his head, Michael bowed to me. "Thank you for that, sister." He gave Arius and abrupt nod and went the same direction Quinton went in.

Troy looked down at Daxx. "So, about these boots…"

She nodded. "Yes, come help me get out of them."

He laughed, "That wasn't quite where I was going, but whatever you wish." He hugged her and looked at me. "Best coronation anniversary ball so far. Can't wait for next year."

I watched them walk away. I looked up at Arius, his eyes were on me and not the couple walking down the hall.

"I can't believe you danced out into the crowd after those guys."

I shrugged, "I didn't want to tip them off." I bit my lip. "Troy will find out what they were planning won't he?"

He nodded. "Most definitely. They ruined Daxx's dancing." He held out his hand.

I put mine into his. We started walking. "I had a lot of fun. The start was tense for me, so many people staring and bowing. It was—never in a million years would I ever thought that something like that would happen to me."

"They loved you." He said softly. "You were amazing. Graceful and polite when needed, glaring at people cringing from me, and you just rocked half of the realm." He stopped and looked down at me. Tilting my chin up, his eyes searched my face. "I can't believe how lucky I am. I don't know what I did for fate to bring me you, but I will never complain."

My heart beat so fast in my chest, I almost felt dizzy.

"Get a room." Quinton walked by carrying a tray.

"We have plenty." Michael walked by with a grin. "If you're restless Arius, we're going to binge watch some movies."

Arius looked at them, then back down to me.

"Arius is busy tonight." I said loud enough they'd hear, but my eyes never left Arius' curious look.

I gave him a nervous smile. "First, we should probably get out of the hallway."

He blinked, then hugged me and we were in his room.

"You really need to start giving me some warning." I put my hand on my stomach. "The sudden butterflies thing is weird."

"Sorry. I didn't want to take the time to walk all the way here." He tilted his head and looked at me. "What do you mean I'm busy tonight?"

"I thought I'd stay with you tonight."

He made an odd noise in the back of his throat. "You know I'd love that, but since I've been having so many problems controlling—myself, I don't think that's a good idea."

I nodded. Lifting my arm, I looked at the gown. "Can you help me figure out the secret to this? I have no idea where the catch is to get me out. As pretty as it is, I don't think wearing it until tomorrow when the seamstress is around will be comfortable."

He smirked, "I won't mention if you got tangled in those skirts while sleeping, you may never get out." He looked at the back of the gown, running his hand along the fabric. "I don't miss all the big skirts and thirty layers."

I grinned. "I forgot you'd have seen that."

His brow creased as he looked at the gown. "I've seen some ridiculous fashion ideas. Maybe there's a zipper hidden behind the bow."

I chuckled. "Can you see Troy and your brothers trying to get their mates out of these?"

He shrugged. "Serves them right if they have to work for it." He stepped around front again and shook his head.

I lifted my arm, so he could check the side of the dress. "They were yanking at the bodice so much, I don't know where it is. Felt like I put it on and they twisted it in a circle."

He smirked. "I could just cut it off, but I think Mitz would get upset by that."

I nodded. "Yeah, not a good idea, that."

"Found it. It's hidden in a pleat." He sounded elated finding a clasp.

"Maybe it was your secret challenge." I laughed.

"If that's the case, we passed. I don't see my brothers faring so well." He unhooked it and pulled the zipper down about two inches, then stepped back and tucked his hands into his pockets.

"Thank you."

He nodded but didn't speak.

"Did you need to feed?" I'd been asking him often since he was hurt. I still didn't understand all there was about his man in front of me, but I was trying.

His gaze moved to my throat. "Need? I've wanted to since I saw the neckline of that gown. It's been torture with your shoulders and neck completely exposed."

I tilted my head to the side a bit. I could see his eyes close to turning red.

He didn't move.

"Arius."

"I shouldn't tonight." His eyes flicked from my face to my neck again.

I nodded. "I understand." Reaching, I pulled the zipper down. Holding the front, I pulled my arms from the tiny cap sleeves that were barely a ruffle from my shoulders. Dropping the dress to the floor, I stepped out of it and stood there.

His eyes were red now, but he didn't move.

Walking over, I reached up and undid his bowtie. I pulled it off and tossed it over my shoulder. Stretching up, I shoved his jacket off his shoulders. He pulled his hands out of his pocket and let it fall to the floor. I reached around him and undid the cummerbund around his waist. I started on the buttons of his shirt. His eyes never left mine. "You can touch me." I said and undid another button.

"I'm afraid to." His voice was barely a whisper. "I don't want to hurt you."

I reached his waist and pulled the shirt out of his pants. Running my hands back up his bare chest, I molded them over the muscles I'd only admired before.

He inhaled a deep breath. His red eyes were moving over my face, searching.

I reached for his hand and undid one cufflink, then moved to the other side.

He shrugged out of the shirt.

I pulled his braid around and took the tie from the end of it. Running my hand through his thick hair, I loosened the braid, so it would fall out. "I want your hair loose, we'll braid it later before sleep." I said softly.

Running my hand back over his abdomen, he caught it and held it still.

I looked up at him, could see the doubt in his eyes. "I'm making the clothes rule fair," I motioned down my body. I was only wearing a strapless bra, underwear and boots. "Make it even." Bending forward I kissed his hand, then pulled mine out of it. I undid his belt and pulled it free and dropped it to the floor.

When I reached for his pants, he grabbed both my hands. "I need you to define what is happening."

I gave him a surprised look.

"Words, babe, I need words." His eyes were a deep red.

The same red they'd been after he was hurt. I realized how close he was to being the beast he feared.

"You want me to write it down for you?" I bit my lip.

His expression lightened ever slightly. "Say it." His voice was a hoarse whisper.

Stretching up, I ran my hands up his chest and then kissed a trail behind them. "I'm there." I whispered.

He cocked his head to one side and looked down at me, his gaze holding mine, searching. His hands were shaking as he cupped my face. "You're sure." I could see the self-doubt in his eyes.

My heart hurt, to think he'd lived so long thinking he was unlovable, unworthy of the simplest thing as having someone meet his look. "I'm sure. Man, warden, prince, beast—" I shook my head slowly, "I don't care what others think of you, I just know you're the most honorable man I've ever met, and I'm so lucky and proud to be your mate."

His breathing grew faster. "I will never make you doubt me." Leaning down, he brushed his mouth over mine.

I could feel the emotion, through the bond, like he'd finally released his hold on it. It was almost overwhelming, the love, pain, lust and fear coming from him. Then I felt his hunger. It was the strangest sensation.

When he lifted his head, I moved my head to the side. "Feed," I whispered.

With his fangs clenched together, he looked down at me. Bending his legs, he wrapped his arms around my hips and lifted me off the floor.

I clutched his shoulders and squeezed his waist with my knees. When he started nipping along my skin, his fangs pinching lightly, I forgot to breathe. I wanted this.

Reaching behind me, he pulled one of my boots off, then the other. At the same time my bra was undone and removed from my body. His mouth hadn't paused once.

Lifting his head, he looked at me. "You're not afraid." He sounded surprised.

I gave him a blank look, "no, but if I get any more turned on I'm going to scream and bite you."

His lips quirked. "You are so fucking perfect." He moved and pulled his shoes off. Kicking the second one across the room, he grasped the back of my head and pulled me closer then bit into me without preamble.

I moaned in the back of my throat and grabbed his long hair, holding his head close.

Licking over the bite, he lifted me higher then licked over one breast then the other. Closing his mouth around one nipple, I could feel his fangs and my whole body shuddered with the erotic sensation. Moving his mouth again, he pulled my face to his and attacked my mouth. I was right there with him, trying to consume him.

He moved us toward the bed and lowered us both down onto it without breaking the kiss. Tearing his mouth from mine, he looked down at me for a moment. "I'll try to do this gently, but I can't promise. I've been losing my mind since I first saw you."

Reaching up I grabbed handfuls of his thick hair and pulled his face back down to mine. "If I needed gentle, the idea of your fangs biting into me wouldn't turn me on so much." I bit his lip, hard enough I tasted blood. I sucked on it. "You can heal any marks of passion later."

He growled in the back of his throat and raised up above me. Leaning down, he moved slowly down my body, leaving a trail of teasing bites along the way.

He used just enough pressure to not break the skin. His hair brushed against my skin. I was losing my mind. I could feel what my reactions were doing to him through the bond, and there was an inferno of passion building inside me. When his mouth moved down my stomach, I grabbed the bedding, so I wouldn't reach down and rip his hair from his head.

His red eyes never left mine once as he moved down my body. When he reached my underwear, he leaned down and bit the thin elastic. It broke. He repeated that move on the other side.

Letting go of the bed, I sat up and grabbed his hair. "Foreplay later." I attacked his mouth.

Pulling back, he glanced down at his body.

I paused and looked to see he still had all the clothes from the waist down, on. I released his hair and lay back. His gaze held mine as he stood and undid his pants. Reaching around his waist, he pulled the knife off and dropped it to the bed. My eyes left his face when he dropped his clothes to the floor. The rest of his body matched the sculpted chest and arms. If I hadn't already been on the brink of insanity from lust, one look would have done it for me.

As he moved onto the bed, he picked up the knife.

I pulled it from his hand as he lay beside me. Turning on my side, I looked at his chest. He nodded. My hand shook slightly as I pulled the blade across his flesh. Flinging it behind me to the floor, I leaned close and wasted no time sucking on the cut until it sealed.

Lifting my head, I stretched up against him and bit into the thick corded muscle in his neck.

He growled and grabbed the back of my head. "If you had fangs, we'd end up bleeding each other to the brink of death." He crushed my mouth beneath his as his hand moved down my body, caressing each part of it.

I gasped, breaking the kiss as he reached between my legs.

With a sound in the back of his throat, he grabbed my hips and turned me quickly, so my back was against his chest. His mouth was on my neck, his hand touching me everywhere.

I shook my head when I realized why he'd turned us this way. "I want to see your eyes." I turned so I was on my back and touched his face. "You're not my trophy."

He opened his eyes and looked at me. Moving, he lay between my legs and kissed me tenderly. "So perfect." He whispered against my mouth. Raising up, he nudged my left hand, so I'd raise it above my head. When I did, he clasped it with his. "I never thought I'd have this." He said quietly and squeezed my hand.

Our eyes were locked on one another as he entered me, we both moaned. I could feel the connection between us with the bond as his barely contained passion flooded into me. "Claim me." I told him and leaned up to bite his shoulder.

With a growl, his movements became fast and rough. The onslaught of emotions swirling inside me now were euphoric. Reaching under me, he lifted my hips up and as he bit into my neck, and my whole body began to quake beneath him. My arm burned, only increasing the other sensations more.

I grabbed his hair and pulled his head to mine, kissing him and fighting to keep my eyes open to look into his.

He groaned loudly into my mouth, his whole-body stiffening then slowing. The movement slowed, but he didn't stop.

Our breathing was erratic and scarcely there when he suddenly moved to his knees, bringing me with him. I wrapped my arms around his neck, then paused and noticed the markings down my arm. It was an intricate design of swirls and curves.

Arius glanced at it and growled against my throat. He pinned me against the headboard and began moving again.

I held on, barely able to think I'd wanted the beast, and now he was here and all mine.

Chapter Twenty-Two

In an exhausted sleepy haze, it registered that Arius was patting my hip and kissing my neck. "I need to show you something."

I smirked. "I think I've seen it already."

He chuckled. "Not that, after this."

I dropped my arm from my face and rolled to look at him. His hair was all over the place. The shower and more playing in bed had been a bad idea. "Your hair is going to be a challenge."

He nodded. "I know." He leaned over and kissed me quickly. "Get dressed."

I rolled my head to the side and looked at the gown. "I don't have clothes here."

He looked around the room. "Okay, let me get dressed and we'll pop to your room. It's almost dawn, so we need to get moving."

"Dawn? Where did the night go?" I sat up, every muscle in my body buzzing from the long night.

He turned and looked at me over his shoulder, sending me a shot of passion through our bond.

I shivered and blushed.

I watched him pull on some jeans, then pick up his phone and tuck it into the pocket.

As he pulled a shirt out he motioned to the other side of the room. "We'll get you a bigger sound system and set it up over there." He put the shirt on then looked at me again. "Just as long as you promise not to try and teach me how to dance."

I grinned, "Oh you have rhythm, and there's no music required."

He paused, then continued trying to pull his hair into a loose, tatty braid. "Don't distract me."

I got up on my knees, dragging the large sheet with me, watching him quickly put on socks and head to the closet. "You dress faster than I do."

He smirked as he came back out of the closet. "Take my age and figure out how many times I've gotten dressed in my life."

I opened my mouth then frowned. "Good point." I jerked the sheet and stood up. "So where are we rushing to?"

Walking toward me, he smiled. "You'll see." He grabbed me, then we were standing in the closet in my room.

"Uh," I touched my stomach, "warning."

He walked along the row of clothes, grabbed some jeans and a simple black top. Turning, he handed them to me and cocked his head to the side, "no need for underclothes." He grinned.

My cheek grew hot, but I took them and quickly put them on. As I struggled into a pair of running shoes, I paused and ran my hand over the pattern on his arm. "That looks good on you."

Leaning down he kissed me. "And only you could have put that there."

I smiled up at him. "I like that."

Hugging me, he kissed the top of my head. "Porting." He said quickly.

I opened my eyes and we were standing on some sort of stone balcony. I looked around. "Where are we?"

He hugged me against his chest. "The old palace." He motioned so I'd turn and look. "You can see so much from here."

I turned and looked. We were on top of a mountain. I moved closer to him and looked out as the sun started to reveal the land below. I could make out small towns and larger ones, miles of countryside. "Wow."

He leaned down and kissed my cheek. "This is your new realm." He hugged me. "You can walk all the way around this balcony and look in any direction."

"Why doesn't the family live here still?" I looked down. "Other than the whole way up in the air thing."

He put his arm around me and walked toward large glass doors. "It was too hard to keep secure. My great-great—" he shrugged, "I don't know how many generations back started building the tunnels to keep the royal family safe. It kept getting expanded into what it is now, with each king." He paused and stood in the middle of a huge room.

I looked around, it may have once been a ballroom, or similar.

"Some still lived here while the younger ones moved to the underground chambers." He took my hand and started walking to the open doors on the other side of the room. "Once the twin kings came to be, the whole family moved. Too many felt if they died, the throne was open."

I frowned, "Troy and Chase? People wanted them dead when they were babies?"

He nodded. "There has always been one main family to contest my family over which was the true royal family." He shook his head. "Willis Hubert's family." He motioned down the long hallway, where the faded outline of portraits would have once hung. "Hubert is older than the elders, I think it was his grandfather that fought in the first challenge for the throne." He started walking again. "That's when it was discovered that royal blood heals. And that only we could port without a device." He smirked, "how you can contest that, I don't know. No other line has that ability."

"It's like a neon flashing sign that the gods chose the royals." I said in awe.

He nodded. "Exactly." With a quick shake of his head, he opened a door and we began to walk down a winding staircase. "We didn't ask for this responsibility, but for as far back as history goes, my family has always held the position and the burdens that go with it." We reached the bottom and he slowed his pace, so I could look around at the tall pillars and molded stone arches. "We do so with as much honor and integrity as possible, despite the pain that goes with it." He shrugged, "it's a thankless task. My brothers and I, early on, decided we weren't going to rule from a gilded platform and that we would personally see to the armies and protection of our realm and the other."

I hugged his arm. "That's so unlike most."

Arius looked down at me and smiled, then his brow furrowed.

I turned to see what he was looking at. There were some crates in the corner, set up like a table and chairs. "Wow, that's some ambitious teens, hiking all the way up here to hang out."

He chuckled. "I was never that energetic." He motioned to it. "I suppose if they got it up here, I can allow them the bragging rights that they accomplished it."

Tugging on my hand, he pulled me toward large ornamental doors. "*The* original throne room," he bowed dramatically, "Princess." He smirked. Reaching for the door, he jerked his hand back when purple sparks flew from it. He backed up, pulling me with him. "Son of a bitch." He hissed.

Going over to the crates he kicked the table and it flipped over onto the floor. Grey material fell out on the floor. Reaching down he held up a grey jumpsuit.

I held my hand to my mouth. I knew that jumpsuit. They were bringing captive women here.

Grasping my hand, he turned to a door. With long strides, and me almost running to keep up, he was out the door and standing on the stairs that would have been the main entrance. He looked down the long winding road and cursed softly.

I looked at it, trying to see what he saw.

Pulling my hand gently, he went around on the balcony until we were around the corner. He pulled his phone out and tapped it with jerky movements. Putting it to his ear, he hugged me close to him.

I watched the direction we had come from, my hand raised from my side.

"Yeah. I think I know where Hubert has been hiding." His tone was quiet. "Don't tell Michael until we know for sure. I just hit a barrier when I went to show Paisley *the* throne room." He smirked. "Where else is there a throne room, Leone? Get everyone together, we'll be there soon."

He hung up and looked down at me.

I could see the vengeance in his eyes and reached up to touch his cheek. "Guess you better show them my beast."

KEEP READING FOR AN EXCERPT OF

The Warrior

Alterealm Series

Book 6

By J. Risk

Prologue

I stepped out the back door of the gym, rolled my shoulders and took a moment to appreciate the quiet of the neighborhood. I liked this time of day. It was silent, with no noise from traffic or the bustle of people. Times like that in the city were rare.

Stretching from side to side a few times, I zipped up my sweatshirt, then pulled up the hood and started a slow, steady jog.

This is how I started every day, just as the sun was appearing in the sky. I ran through the alleys and reminded myself that although I came from the streets, I'd fought hard to stay off them. Each day seeing where I came from was my reality check.

I rounded the corner by the old restaurant and slowed my pace to watch the old woman, I think she called herself Betsy, roll up her blankets. I waited until she spotted me before I spoke. "The kitchen will have breakfast started soon, if you go now and ask for Albert, he'll give you some hot coffee."

The only acknowledgement I got was a slight nod, before she looked back to the pavement. Betsy never made eye contact for long. I would have liked to know her story, but that was for her to share, not for me to ask.

I picked up my pace again, making short jabs with my hands as I went. I felt good today. No aches or gripes from my muscles. It had been a week since my last fight, and this may have been the longest period in my life that I wasn't injured on some level.

Someone stepped out of the shadowed doorway in front of me. He lifted a hand in hello, and then was invisible in the low light before I went by him. Living in the shadows was a hard life, not knowing who to trust and who not to. I had a roof over my head now, but those feelings that tell you to run would never go away, I thought, not that I'd want them to.

The only sound I could hear was my shoes hitting the pavement in a steady rhythm. It was just loud enough to warn any in hiding that I was present, and to scare off any rodents or lost pets living in the area.

A clatter to my left had me turning fast, ready, just in case. Relief washed over me when I saw it was only the old guy with the cane. He was struggling to get his wagon out from under the fire escape ladder. He'd probably slept there last night. I stopped to go over and duck under the metal ladder, pulling his wagon free, so it would clear the obstacle. He grinned his toothless smile and patted the red hat on his head. I'd given it to him a few months ago when we had cooler weather. "Kitchen will be open soon. Make sure you fill your water bottles with clean water." He nodded and turned to pull his creaking wagon down the alleyway.

Rolling my shoulders, I resumed at a slower pace, in no hurry to finish my run today. I hadn't been to the south park lately, I should probably drop by later today and see if anyone was around. I'd been so caught up helping the guys in the gym, I hadn't taken the time. Guilt rode me hard for that.

The stench of the dumpster I passed had me wrinkling up my nose until I was clear of it. That was one thing I would never miss, the odors that went with living on the streets.

Turning right into the next alley, I grinned to see the light from the rising sun shining down. If there was any way to see this deserted space as beautiful, this brief moment each day was it. It made you forget that rats and the homeless lived here in this dirty space that others used to toss unwanted things in. For a brief time each day it glowed with the chance to be something better, something more than it appeared to be.

Walking toward me quickly was the woman that lived in this alley, I didn't know her name, but everyone knew her as the lady that sings. She was always singing. I frowned, she wasn't today. Her expression was one of fear. I slowed down as she reached me.

"No, no. Go back." She said quickly and ran past me.

I jogged on the spot and watched her keep going. That was unusual. I looked around, there was no one else around that I could see. She turned down the dark alley I'd come from and was gone. Odd. I'd have to swing by the kitchen later, after I opened the gym, and see if the guys there could shed some light on what was bothering her.

I grimaced when a sharp pain traveled down my left calf. That would teach me for skipping my stretching this morning. Muscle strains were a tricky thing. Feeling a bit breathless, I turned to keep moving. Getting tired and dizzy before I was half-way through had me mentally scolding myself. One chocolate bar the night before messed up a carefully maintained metabolism.

I wasn't one to quit. I'd keep going through the light-headedness until I burned that artificial garbage from my system. I glanced up, blinking to focus, gone was the bright sunlight as blackness closed in.

Chapter One

The blood trailed down his face, dripping from his nose as he came at me again. As he widened his stance, I knew there was no chance I was sweeping his legs out from under him a second time. My movement was restricted by the bagging clothes they made me wear, otherwise a roundhouse kick would knock him flying. I'd learned the hard way yesterday that it constrained my movement and I couldn't follow through. The bruises on my arms were proof of that.

"Told you it wasn't going to be easy." Blondie said to him from the doorway. His face was sporting a black eye from the day before. He rattled the chain in his hand. "Just grab her and I'll get these on her legs."

The other guard wiped the blood across his face and gave an abrupt nod, then stupidly started toward me again.

When they'd dragged me in the day before and tossed the jumpsuit at me, I thought I'd been wrongfully busted. After a few moments of trying to justify the error I'd realized this was not a jail, they were not cops and I was in a different kind of trouble. The kind of trouble that wasn't on any books, had no laws, and was a matter of life and death.

People usually react three ways in situations like this. Fear, that causes them to comply. Shutting down and doing nothing or freaking out. I wasn't big on screaming and crying.

Fight or flight. In my case I had to do the fight the part to get to where I could run. Fighting. That lead to a much larger problem, considering the size of these guys. I'd fought big men before, but these s were taking that to the extreme. I couldn't execute a good elbow-knee combo if I couldn't reach anything vital to hit.

I could taste the blood from my mouth and it made me want to break his nose again. He knew it too, and was shielding his face better now. If I could just get past him and drop blondie at the door, I might be able to find a way out of here.

"There's nowhere to go." He growled, hunkering down further, his arms out.

It was a perfect position for me to inflict damage. I sneered at him. "What are you waiting for? Come and get me." He charged at me, I ducked his arm and jumped up to land an elbow on his temple. He grunted and swung out, catching me in the side of the face. The pain radiated up through my eye. I hated face shots, they hurt more than a blow to the kidneys.

"What is going on?"

The guard stumbled back and turned toward the door. Blondie was now standing erect and looking straight ahead.

I wiped the blood off my mouth and stared at the tall woman in the doorway. She had long red hair and her aura and expression both spelled out the same thing, bitch with a capital B.

"You're supposed to be transporting her, not fighting with her." She looked from one guard to the other. "No one is going to want a pulverized woman. It's going to take a week for those to heal."

I backed up, trying to decide if I could make it through the three of them. The words were echoing through my mind. My heart started thrumming out of control. I'd been abducted by human traffickers.

"Sorry, ma'am. We can't get near her long enough to transport her." Blondie said, still looking straight ahead.

She turned and looked at the man dripping blood all over the floor. "Go get that dealt with."

Holding his nose, he moved by her quickly.

Turning, she looked at the chains in the other man's hands and then to his face. I wasn't sure, but it looked like she smirked when she saw my handywork.

I didn't feel bad about his black eye. He'd walked up to me the day before and grabbed my arm. No one grabbed me. No one touched me if I didn't want them to.

With cold eyes, she looked at me. "Look, Autumn—"

I scowled, she knew my name.

"While I admire your fighting spirit, I simply can't have you beating up the guards and giving the others any ideas." She gave me a tight smile that looked more like she was in pain.

I glared at her, if she was waiting for me to throw my hands up, apologize, and then comply, she was in for a big surprise.

With a slow nod, she sighed and looked at the guard. "Sedate her, get those on her," she looked back to me, "you may want a pair for her hands as well. Then transport her." She snickered. "After the walk, she'll be too tired to fight." She walked away without another word.

The guard slammed the door. I heard the lock click into place.

Exhaling, I slumped my shoulders forward. My face was throbbing. I'd baby my injuries later. Now, I had to come up with a plan. If they thought they were sticking some needle in me to knock me out, they were in for a world of hurt.

The door opened.

I spun toward it, ready.

Blondie smirked, then raised a gun and pulled the trigger, then the door closed.

The sting registered in my leg. I looked down to see a dart sticking out. I pulled it out and tossed it across the room. My head felt weird. I blew out a breath and hopped up and down trying to shake it off. The room tilted, and I stumbled and hit the wall. Sliding down it, I glared at the door.

The door started to blur, I shook my head but everything felt like it was in slow motion. My body was slipping sideways—I think, everything was too fuzzy to be sure. I couldn't command my arm to stop the fall. I blinked, trying to focus, it was like someone was playing with the light switch and dimming the lights in the room. I tried to fight the darkness. I was going to have to teach blondie a lesson was my last thought.

About the Author

J. Risk is a pseudonym used by Jacqueline Paige

I wanted to write a story that would fit into new adult levels as well as adult. Something that was serious with fun elements-- paranormal / fantasy that everyone could read and enjoy.

I've decided to use J. Risk as the pen name for this to separate this series from my other writing which is definitely adult reading material.

Jacqueline Paige lives in Ontario in a small town that's part of the popular Georgian Triangle area.

She began her writing career in 2006 and since her first published works in 2009 she hasn't stopped. Jacqueline describes her writing as *all things paranormal*, which she has proven is her niche with stories of witches, ghosts, psychics and shifters now on the shelves.

When Jacqueline isn't lost in her writing, she spends time with her five children, most of whom are finally able to look after her instead of the other way around. Together they do random road trips, that usually end up with them lost, shopping trips where they push every button in the toy aisle, hiking when there's enough time to escape and bizarre things like creating new daring recipes in the kitchen. She's a grandmother to eight (so far) and looks forward to corrupting many more in the years to come.

Jacqueline loves to hear from her readers, you can find her at

http://jacquelinepaige.com

www.ingramcontent.com/pod-product-compliance
Lightning Source LLC
Chambersburg PA
CBHW021138110726
47900CB00002B/402